What people are sayir

The Village

T0169198

The scars of the Second World War are not deeply hidden or fully healed on the island of Crete. Philip Duke, in his terrific evocation of the battle for Crete and its aftermath, does a masterful job of showing why. *The Village* of the title stands for many villages, where the German invasion was met with little more than aged hunting rifles and kitchen knives. Cretans, invaded serially over the centuries and most recently by the Ottoman Empire, fought back bravely against the Germans and were met with terrible reprisals.

We see this story told through the eyes of a British soldier stranded in Crete, a German member of the Hitler Youth, whose ideals become tested by the realities of brutality, and the ordinary folk in a Cretan village living through extraordinary times.

Duke evokes the gaunt splendour of Crete and the raw courage of those who defended its liberty and were never completely subdued. It is a moving story, well told, and we see it from multiple perspectives, reminding us that in the end there are no winners in wartime. This is a great example of how to learn history, through a well-told tale resting on excellent research.

Murray Morison, author of *Time Sphere* and *Time Knot*

As a writer of non-fiction, I am deeply envious of those with the imagination and talent to produce first-class fiction, and *The Village* certainly falls into that category. Not only does it deal with an aspect of the last war with which I was entirely unfamiliar, but its characters and story are so compelling that I read it almost at one sitting. The author's familiarity with the

locations and the facts behind the story give the book that vital extra ingredient which raises it to the level of a truly great read.
Paul Bahn, archaeologist and free-lance writer. Author of *The Archaeology of Hollywood*

The Village is a character-driven novel and a thoroughly good read — from beginning to end. Philip Duke's four main characters are distinct, well drawn, believable, and sympathetic. Duke delays many details describing Anastasia, Yianni, Paul, and Dieter until they're pertinent to the plot, making me feel as if I am coming to know them as they come to know themselves. What happens to Yianni and Anastasia because of the war fought in Crete provides a wonderful contrast to what happens to Paul and Dieter when they mature into soldiers sent to the island. Before they finally appear together in the central village of the book's title, Duke has hauntingly reminded us of the essential, personal tragedies wrought by war.
Shaila Van Sickle, Emeritus Professor of English. Author of *Seven Characters in Search of an Author*

The Village

A Novel of Wartime Crete

The Village

A Novel of Wartime Crete

Philip Duke

Winchester, UK
Washington, USA

First published by Top Hat Books, 2019
Top Hat Books is an imprint of John Hunt Publishing Ltd., No. 3 East St., Alresford,
Hampshire SO24 9EE, UK
office1@jhpbooks.net
www.johnhuntpublishing.com
www.tophat-books.com

For distributor details and how to order please visit the 'Ordering' section on our website.

Text copyright: Philip Duke 2018

ISBN: 978 1 78535 910 1
978 1 78535 911 8 (ebook)
Library of Congress Control Number: 2017961319

A CIP catalogue record for this book is available from the British Library.

Design: Stuart Davies

UK: Printed and bound by CPI Group (UK) Ltd, Croydon, CR0 4YY
US: Printed and bound by Thomson-Shore, 7300 West Joy Road, Dexter, MI 48130

We operate a distinctive and ethical publishing philosophy in
all areas of our business, from our global network of authors to
production and worldwide distribution.

To anybody who has spent some time on Crete, it will be readily apparent that within the broadest parameters certain elements of the geography of western Crete are fictionalized. This was deliberate in order to accommodate the trajectory of the story. All characters in this novel are fictional, and any similarity to individuals, either living or dead, is entirely coincidental, with the obvious exception of certain well-known historical figures.

Main Characters

Cretans

Anastasia Manoulakis (née Andrakis). Inhabitant of Ayios Stefanos.

Antoni Manoulakis. Husband of Anastasia.

Yianni (PRON. Yanni) Manoulakis. Widowed son of Anastasia and Antoni.

Elpida Manoulakis. Only daughter of Yianni.

Kosta Vlakakis. Inhabitant of Ayios Stefanos. Also known as The-Man-Who-Walked-Backwards.

Papa (Father) Michali. Village priest of Ayios Stefanos.

Christo Papadakis. Best friend of Yianni Manoulakis.

Sophia Theodorakis. Closest friend of Anastasia Manoulakis.

Eleni Apostolakis. Young and widowed inhabitant of Ayios Stefanos.

Anesti Mandrakis. Cretan resistance fighter and Paul's translator.

Alexi Doukakis. Teenage resistance fighter.

Aristotle (Ari) Hatzidakis. Resistance fighter, employed primarily as a runner.

British and Allies

Paul Cuthbertson. Gunner, Royal Artillery.

Terry Hendricks. Gunner, Royal Artillery.

Fred Drake. Sergeant, Royal Artillery.

Captain, the Lord Cranford. British intelligence officer.

Bill Presley. Sergeant, New Zealand Expeditionary Force.

Germans

Dieter Lehmann. Private, Fallschirmjäger.

Hans Becker. Private, Fallschirmjäger.

Kurt Maier. Lieutenant, Fallschirmjäger.

Gerhardt Schneider. Lieutenant, Wehrmacht.

Manfred Schulz. Sergeant, Wehrmacht.

Greek family Terms

Baba - Dad

Kyria - Mrs

Kyrie - Mr (these two terms also used in greeting, as in Madam or Sir)

Papa - Father (as in priest)

Papouka - Granddad

Pappous - Grandfather

Pedhi mou - my child (a common form of greeting, often used not just to address a child but also as an informal greeting to friends, along the lines of 'mate')

Yiayia (PRON. Yaya) - Grandmother

Yiayiaka (PRON. Yayaka) - Grandma or Nana

Prelude

1990

The village of Ayios Stefanos sits on the northern flanks of the White Mountains. It is far enough away from the sea not to have been constantly threatened by the corsairs and other raiders who have pillaged Crete over the centuries, nor does it crown a hill so high that escape is impossible should the worst happen. At its feet, the village's olive trees spread out towards the sea, their green canopy assuaging the rockiness of the soil from which they grow. To the south, small gullies quickly turn into sharp-sided canyons inhabitable only by goats and fed each spring by the torrents of water that cascade from the mountains. There is nothing to single the village out from so many others. Its location, size and composition are common in that part of the world.

The poets tell us that history is a tide that washes over every man. But on this island history is a tsunami, transforming and sometimes destroying all it confronts. The men and women of the village know the oceanic forces of history, have experienced them in person, have been told of them down the ages: first the Venetians, and then the Ottomans whose cruelty was as unspeakable as anything they had suffered before, but made worse it seemed by their alien religion. Even the latest of the island's invaders, the Germans, ostensibly all Christian, brought their own brand of barbarism to the island.

When good things happened to the island, the villagers hardly noticed, so small was the bounty. The best of them left, lured by the promise of riches abroad, the money they sent back to their relatives only heightening the realization that the village and all in it had been abandoned, left defenceless as always to the whim of forces they scarcely understood and to which they have no earthly response. For centuries, poverty has stalked

1

this village like an ever hungry wolf, always probing, always searching, always ready to devour the weakest in the flock.

One source of comfort, constant if capricious, remains for them: the Church. Daily the men and women pray for relief, if not in this world then the next. But too often their prayers are unanswered. Why do they persist in this futile exercise? Because they know that their God hears all their prayers, and although sometimes—most times—He refuses to answer them, He knows all and what is best for them. And so they persist, refusing to give in, refusing to accept that life will not get any better, and buoyed by the inexplicable belief that if they can only confront the new obstacle in front of them, their suffering will end and they can live as they hope their God intended them to.

The stranger enters the village. He stops to catch his breath and lets his eyes take in the view. He is confronted by nondescript and, were he to be honest, cheap and rather ugly houses whose faded whitewashed walls face outward to the streets. The few windows are curtained, as though discouraging intercourse, as do the empty balconies, some of them draped with laundry, others sheltering rough wooden chairs or a table covered with the chipped cups of last night's coffee. Only the strident barks of the dogs indicate that perhaps life does go on here, albeit in an attenuated and unknown manner. As the stranger continues his journey, a large plane flies overhead, bringing in, he surmises, another crop of tourists, seeking sun, sand and whatever other pleasures of the flesh the island can offer. It is a reminder, despite the evidence of everything else around him, that timelessness is an illusion.

At last the stranger arrives at the plateia, the centre of the villagers' little universe, for here in this square ends the myriad of streets and alleys that curve through the houses, confusing to all but the villagers themselves. He stops at the edge of the square, unsure of where to go. He is old and glad to take another rest for his walking cane can bear his weight only for so long. The small plateia is dominated by a church, its faded whitewash sparkling in the afternoon sun, and a kafeneio boasting a small patio, its tables and rush-bottomed chairs shaded by a luxuriantly foliaged plane tree. The old men, placidly drinking their coffee, look at the stranger with indifference. They stare lazily at him as though foreigners come to their village every day; perhaps they do but they will never tell him. They show the same level of interest had an oddly coloured dog or cat walked in front of them. The stranger is merely a distraction, a brief change in their accustomed landscape.

Forcing himself on, the stranger absent-mindedly rubs a scar on his cheek and walks over to where the men are sitting, ignoring as best he can their hooded stares. The aroma of roasting coffee draws him in and he sits down—gently, for his chair creaks alarmingly—and gestures for a coffee. The owner, a small, dark-skinned man, orders the serving woman to bring him a cup of the strong, bitter liquid and a glass of water. The stranger drinks slowly, trying to negotiate a greeting with the few words of Greek he knows. He sees the men turn to him with new interest, listening as he struggles with their alien language. They nod, whether in comprehension or appreciation of his efforts he doesn't know, but heartened by their response he continues haltingly. Unmoving, they sit at their tables, sipping their coffee in silence, as he speaks, of everything and nothing.

A villager stirs. He is the same age as the stranger, perhaps a little older, for old age is kind in one way at least and dilutes the differences of a few years. As the stranger speaks, the man looks at the other villagers. His eyes flick from one to the next, probing for anything that might help him understand his feelings. A tic flares on his cheek and he massages it with his hand. But there is nothing from the others to give him guidance, and confused by what is happening the villager stands up, grabs his cloth cap, mutters a low goodbye, and leaves the kafeneio. He turns to look at the stranger one more time, and his eyes suddenly empty of life as his memory jogs itself into action.

March 1941

Chapter 1

Anastasia Manoulakis loved cats. She didn't tolerate them like the other villagers did just because they ate mice and the rats that attacked their chickens. No, she loved them with all her heart, for cats were her constant reminder that she, Anastasia Manoulakis of the tiny village of Ayios Stefanos, had once been cultured. As she heard her current favourite cat Wawa—she called it so after its distinctive meow—scream at the top of its lungs, in the throes, it seemed, of a permanent mating, the caterwauling took her back to that special time many years ago when her parents had taken her to a concert by a travelling operatic troupe. The group of artists, so far as she could remember, consisted of two singers, a man and a woman, both of them fatter than she could imagine possible, and a young man whose lack of expertise on the accordion was surpassed only by his inability to keep time with the singers. Anastasia had no idea what the two were singing about but they kept clutching each other as if they were afraid the other one would flee the stage. And even though the high notes had reminded her of the village cats fighting over kitchen scraps, the little girl sat there and listened in rapture. Her father had told her that the troupe had travelled all over the world— or at least as far as Iraklion 140 kilometers away—and that she should never forget this moment. At the end of their final piece the crowd stood up and gave the performers round after round of applause. How Anastasia squealed in delight, how everybody shouted bravo, bravo, bravo.

Now, many years after her one and only introduction to high culture, Anastasia was a small and slightly stooped woman, the result of years of unremitting toil. Her grey hair was pulled back into a bun held tight by a small clip and the grease that she was able to wash out far too seldom. In the right—or wrong—light there was a trace of a moustache, a grey colour that matched the solitary hair that sprouted from the mole on her right cheek. She wheezed and gasped for breath at even the slightest exertion, but so far, God willing, she had not been called to meet her beloved parents at the right hand of their Lord.

Anastasia heard Wawa wailing again and smiled at the memory of that wonderful musical evening. But even as her little cat screeched on, now joined by the rest of the Manoulakis feline menagerie, the old woman was forced back to reality by the patter of raindrops outside, as a late winter storm, at first haltingly and then ferociously, blasted in. She sighed. How many times, she asked herself, had she seen this happen, and with the washing still wet and hanging out to dry. She put down the spoon she had been stirring the evening soup with and went outside to her little garden to pull down the laundry from the line. She made a mental note to sew up the hole in her husband's shirt again, for he was always putting his elbow though it.

She was glad she had come out when she did for the wind was from the south and already the brown sand of the Sahara was beginning to wipe out all of her hard work and even to coat the houses a yellowish brown. The wind slashed through the village, blowing shutters open, ripping shirts, trousers, and skirts off clotheslines to leave them snared on the branches of the trees, and whipping up the dead leaves of last summer into brown vortices that danced through the lanes and across the fields. Taking time to look around her as she hitched up a stocking that was falling to her ankle, Anastasia pulled the last remaining clothes off the line, promising to have Yianni climb the tree in her little garden to recover the rest of her laundry. High clouds were beginning to scud in from the west, still light grey but ominous nonetheless. To the east huge boiling mushrooms of black clouds filled the sky, and to the south the White Mountains rapidly were disappearing in a wreath of mist. And then the rain began in earnest. Anastasia hurried indoors, grateful to be dry but worried that Elpida, her granddaughter, her husband Antoni and son Yianni, would not be so lucky. Now, sheet after sheet of rain, so dense she could scarcely see through them, blasted against the house. Streams of water cascaded off the houses into the alleys and coursed down the streets, cutting deep gullies in their hungry search for the sea, as though the village itself was dying from a thousand slashes. Harsh winds continued to hurl in from the mountains, roaring down the valleys and gullies, and blowing away everything that was not tied down. Sheet lightning flashed over the sea, now barely distinguishable from the pall of clouds embrowning everything. Thunder rocked the very foundations of the house. A violent gust of wind coughed down the chimney and the smoke from the fire petulantly kicked back into the living room for a moment but then, as though remembering where it needed to be, continued on its course up the chimney.

Anastasia turned to the sound of footsteps followed by a slither as someone slipped in the mud outside. The heavy wooden door was thrown open and her husband, Antoni, stormed inside, water falling in large globules from his clothes. He was followed by the source of the slithering, Yianni, his clothing covered in thick mud. Anastasia stifled a laugh. 'Take this, Husband, and you, too, Yianni,' she ordered, and threw two rough cloths at them. The men stripped down in front of the fire, the steam rising from their bodies and the rain dripping onto the hard earthen floor to create little craters of mud. Anastasia averted her gaze as they pulled off their trousers; she had never seen a man naked, not even her husband, and she did not intend to start now. Retrieving dry clothes from the other end of the house, Anastasia handed them over and at last they grunted that she could face back to them.

'Well, at least the sheep are in the cave, not that they would give a damn,' Antoni grunted. Like most Cretans, he was a small man. His bald head was compensated by a luxuriant moustache that knitted imperceptibly into a thick field of nose hair. He scratched his weather-beaten face, its bristles a perpetual presence except for Sundays when all the villagers smartened themselves up for church. 'We got them in, Woman,' he continued, 'and we were halfway back when the heavens opened. So, there we were stuck in the open and figured we just had to run like hell, which we did.' He sat down in front of the fireplace and drank the coffee his wife had given him.

Yianni joined him, luxuriating in the hot drink. He alternately cracked his knuckles, a habit he continued with despite his daughter's protestations, and rubbed the side of his large, hooked nose. He stared into the fire with a mournful look that never seemed to disappear completely. He shook his head, dragging himself back to the present. 'Where is the little girl, by the way, Mama?' he asked.

'At the church, helping Papa Michali with the cleaning,' his mother replied.

Yianni shook his head. 'She spends too much time at that place. She should be playing more with the other children in the sunshine. If we ever get any.'

'She's fine, my son.' She paused. 'So, tell me,' she asked the two men. 'You were at the kafeneio earlier, what are you hearing?'

Yianni and Antoni looked at each other, and their silence worried Anastasia more than if they had spoken. Antoni took three long drags on his cigarette. 'Woman, it appears that our army up north has been victorious against the Italians. But, and this is only a rumour, if the Italians are truly beaten, then the Germans will have to come to their rescue. And that will be a totally different fight. If that happens I don't know.'

Anastasia stared at the fire as it crackled in the hearth, playing with a scab on the top of her forehead until it began to bleed.

The sloshing of light footsteps coming up to the house broke the old woman's spell. 'It must be Elpida. We'll talk later,' Anastasia said.

The rain had already lessened, and when the little girl opened the door, the sweet smell of wet clover and olive trees wafted into the room. Elpida was eight years old with jet black hair and piercing, green eyes. She had never known her own mother, who had died in childbirth. But as she told her family once, with a maturity that shocked them all into silence, 'How can I miss something I never had?'

Elpida sat down in front of the fire, but Yianni said sharply, 'Little girl, help Yiayia. Pick up those cloths and rinse them out. I don't know what you young ones are coming to.' Elpida opened her mouth to say something, but a furtive shake of Anastasia's head silenced her.

The storm blew through quickly, as they so often did on the island. The clouds dissipated and the sky turned first a washed-out and then a deeper, almost luminous blue. Yianni went back to the kafeneio for coffee. Anastasia and Elpida cut vegetables at the kitchen table, made from a roughly hewn single plank of olive wood, while Antoni sat outside smoking his cigarettes.

When Elpida had gone to bed for the night, Anastasia joined her husband. They had been married for more years than either of them could remember. Although the marriage had not been arranged in any formal sense, their two families had gently nudged them together so that his proposal and her acceptance seemed part of the natural order of things. Anastasia had long ago realized that they would never achieve the type of love the poets wrote about, with white doves flying and gentle music playing, but they had reached a level of affection and tolerance that many others of their age could only wish for. They were, she knew, in a word, happy, or as happy as an old couple had a right to be. Now she turned to her husband for reassuring words about the war on the mainland. But for once, Antoni could find none, and the two of them held hands in silence, each trying to dispel their fears for the future.

Chapter 2

Paul Cuthbertson, eighteen years old and unemployed since he had left school four years ago, was grateful for his local library, for here he could find refuge from his house and the solitude — and books — he craved. The library was a small brick and stone structure in a working-class section of Liverpool, made possible by an American benefactor many years earlier. Its main hall boasted a huge glass ceiling dome where light flooded in even on dark winter days. Paul's favourite room was the small annex to the main hall, for this housed the history section. Why he liked reading about the past so much he never could quite fully figure out, beyond its being a lot better than his present. He liked to think that he was fairly smart — at least if the other boys in his class were to be believed — but why he did not know. His parents didn't seem particularly bright to him, and it certainly wasn't because of his schooling, for Paul had realized years before that the school's only purpose was to prepare him and his mates for a life of unremitting drudgery in one of the many factories that surrounded his house.

The library clock struck five and told him it was time to go, for the library closed as soon as the blackout was observed. He put on his thin raincoat and cap and walked back to his home a few streets away. The terraced houses of his neighbourhood had already borne the brunt of the Luftwaffe and no doubt, Paul was certain, would suffer more. He passed the greengrocer's shop where his mother worked. The plate glass had been blown out, and she had spent a cold week selling the fruit and vegetables through the shop front as the women stood in line with their ration books. A gap in the row of houses was all that was left of where the McGinleys had lived. A landmine had made a direct hit on their home and taken it out in one earth-shattering explosion that had rocked the foundations of the surrounding houses and even made a huge crack in the concrete roof of the air-raid shelter where Paul and his family were hiding. Paul had dug through the debris the next morning with the other neighbourhood men. The concrete and bricks made an almost impenetrable tangle and Paul breathed heavily and had to stop often to catch his breath, the result of years of eating too little food and living in a city where all the buildings were black from the soot that thousands of chimneys daily belched into the air. It was Paul who had found Mary McGinley. He had gently uncovered her face, but as he moved the debris around it he realised that the head was all there was. He still remembered the bitter taste of the bile that he had vomited up. It took another three hours of sifting through the unstable debris before they found the rest of her, together with her husband and two daughters, each of them in one piece, but dead all the same.

Paul hurried on through the early evening, drawing his coat in tight as a fog began to seep in from the Mersey. With no streetlights and the fog getting worse by the minute, Paul needed to rely on recognizing the individual housefronts to keep his bearings. There was the Rossiters' house, identifiable by the heavily sandstoned front step that Lizzie scrubbed every morning without fail. Then past the elm tree that he and Billy Boyd used to swing from until the rope snapped and poor old Billy fell down and broke his leg. Finally, his own front door, painted a sickly lime-green colour. His father had said he'd got the paint cheaply from a pal in the pub, but Paul suspected that it had fallen off the back of a lorry, to use one of his father's favourite phrases.

Paul let himself in, catching the familiar smells of coal and cigarette smoke and his mother's own unique blend of cooking, which now had to rely mostly on a chip pan, potatoes and large quantities of lard. He hung up his coat and hat in the hallway but kept the scarf round his neck. In the living room his parents were sitting in front of the coal fire, drawing from it as much heat as they could, for coal was expensive and the Liverpool weather always seemed to create an inescapable dampness. The house was draughty and the blackout paper and curtains stirred in the breeze. Paul coughed; the air was thick with smoke from the coal fire and the cigarettes that Paul's father lit up like clockwork. As usual they did not say much, the three of them, but after Paul had warmed his hands in front of the small fire, his mother said softly, 'Paul, over there, on the sideboard, there's a letter for you. It looks government, like.' Paul knew, they all knew, what was in it.

Paul picked it up, looked at the front, turned it over to look at the back and then inspected its front again, as though he had never before seen such a wondrous object as a letter. He pushed back the hair from over his eyes. His parents remained silent, but in deference to the occasion his father put down his cigarette in the ashtray, a heavy, bright orange ceramic dish, a souvenir of a pre-war Whit Monday excursion to Southport, just up the coast. In her own concession to the solemnity of the occasion, his mother turned down the radio, though not so far as to make it inaudible. Paul opened the envelope and read the letter. 'Dear Mr Cuthbertson, blah, blah, blah, you are requested, blah, blah, blah...'

'Well, love?' his mother asked him.

'Saighton Camp, Chester. Royal Artillery,' Paul replied.

'It could be worse, son," his father spoke up. 'Coulda' been infantry. I was with the Fusiliers last time the balloon went up, Lewis gunner. Bloody artillery were so far back they might as well have been in England. Come on, son, it's time you had a drink with your old man. Ivy, we're off to the Prince Alfred.'

Paul settled himself into a corner of the pub and waited for his father to return with the beer. His father put Paul's drink on the table and looked around the pub's smoky bar. 'Son,' his father's tobacco-gravelled voice could hardly be heard above the talking, 'I just need a word with Harry about next week's darts match.' Paul nodded, surprised but grateful for his father's perceptiveness in allowing him to be alone. Paul continued to nurse his drink, rubbing his hand over what passed for a beard—his father called it 'bum fluff' and wondered why his son even bothered to shave. Paul reflected on what lay ahead. He harboured no illusions that his generation of Englishmen would be spared war, but it was still difficult for him to come to terms with the possibility that he might very well die, and die very soon, and perhaps die quite gruesomely, too. He had read once, in the library, a memoir from the Great War, the one his father had fought in. The writer had said that youth offers a shield of invincibility to a soldier: the conviction that while everybody else might die, he himself would survive. In the coldly logical atmosphere of the library, Paul had agreed with the sentiment; he himself might go to war but he would with certainty emerge unscathed from it. Now, as he drained the last of the beer and moved to the bar for another pint, he was not so sure. Still, as his father had reminded him, at least he would be in the artillery and with luck might never even see the enemy let alone face any danger.

Paul's Uncle Arthur came in. He had missed the Great War because of poor eyesight and now he worked on the docks, although the nightly pounding by the Luftwaffe hardly made his job a cushy one. Paul waved him over, and his father rejoined them in a second round. 'Your mam just told me, Paul. About gettin' called up.' He turned to his brother-in-law. 'Well, 'ere we go again, eh, Alf. Whatever happened to a land fit for heroes? That's what I wanna know. This country's a bleedin' joke, and that Chamberlain. Mind you, I don't think this feller Churchill's any better, for all his struttin' and talkin'. They're all bloody swine if you ask me. '

Paul's father shrugged. 'So what's new? The politicians always mess things up and it's the likes of us who've got to sort it out for 'em. Mind you, that bloody Hitler does need sortin' out and no mistake. And if we don't do it, who will? The French? Don't make me laugh. They didn't last five bloody minutes. Anyway, Paul, you'll be in the artillery. You'll be fine.'

Paul gave a half smile and their talk drifted to other, more immediate topics, like the weekend's football results and the upcoming darts match against the Black Horse.

The next week was a blur for Paul; not because he was busy preparing to leave but once he'd decided on what few clothes he could take with him, there was nothing to do but wait. Each day was a blur of sameness. His mother told him to go to the library, but reading seemed pointless, and so he just hung around the house, as though he wanted to wrap himself in its familiarity for future reference. On the night before he left, he packed his small suitcase and went to bed early. Early the next morning — an hour before the time his parents had agreed to send him off — Paul slipped out of the house, leaving his parents asleep upstairs. He walked along the main road for thirty minutes before he was able to catch an early tram that took him to the ferry to Birkenhead. Seagulls wheeled around the masthead of the dumpy little boat as it battled against the tide and the wakes of the myriad vessels that made Liverpool the most important seaport in the British Isles. Up and down the river, merchant ships were unloading their goods after their Atlantic crossing and destroyers *whoop-whooped* in circles as they and the tiny corvettes finished their shepherding. Paul sniffed the familiar mix of river, oil and smoke and wondered when he'd smell it again. The ferry bumped against the Birkenhead landing stage and Paul waited with the other passengers until he could disembark. A short walk took him to the railway station where he bought a ticket for Chester. Three hours later he stood, alone and rather forlorn, on the platform at Chester's railway station, and after asking a porter for directions, Paul walked the few miles south to Saighton Camp. An icy rain had begun to fall and the wind cut through his thin coat. Paul felt his stomach rumble and he remembered the carrying-out his mother had made for him the night before. Like an idiot, he'd left the cheese sandwich on the kitchen table and he hoped that food was waiting for him at the camp. He was not optimistic.

At the entrance to the camp a tall, immaculately uniformed corporal, complete with blancoed belt and holster, checked Paul's papers and opened up the gates to let him through. Paul felt small, for reasons he could not explain; perhaps surrounded by all the military uniforms and air of general efficiency his cheap brown suit and small cardboard suitcase simply made him feel as insignificant as he had ever felt in his life.

Paul was assigned to a billet in a hastily constructed Nissen hut, its end windows moving in time to the violent gusts of wind that blew through the camp. His bed was a thin mattress covered with threadbare sheets and blankets. Paul sensed the other recruits were as nervous as he was, their banter barely masking their fear of the unknown. They waited, not knowing what to do, until a sergeant appeared and led them off to the mess hall for dinner.

Paul found the meal better than he expected. The mashed potatoes were runny but the corned beef was edible at least. Another young recruit sat down next to him. Paul learnt he was from Birmingham and like him a rabid football fan.

'My name's Terry Hendricks, by the way,' his nasal accent even worse, to Paul's ears, than his own thick Liverpudlian.

Paul introduced himself. They found little else to say and contented themselves with trying to smooth out the lumps in the custard.

That night, lying in his bed, Paul stared at the ceiling, listening to the snores and heavy breathing of the other recruits and wondering if they all felt the same way. He was alone—that he did not mind so much—but the loneliness led him to a place of fear. A fear of whether he could survive, not just the next few weeks of training, but—most of all—the indefinable future ahead of him.

◊

The weeks of basic training passed, each day starting with the ritual cleaning of an already spotless latrine, then an inspection of hair length and a quick march to the barber's if it offended the sergeant's overly developed sensibilities, and endless uniform inspections—Paul's uniform did not fit him, though nor did anybody else's—and hours of drill on the parade ground. The repetition, before the recruits were even allowed to fire an artillery piece with live ammunition, turned his mind—temporarily he hoped—into a sponge that absorbed little else but how to work the gun. Yet some things did impress him even if he could recall some of them fully only after he had left the camp. He was given rifle and bayonet training and learnt how to stick, twist, pull; stick, twist, pull; stick, twist, pull. He wondered if a German would be quite as compliant as the straw figure he now could efficiently skewer. And all through his training, he never got over the inordinate attention his drill sergeant, an almost incomprehensible Cockney, paid to the creases of Paul's trousers or the shininess of his boots.

One morning, Paul and his squad lined up for the morning inspection. The sergeant moved along the line, swinging his swagger stick. He stopped in front of Paul.

'Cuthbertson,' he shouted, peering down at Paul's wiry frame and jamming his nose six inches from Paul's. 'Do you know why your badge is the laziest in the whole army?'

'No, Sarge, not really. Never thought about it.'

Well, let me tell you, Scouser. It's because it's got a crown that's never wore, a gun that's never fired and a wheel that never turns.'

The drill sergeant thought this joke equal to anything that had ever come out of Tommy Handley's mouth and he laughed until spit and bits of tobacco were spraying Paul's previously pristine blouse. Paul was slow on the uptake and instead of laughing along with the sergeant, as he would have done just a few weeks later, he looked quizzically at him. The sergeant took this to be a mortal insult and got his own back. Still inches from Paul's face, he screamed, 'Polish those fucking boots, soldier, and report to me at five o'clock. You're cleanin' the latrines...again. Now, piss off, I'm sick of all you Scousers. No fuckin' sense of humour.' Paul had, however, learnt a valuable lesson. Any joke was funny if a superior told it, and since Paul was the lowest of the low he realized that from now on his stay in the army was going to be a veritable barrel of laughs.

Paul and Terry Hendricks were placed into a light anti-aircraft training battery, and although, like them, only a trainee gunner, Paul noticed that the other members of his gun crew often looked to him for guidance. Yet despite the need to work as part of a team, Paul remained at a distance from his fellow recruits with the exception of Hendricks. While he enjoyed being part of a competent gun crew and always laughed at their jokes even when they weren't funny, he would find excuses to shrink away from them once their talk became too intimate—when they began talking about the local girls, who would do what and for how much, who would do it just for fun and who would run a mile. His comrades all seemed sexually experienced, although Paul knew that a lot of it was just banter and that most of the recruits, if not all, were as inexperienced as he was. Only when the talk turned to football did Paul feel comfortable enough to join in. But still he felt an enduring distance from them that gave him a barely conscious source of pride as though he was capable of living an existence separated from, albeit partially dependent on, those around him. But still, like a cat prowling a back entry, in the back of his mind always was the fear.

Chapter 3

Seven hundred miles from Liverpool, in a spacious mansion that fronted a wide, tree-lined boulevard, the two males of the Lehmann family were in the middle of one of their all too frequent arguments. The family patriarch Heinrich, a successful Berlin banker prominent in the local church, sat at a huge oak dining-room table, across from his twenty-year-old son, Dieter. Both of them were for a moment silent as they reloaded their rhetorical shotguns, so Karla, Heinrich's wife, and their twelve-year-old daughter, Liesl, took advantage of the cease-fire to clear up the dinner plates and retire to the kitchen to watch Magda, their maid, dump the slops into a compost bucket before the laborious task of individually washing every plate, cup and piece of cutlery. Magda felt Karla's eyes watching her every move and she was glad that the argument in the other room was even more vociferous than normal as it perhaps would give her mistress more important things to worry about than her own efficiency.

'It still bothers you, doesn't it, Father, that I am a paratrooper.' Dieter broke the silence.

His father remained silent and stared at his son as though he were a stranger.

Then the tempers flared and the shouting began again. 'Admit it, Father, admit it.' The young man continued, his voice rising in pitch, as it always did when he was angry. 'Admit that we are better off under the Führer than before he took power. Our countrymen are employed again. Europe and the world respect us again. What is so wrong with that?' Dieter's face was red and spittle flecked his lips as he shouted at his father.

'Dieter, why do you speak like this?' Heinrich kept his voice low and unhurried. 'This is not how we brought you up. You were always such a polite young man. And now, since you started to wear that damned uniform, you act like everybody is your enemy, especially your own family. First it was the Hitler Youth and now...'

But Dieter cut him off. 'Father, I am not always angry, but I do get frustrated when you refuse to acknowledge what the Führer has done for our country. And don't you think you are being more than hypocritical? You sit in this magnificent house only because the Führer has made this country prosperous again. All the other political parties were corrupt beyond redemption. Only the Führer could restore Germany's greatness, its very purity. And he has done that. Now the whole world is afraid of us. The Führer is our destiny. And besides, Father, you say you hate war, but you loved telling all your own war stories when I was little.'

'That war was different, Dieter, and you know it. We were only protecting the Fatherland,' Heinrich retorted. 'And don't give me a history lesson. I saw what the French and the British did to us at Versailles. And I remember the Weimar Republic when nobody could afford anything. So, no history lessons from you, young man. Only a fool states the obvious, and I know you are not a fool.' Now Heinrich's voice was louder, and Karla slammed the dining room door shut.

'Dieter,' his father persisted, so involved with his train of thought that he did not even glance up at the sound of the dining room door rocking on its hinges. 'Don't you see, Dieter, it's all come at a cost? Surely we Germans could have thought of another, better' — he searched for the right word — 'less violent way to regain our rightful place in Europe.'

'Father, all revolutions —'

Heinrich cut him off. 'No, Dieter, I know what you're going to say. Some things simply cost too much. Do you really want to live in a state where everything, our thoughts, our ideas, the books we read, even the God we worship, are all controlled by the Führer? Did you have any choice with the Hitler Youth? No, the Führer forced you to join it, like he did every other Aryan.

And now you are just another parrot, Dieter, simply repeating empty words you do not fully understand. They've corrupted your mind, Dieter. All those evening talks about Nazism you attended, the readings from *Mein Kampf*. I suppose your schoolteachers were all party members, too, eh.'

Heinrich's upper lip curled. 'My God, son, did we pay all that money on your education just for you to stop using your brain?'

'Father, you've been listening to those so-called intellectuals down at the Confessing Church, haven't you?' Dieter said.

'And why shouldn't I?' Heinrich said. 'Why should Nazism tell us how we worship? Or whom? Oh, perhaps I shouldn't have said that.' The old man did not bother to hide the sarcasm in his voice. 'Perhaps you'll denounce me, get a promotion.'

'Maybe I will,' Dieter snapped back. His face turned red. 'I am sorry, Father, that was uncalled for. Of course, I would never do such a thing.'

Heinrich nodded. 'But, Son,' he continued quietly, 'I know things are better off now. But again I say to you. At what cost? The state police go too far in repressing opposition. And look at our treatment of the Jews, some of whom had sat at this very dining room table. It is immoral, and one day we will pay a terrible price.'

'Father, I know this is difficult for you to understand, but I truly believe that what the Führer is doing is not only right but necessary. I truly believe that the Jews nearly destroyed our country. They stabbed us in the back in 1918 and they will keep doing so unless we stop them.' His voice rose an octave. 'I could hardly bear their company whenever they dined here, acting as though they were not to blame for the Fatherland's ills.'

His father turned away, sickened by the words his own son was speaking.

Dieter stood up and strode to the window, his body quivering. He carefully poked his head around the heavy chintz blackout curtains so as not to let out any light. He looked out across the manicured lawn to the boulevard. An inky blackness enveloped the city; there were no street or house lights anywhere, a restriction enforced ever since the British Air Force had started their bombing raids. Dahlem, the suburb in which the Lehmanns lived, was far from the industrial core of the city, but the blackout was still strictly enforced. Even Dieter had been angry when Reichsmarschall Göring's promise that no enemy bombs would ever fall on Germany had been exposed as a hollow boast. His father's words had affected him, as they always did. He realized his vitriol against the Jews had not been entirely sincere. He experienced an unwanted feeling of guilt over their treatment, the yellow stars pinned to their chests, their property wantonly destroyed or confiscated by the state. But, he forced himself to conclude, if this was necessary for the good of Germany, then so be it.

The creak of the kitchen door opening was quickly followed by the clink of coffee cups, and Dieter looked over his shoulder to see the whole family at the table waiting for him to join them. Liesl walked over to her brother and took his hand. 'Please. Please, do not be angry.'

As always, his little sister had a way of calming him, and he picked her up and hugged her. He gently placed her on the chair and walked over to the family photographs neatly arranged on the grand piano. He picked up one in particular. He had been so proud when his mother had snapped that photo the day he had been inducted into the Jungvolk, and he smiled wistfully at the pimply faced ten-year-old who looked back at him. The black-and-white photograph hid his oddly coloured eyes—one blue, the other a smoky gray—that had been the butt of many jokes during his childhood. He looked at the long scar on his right cheek, and smiled at how he had imagined that it was the result of a grand Junker-style duel, not a simple bicycle accident, courtesy of Otto, his best friend since childhood. His uniform was slightly too big and it hung on his frame making him even more puny than usual, for unfortunately the uniform could not hide his knobby knees, which poked out between his trousers and stockings like two—how had Otto described them—like two undernourished jellyfish.

Liesl called him to come to the table, and he placed the photograph back in its place and rejoined his family. The three adults sipped their coffees, and Liesl dunked a biscuit into her glass of milk until it was soggy enough for her liking.

Dieter was still angry at his father's obstinacy in not seeing the truth but he contained himself. Surely, Dieter told himself, it would all be worthwhile if Germans could avenge their humiliation by the British and the French and regain their rightful place as the most powerful nation in Europe. He managed a smile for his little sister who now sported a thick white moustache. 'Mother, Father,' Dieter said, 'I apologise for losing my temper. I did not want this evening to be like this. Look, I even wore my Sunday suit, even if it is much too small.' Since leaving school and eating the best food, courtesy of the Parachute Regiment, the young man had added inches to his height and even his chest now threatened to burst through his shirt. Heinrich drew on his pipe and nodded, the closest, Dieter realized with amusement, that his father could ever get to an apology.

'I came here tonight not just for your wonderful cooking, Mother, but to tell you that my battalion is moving out. They have not told us where or when for obvious reasons, and of course I could not tell you if I did know, but I believe it will be happening in the next week or two. We have all completed our training and we are all now fully qualified paratroopers. I do not know when I will return. You know how the army is, Father.' Heinrich smiled at his son, another small act of reconciliation.

There was silence as the family let the news sink in, that now it was their turn to sacrifice for the Reich, whatever that sacrifice might be. His mother very gently blew her nose and dabbed her eyes, and then she looked up as if embarrassed. Liesl came over to her brother and climbed onto his lap. She gently kissed his cheek.

Heinrich coughed and then spoke. 'Dieter, I knew that one day this would come. You know, I've been angry with you since you became a Fallschirmjäger. You could have stayed in the Luftwaffe, and silently I hoped that the regiment would reject you. When you went for your physical examination, I hoped your eyes might convince them you were not sufficiently Aryan. But no, you passed every test they threw at you. It was as though you were pushing yourself beyond some boundary that only you knew about, whether to prove something to yourself or to us it has never been clear to me. And I could never understand why the Paratroopers, one of the most dangerous regiments you could pick. Sometimes I have even thought that you volunteered just because you knew it would make me angry.' Dieter started to speak but his father waved him down. 'But...' He hesitated. 'But, at least you are a member of the best trained and best equipped regiment in the country. And that has to count for something, I suppose.'

Dieter's face reddened. He rarely heard his father speak in this way, his normal authoritarian brusqueness blending with paternal compassion. Dieter gently put Liesl back onto her chair and stood up. 'I too knew this would happen, I even rehearsed what I would say, but now I cannot find the words.' He grinned lopsidedly and his mother fleetingly saw in that smile the little boy whom she loved more than life itself. He glanced at his watch. 'I should go.'

'No, no, Dieter,' his mother said hurriedly. 'You must stay, at least for one more coffee.'

'Really, Mother, I must go. I mustn't miss the last tram,' Dieter said and stood up.

His father walked over to him. The two men shook hands, Heinrich going so far as to grasp his son's right arm. He withdrew to allow his wife to embrace her son. Then Dieter picked up Liesl and kissed her on the nose. 'Now remember, Liebchen, you be good for Mama and Papa, or your big bad brother will hear of it and come back and tickle you till you can't stand it.' He kissed her again and let her down. He looked at his parents and almost in a hurry said his farewells and rushed out of the house, lest they see the tears in his eyes.

The dining room seemed impossibly empty. The two adults looked at each other and Liesl tugged on her mother's dress until she was lifted up. Magda came in. 'I heard what Master Dieter said, and I will pray to God for his safe return.'

'Thank you, Magda. That is very kind of you. Could you, just this once, help Liesl to bed? I know I always do it, but tonight…' Her voice trailed off, and Magda took the little girl's hands and led her upstairs.

'Well, Heinrich, that's that then. Finally, it has happened to us.'

'Yes, and I feel angry that we argued, but he just provokes me so, and if I'd known I wouldn't have jumped, but—'

'You two men, really,' Karla interjected. 'Young men should argue with their fathers. It is part of growing up, of striking out to find their own independence.' She placed her arm around her husband. 'You know, don't you,' she continued, 'that deep down he is still the innocent little boy we raised. There is still goodness in his heart. He is like a magpie, just plucking gaudy phrases like tinfoil from wherever he hears them. He will grow up. Believe me.'

'I hope you are right, my love,' Heinrich said. 'But still I worry. I just hope that he will be able to find a path between the Hitler Youth and what I, you, taught him. I know that there still exists a good and moral being in Dieter. And I pray that one day he will be able to rediscover it.'

'Don't worry about tonight,' Karla said. 'We've got something much more important to worry about now, wouldn't you say?' Her husband nodded, and the two stood in silence, looking at the doorway and knowing that it had not been just a bad dream.

April 1941

Chapter 4

Twilight shaded Ayios Stefanos, and Anastasia took her first real break of the day. Slumped on a bench in the garden, she admired the first fruits of the season beginning to show themselves on the trees. Soon, she would savour again the sweet juice of apricots and plums and enjoy watching her granddaughter as she picked the medlar bushes, the little girl's own special treat, for the adults could never bother with such a tiny fruit. She smiled as Elpida busied herself building a wall of twigs to try to stop a line of ants from reaching their hole.

'Elpida, really what will you think of next?' Anastasia gently chided her granddaughter. 'Come on, little girl, time to get back to work. And wash your hands first before you touch any food.'

Inside, Anastasia pulled an onion off the bunch hanging from a nail on the wall and peeled off the skin. She was about to start slicing when the front door was thrown open and Antoni rushed in.

'Drop everything, Ana,' he cried. 'The Papa wants us all down at the church. Something big is happening. Come, hurry, Woman. Yianni is already there. Bring Elpida, too.'

The three of them dashed out of the house and joined the other villagers already spilling out of the church and onto the square as the church bell summoned them. The odour of incense and candle smoke wafted through the doorway and mingled with the men's tobacco smoke, their cigarettes twinkling in the dusk of the evening. The whole village had shown up: old women in funereal black, old men leaning on gnarled shepherd's crooks, women cradling children in their pinafores, men just rushed in from the fields and still breathless. Different ages, different sexes but all bearing the marks of a hard life; the dirty hands, the etched faces, the ragged working clothes. Antoni grabbed a chair from the kafeneio, and Anastasia nodded her thanks as she plopped down onto it for the rush to the square had left her breathless and she could feel her heart beating through her chest.

There was a surge of villagers from inside the church as Papa Michali, the village's priest, ordered them outside into the square. 'There now all of you can hear me, that's much better,' the priest shouted. He was a portly, middle-aged man, and he wheezed as he tried to make himself heard over the hubbub of the villagers. 'But I want to tell you what has happened. I heard it from the bishop in Chania just this morning. And I believe him, but it is still only rumour, I want you to know that. Still,' he hesitated, 'it does make sense but we can't be sure for certain.'

Antoni whispered into his son's ear. 'Our priest is a good man, but, I swear, he could turn the Ten Commandments into the Erotokritos. My God, he can go on.' Yianni smiled at his father's quip and was about to reply, but the priest was getting at last to the nub of the meeting, and so the young man kept his silence. The two men had to crane their necks to hear him clearly and even Anastasia was forced to stand up if only to snatch the odd word or two. Elpida contented herself with standing on her grandmother's chair.

'The Bishop,' Papa Michali said, now with the crowd's full attention, 'the Bishop told me that the Germans have invaded our sacred homeland, and we have suffered lots of deaths. I know that many of the dead soldiers come from our own small island, God rest their souls. And let us pray our village at least has been spared the misery of fallen children. Now the English and our own brave army are being pushed back by the Germans, and we cannot stop them. The English are holed up in Athens and the German planes are bombing them all the time. I think nothing can stop the Germans from overrunning the mainland and when that happens the English will abandon our country.'

As the import of the priest's words sank in, the villagers were too afraid to believe him and at first cries of denial arose. But Papa Michali was an educated man, the only one in the village and they knew he could be trusted. Village lore even had it that as a young man he had been ordained in Athens and was destined to go to Constantinople for further studies. He was to be a great man of the church, but the lure of the village of his birth had been too much and he had happily applied for and accepted the post of priest of Ayios Stefanos when it had opened, much to the anger and disappointment of his superiors.

Antoni sidled to the front of the crowd. 'But that's good, isn't it,' he asked, his voice quivering. 'That the English are being kicked out of Greece? I mean if the mainland falls, then the Germans won't need to bother with us.' Some of the men murmured in agreement.

The priest continued, as though Antoni had not spoken. 'Our Bishop also says that the English will come here, to Crete. I agree with him.'

But Antoni persisted. 'Papa, with respect, that makes no sense. We're a tiny little island. We've got nothing the Germans want.'

'This is wrong. You're all wrong. Every one of you.' The strident voice of young Christo Papadakis broke through the clamour of voices. Tall compared to the other islanders and forced at a young age to look after himself after his parents had died, Christo had always been an outsider, looked on as something almost freakish, a status sharpened by his always wearing the traditional Cretan costume of baggy trousers, boots and cummerbund, even when he was working in his fields. And he held markedly different political views from the other men, with their conservative and, in his opinion, self-defeating attitudes. 'This is wrong,' he continued, his voice growing louder with each word. 'Why should we give a damn what happens to the English? They don't care about us. They're all filthy, robbing capitalists.'

A groan rose from the men. One shouted, 'Shut up, Christo, just because we don't love your hammer and sickle, you think we're all stupid.'

But Christo would not be silenced. 'I tell you, if we help the English they'll turn their backs on us when it suits them and then we'll be worse off. No, I say let's stop the English from coming to this island, then let's take the Fascists on by ourselves and we will win.'

Papa Michali opened his mouth to respond, but a scuffle of feet and the *tap-tap-tap* of a stick at the back of the crowd made him pause. Walking through the villagers towards the priest, or more accurately walking backwards towards him, was Kosta Vlakakis, a small man in his sixties with a slight hunchback that the children made fun of when he was not around to shake his walking stick at them. Most of the children didn't know his real name; to them he was simply The-Man-Who-Walked-Backwards. When he had adopted this habit many years ago, the villagers had simply decided he was crazy, and perhaps he was, though only a little, and they had gradually become used to it.

Anastasia moved her chair aside to let him pass. Many years ago—exactly when she could no longer remember—she had turned a corner on the outskirts of the village and bumped headlong into Kosta's back. The bag of eggs she was carrying fell to the ground and splattered into the dirt. She confronted the man, telling him that this walking backwards was just silly nonsense and he should act like an adult for once. He just stood in front of her and apologized for the accident. But as the preternatural calm of the man engulfed her and her anger melted away, she had quietly asked him why he always walked backwards. Kosta slowly pulled on his cigarette and leaned on his shepherd's crook. With a trace of a smile he had told her that looking back meant he never had to face what was coming up, and since the past was always more comfortable than the future if only because it was over, this preferred mode of approach suited him to the ground. It was then that Anastasia realized that The-Man-Who-Walked-Backwards was a lot cleverer than he appeared.

Kosta stopped next to Papa Michali. He looked for permission to speak, and the priest nodded. Kosta hesitated and pulled up his trousers, adjusting his thick brown belt so it was more comfortable. He then cleared his throat and spoke almost in a whisper. 'You think I'm a little crazy, but I'm not. I listen to everything and I see most things.' He took a sip of the wine Papa Michali offered him. The men and women stared at him transfixed, silent, for Kosta only spoke when he had something to say. 'First of all, Comrade Christo,' he continued with a sly smile, 'I know passion burns in your soul, and that is a good thing in a young man. And perhaps I agree with you, the English are no friends of ours despite what our betters may tell us.

'But Christo, don't you see?' His voice was low but still it cut through the crowd. 'You think the English are just as bad as the Germans.' Christo opened his mouth but Kosta impatiently waved him down and continued. 'But you are wrong.' Kosta raised his voice and stared at the young man. 'You are wrong. The Germans are coming. And God help us. You've heard what they did to our army on the mainland. They think nothing can stop them. Our Bishop and our dear Papa make a lot of sense. We think we're an insignificant little island but we're not. We're quite the opposite, in fact. You see, once the English are kicked out of the mainland, and they will be, that's a fact, they will have to make for Egypt, and Crete is right between the two. Plus, whichever army controls Crete controls this part of the Mediterranean. So, friends, I think the war is coming to us, and it's coming soon. And Christo,' he said and his eyes narrowed as he looked at the young villager. 'What choice do we have? You know we can't beat the Germans by ourselves. So, let's help the English when they come. They will come, you know. And when the Germans have gone, then we'll worry about the English.'

As Kosta stopped speaking, the villagers broke into individual conversations. Papa Michali gave up trying to bring some order, so he sat down by the altar, wiped the sweat from his brow with a faded linen handkerchief and gulped down the large glass of wine his wife had filled for him.

Ten minutes later, as the villagers again turned their attention to him, Papa Michali wiped his beard of excess wine, belched and stood up. 'Please, listen to me, please,' he shouted. 'I agree with Kosta. I studied in Athens, when I was a young man, I know,' he said with a smile, 'many years ago. And I know people, people who perhaps are a little wiser than us. And I believe them about the Germans coming. Look, do we have a choice if the Germans come? We will need all the help we can get, and the English are our friends, that I believe.' He hesitated. 'This is very important, please listen. This is very important. If the Germans come, they will not be our friends. I've heard enough to know that they are monsters and yes, I am afraid that we will have to fight them. I will pray it does not come to that. But I promise that I will let all of you know what is happening as soon as I know. In the meantime, just in case, I ask you to gather together your guns and anything else you might have to fight them with. I will not ring this church bell again unless something terrible has happened. If you hear the bell, drop everything and come to the plateia ready to fight. Now, let us all pray.'

Christo pushed himself forward. 'Pray, that's all you fools do, pray. God has really listened to you in the past, hasn't he?' The villagers crossed themselves at Christo's words, and shouted at him to be silent. He stalked off by himself, muttering that they were all fools.

The villagers dispersed, and Elpida gripped her grand-mother's hand as the family made its way back home. For while the little girl did not understand what had happened in the church except that something was wrong. But she was afraid to ask, and her grandmother kept silent. The men too kept their own counsel. Antoni halted as they turned into the alley to their house and told his wife and granddaughter to go on alone. They then walked back to the kafeneio for their evening coffees. The serving woman, Eleni Apostolakis, smiled at Yianni, bowing low so that her breast slightly brushed his shoulder. He said nothing. After she had left, the two men sipped their coffee and helped themselves to a small flask of raki that the kafeneio owner had brought over.

'I am not sure she could be more obvious, Yianni,' Antoni said.

'I know. She's getting worse every day. I just wish she could understand that I'm not interested in her, in any woman.'

'Well, do not go that far, you are still young and every man does need a good woman. Give it time, I know the pain of losing Maria is still there.' Antoni smiled. 'Just make sure it's not Eleni you turn to.'

'Trust me. That will never happen. I do feel sorry for her though, her mother and father both dying before their time, and then losing her children and her husband in that horrible accident. Still, she hasn't made it easy for us to help her. And you know, I'm not the only man she's gone after, don't you? Christo even told me she's thrown her net over some of the other villages, too. I just feel sorry for her. It's all a little pathetic.'

'Yianni,' Antoni said, pulled hard on his cigarette. 'Yianni, I think I was wrong to say what I did at the church. I've thought a little more about what the Papa and Kosta said, and they have convinced me. The Germans will come. So now it is our turn, my son. I am sure that soon we will know of the death and violence that our fathers and grandfathers told us as we sat on their laps in the cold winter nights before the fire. We will be tested, each of us, as they were before us, but we are ready for that struggle. You and I will protect our family, we will protect our island, and, God willing, you shall live to tell your tales to your own grandchildren.'

'Baba,' said Yianni, his brow furrowed. 'I don't think I've ever heard you speak like this before. You sound as though you are at a funeral. Sorry. That was silly of me. But you are serious aren't you, Baba? You really think the Germans will come, and come soon?'

Antoni nodded. 'My God, it's quiet here tonight,' he said. 'Normally this place would be too loud to hear yourself think. But now look at it.' Yianni turned and looked at the men, each of them mostly content to drink their coffee and smoke their cigarettes, wrapped in their own private thoughts, their own hopes, their own fears.

Yet the next day dawned as always. The sun rose over the hills and splashed the village in a heavenly brightness. Men and women had to shade their eyes just to talk to each other, and the heat bounced back from the walls of the village houses forcing everybody to hurry about their business so they could shelter for their afternoon siestas with a clear conscience.

Anastasia and Elpida's morning rituals included fetching water. That morning the two of them made their way through the myriad of lanes to the village fountain just off the plateia, a favourite gathering place for the women of the village. Two large stone benches had been built on either side of the pump head, which was set into a limestone wall. Letters had been carved into the wall. Anastasia had told Elpida that they had been written by the Ottomans many centuries ago. Elpida did not know who the Ottomans were but she liked their writing. It was full of pretty curls and spirals that reminded her of the vine leaves that swirled in intricate patterns around her grandfather's trellises. They found nobody else at the fountain, so Elpida had no choice but to grab the handle—this was always her job, one she never looked forward to—and to begin the laborious task of bringing up the wonderfully cool and clear water from the earth's depths. When the water at last began to flow into the ewers, Elpida and her grandmother were joined by Eleni Apostolakis. Elpida admired Eleni's waist-length gun-barrel hair and her high cheek-bones, her skin still untouched by the wrinkles of age and resignation. She knew the other village women tried to avoid Eleni whenever possible and thought they were simply jealous of her looks. But, of course, Elpida did not know in her innocence—for the little girl was still of an age when beauty spoke of virtue—of the constant rumours that flew around Eleni. Nothing had ever been proven but as in all small communities it was easier, and more enjoyable, to keep the rumour alive than to kill it for lack of evidence. Eleni set down her ewer to await her turn at the fountain. She smiled at Elpida who began to talk to her, but when she saw her grandmother's face harden, she immediately turned away. Anastasia ordered her granddaughter to pick up the water jugs and pushed Elpida away from the fountain and up the street to her home. Anastasia bustled Elpida inside and slammed a water jug down so hard that the old table creaked and dust flew up from the crack in its top.

'For Goodness sake, little girl,' she shouted as her granddaughter sat down. 'Stop playing with your hair. You do it all the time. You'll go bald, and then what man will want to marry you?'

Elpida pushed the unruly lock of hair back from her eyes. 'Yiayia, can I help Papa Michali at the church?' Her voice was choked with tears. Anastasia nodded, and the girl beat a retreat.

Anastasia knew she had treated her granddaughter unfairly and that she should make it up to her. But Elpida did not know, and never would, that Eleni had flirted with her father at many village celebrations, even before his own wife had died, and she thanked God again that only her son's good sense and devotion to his wife had stopped him from falling into Eleni

Apostolakis's web. But on this occasion it wasn't just her anger at the Apostolakis woman. The episode with Eleni had simply been the catalyst, she knew that. It was the meeting last night, and the dire prophecies that Papa Michali and Kosta had spoken of. She felt as though her world was constricting around her, as though something physical was pressing on her, restricting her breathing, even her capacity to think. Anastasia needed time to herself, so she left the house and walked up the road away from the village into the fields. Occasionally, she stopped to pick a bunch of horta for a salad and stuff them into her apron. She saw some snails still sucking in the last of the morning dew, promising that perhaps tomorrow she and Elpida would gather some for lunch.

Stopping to catch her breath, Anastasia leant against a stone wall and looked around her. The mountains still carried the last sprinkling of snow, and the olive-covered hills stretched languidly to the sea, sometimes crossed by gullies full of impenetrable thickets, fed by the spring waters that burst unbidden from the earth or the water that cascaded from the mountains. She recalled a letter her brother Spiro had sent many years ago, not long after he had arrived in America. He described how the flat grasslands of his new country stretched out in every direction, so unbroken that you could almost see the oceans that encircled them. How different that land was from Crete. She believed that it was still the most beautiful land in God's kingdom, despite never having ventured much from her village. But perhaps, she thought, God had visited so much woe on the islanders to remind them of the Sin of Pride and she crossed herself in penance at the thought. Anastasia looked towards the sea: flat, pellucid, beckoning her with its serenity. She knew that soon that same tranquil sea would bring the invaders, just like the Papa had promised. How many times had that happened in the past; how many times would that happen in the future, long after her bones mingled with the dust of her ancestors? Every

Cretan knew by heart the stories of past struggles against the Ottomans, of brave Cretans dying for their island's freedom, of the horrific cruelties the Turks inflicted on any who stood against them, the public hangings, the impaling on stakes, the flaying while the victim was still alive. At least, she comforted herself, the Germans, if they did come, would not be barbarians, for surely no enemy could rival the Turks in cruelty. Anastasia crossed herself again and carried on with her walk.

Her destination was a small, whitewashed chapel that overlooked Ayios Stefanos, a place she sought refuge in whenever life was too hard to bear. She pushed open the wooden door and smelt the familiar mustiness and stale incense smoke. Hanging on the walls were miniatures of legs and arms, looking like dissected children's dolls, some of them carved from olive wood, others moulded in clay. Wrapping herself in the protecting silence of God, she crossed herself and gave thanks to Him for curing her villagers of the afflictions the miniatures represented. Anastasia lit a candle and placed it in the small metal box filled with sand, its delicate flame sending shadows that licked the tarnished silver of the icons. Kneeling at the altar she prayed that she, her family and above all little Elpida would be safe from the coming conflict. She asked God for guidance for what to do in the coming days and weeks, but just like every other time she had prayed for His help, none came.

Chapter 5

Easter is the holiest observance in Greece, more important even than Christmas. As the bell tolled midnight that Easter Saturday, Papa Michali lit the candles that each of the villagers held. They were glad when they were able to light the bonfire and see the flames devour the Judas effigy on top of the woodpile, for a late April wind blew through the village and chilled them. Wine and raki began to flow, and cheese pies were shared. But this year the village's joyousness was clouded by the events across the Aegean. The adults felt little like celebrating; only the children enjoyed themselves as they did each year.

As Elpida ran around the bonfire with the other children, Anastasia smiled at her son next to her. 'I think sometimes that not having a mother has not hurt her at all,' she whispered.

Yianni bent down and kissed his mother gently on the cheek. 'She has a real mother, Mama, you. And no woman could have been a better mama. Little Elpida is happy and loved. And she knows too that her mama is watching over her and waiting for when she joins her in Heaven.' He turned his head away, and after a moment's silence he said, 'Mama, I need to go for a little while. Look after Elpida, yes?' Before she could answer, he hurried away. Antoni walked over and was about to speak, but Anastasia shook her head. He shrugged his shoulders, and took another swig of raki.

Kosta Vlakakis shuffled towards them, the *tap-tap* of his stick announcing his presence. He slumped onto a bench. 'Christ is risen.' He offered them the Easter greeting.

'Truly he is risen,' they replied.

Kosta chewed on a pie. The soft yellow cheese squirted between the gaps in his rotted black teeth and dribbled onto his chin. He licked at it and finally wiped away the sticky cheese with his fingers, which he then snacked on, slowly and noisily.

'Well, that was good.' He burped. 'At my age, food is one of my last pleasures. Glad to know my teeth still work. Not like everything else.' He winked at Antoni and laughed, and more cheese bubbled through his lips. Kosta hesitated. 'Well, we know where he's off to,' he said, nodding in the direction Yianni had taken. He stuffed more pie into his mouth.

'Is it that obvious?' Antoni probed.

Well, of course, it is,' Kosta said, as more half-chewed cheese sprayed Antoni's chest. 'But I wouldn't worry, my friends. Christo and Yianni are the same age, they are both single, they like each other's company. I know you worry that Christo may turn Yianni's head and, yes, Christo does have a big communist mouth but he's still one of us at heart. I think he likes to say things just to get us old folks angry. He succeeds most of the time, but if you ignore him or flatter him or, even better, pretend like you care what he's talking about, he goes away in the end. I think he just wants to be noticed. It can't have been easy being raised by an old aunt, with no father or mother.'

'Well, I hope you're right,' Anastasia said, 'but I'm not convinced. I do worry that Christo is a bad influence.'

Antoni placed an arm around his wife. 'He will be fine.' He hoped he had convinced her even if he could not convince himself.

Kosta looked at Antoni. 'My friend, you didn't agree with the Papa at the church, about what we should do when the Germans come, but last night at the kafeneio, I heard you and Yianni talking about what you would have to do when the Germans come. Why did you change your mind?'

Antoni took a long drag on his cigarette. 'Well, my friend, you and the Papa did make a lot of sense at the church, and I suppose that changed my mind a little. But...' he hesitated. 'But there's something more to it than that. Maybe I'm just an old man and at my age things look blacker than they perhaps are, but I just have a feeling in my bones that the worst will happen to us.' He crossed himself. 'I don't know why. I mean, look, the Germans are bad, and we will fight them, as we should, but their vengeance on us, on the whole island, will be horrible. There is no way out of this for us, Kosta. We've lost control of our fate, not that I really believe we ever had any. And I think that this time we are on our own, truly on our own. And this time, and God forgive me for saying this, I'm not sure God will be enough.'

Kosta chuckled. 'And to think I came over here to cheer myself up. I need another drink.' He stood up and ambled away.

Anastasia and Antoni watched their granddaughter and her friends for a little longer, but the conversation with Kosta had dampened their spirits and they decided to make their way back home. Elpida had protested but as soon as she slumped into the chair by the fireplace she gave a huge yawn and within a minute was fast asleep. Antoni gently lifted her up and placed her on her pallet bed in the corner of the living room. He smiled at the thought that since the bad news had roiled the village, his granddaughter, without explanation had started sleeping there rather than in her father's tiny room. Anastasia and Antoni went outside to sit on the rough stone bench that lined the edge of their house and enjoy the smell of cooked lamb and goat wafting through the village.

Anastasia looked at her husband and slipped her arm under his. 'I am worried, Husband. About Yianni. You remember what Christo said in the church. He is a madman and he will pull Yianni down with him. And I don't care what Kosta just said. About Christo being harmless.'

'You may be right, Wife, you may be right.' Antoni said. He drew deep on a straggly cigarette and delicately picked small shreds of tobacco off his tongue. 'But there's nothing we can do. Yianni is a grown man, out of our control. Yianni will do what he wants to do, and over that we have no control. Still, I will pray for him.' He paused. 'And for the three of us, as well.'

Yianni followed a narrow track that led out of the village. The sounds of the celebrations had become muted when he heard footsteps behind him. He turned to see Eleni Apostolakis. She had let her hair down and the top of her blouse was unbuttoned.

'Eleni, are you all right?' he asked.

'Where are you going?' she asked him.

Yianni stopped. 'Well, to Christo's but why do you care?'

Eleni pushed the hair from her eyes and took a deep breath. 'Ah, yes, little Christo. No, you're right. I don't care.'

She moved towards Yianni, close enough for him to smell the wine on her breath. He stepped back, but she pressed forward and held her mouth up to his. He grasped her arms to prevent her coming closer.

'I am sorry, Eleni. But no. I cannot do this. You may think it stupid but I am still married to Maria. I am sorry.'

Eleni shrugged off Yianni's grip and slapped him hard on his cheek. 'No, that's not the reason,' she shouted. 'Your sweet, little Maria has been dead too long for that. No, that's not the reason. I'll tell you why you reject me. You think like the other men. You think I'm a whore who throws herself at them. Well, I'm not. Though I might as well be.' She spat in his face and ran back up the street.

Yianni stood frozen, staring at Eleni until she disappeared from view. The meeting had ended almost as soon as it had begun. Shaking his head and trying to tell himself that what had just happened actually had, he resumed his walk, down into an olive grove and then to a small shack lit from the inside by a kerosene lamp. The door to the shack was open and Yianni entered. Christo stood up to welcome him, their long shadows playing against the bare walls.

'I won't say, "Happy Easter," my friend.' Christo grinned. 'It's all superstitious nonsense. My God, Yianni, you look like you've seen a ghost. Is everything okay?'

Yianni nodded. 'Something strange just happened. Eleni Apostolakis just threw herself at me.'

'Please tell me you're not complaining,' Christo said. 'I wouldn't mind getting hold of that little beauty.'

'Well, I told her no. And then she got really angry and stalked off. She even spat at me. Spat at me. She was drunk, but still. I don't know what to make of it.'

Christo pulled at his moustache. 'Of course, you do, Yianni. You just won't admit it. I know how you still feel about Maria. But she's been gone a long time. It isn't right for a man to go so long without a woman. And I know Maria would understand.'

'Christo, you are my friend, but do not say that ever again. I mean it.' Yianni's words were sharp.

After a moment of silence, Christo said, 'I am sorry. I did not mean to hurt you. And I am still glad to see you. Are the fools still celebrating by the way?'

'No, not really.' Yianni said. 'Nobody is in the mood. Oh, they're going through the rituals as though everything in our little world is unchanged, but that's about it. Deep down they know what's going to happen. They just won't admit it openly. I can't blame them.' He grinned. 'Even Papa Michali is sober, and you know how he likes to drink.'

'Which reminds me,' Christo said. 'Come and have a drink. I made this raki just last year and it is still good and harsh.'

The two men sat down at the kitchen table, and Christo poured the clear liquid into two small glasses. They ritually rapped the bottoms of their glasses on the table, shouted 'Yiamas' and swallowed the drinks in one gulp.

'You weren't joking, my friend. That is rough. How the Hell can you drink it,' Yianni said between coughs.

'Practice, my son, practice,' Christo said with a grin on his face.

Yianni stood up and gazed through the open door into the blackness beyond. 'Christo,' he said, 'are you serious about what you said? That the English are as bad as the Germans?'

Christo pursed his brow. "Yes, I was,' he said. 'I know you might disagree with me but I really believe that. They want to be our friends now, I know, but the English don't care about us at all. Our little island is just a place for them to try to keep their empire. And if they do win here, nothing will change for the better.'

'My friend,' Yianni spoke slowly, 'none of us can stop the English or the Germans from coming if they decide to. You know that, don't you? My father told me that the Germans are really bad people and that if we have to make peace with the English, so be it. And what have the English ever done to harm us, Christo? Really, why do they make you so angry? And if they come to our island it will be to help us. So I say let's join them and fight the Germans.'

Christo lit the butt of a cigarette and inhaled deeply. 'Because the English enslave the people in their Empire, they enslave their own people. All the wealth they have and still their workers go hungry. Look, I'm not stupid. If I ruled the world, we'd beat the English and then the Germans. But I don't, unfortunately. And so we must choose between two evils and help the English, if only for now. But I can tell you. It will be a Devil's pact. That I know for sure.'

'But why did you say what you said about fighting both the English and the Germans at the church?' Yianni pressed him.

'To piss them off. That's all.' Christo smiled. 'The men in our village are so smug, they really think that it's just us versus them, good versus bad, right versus evil. And it's not, it's a hell of a lot more complicated.'

'So, you will fight the Germans?' Yianni asked.

'Of course, I will fight, you idiot. I love Crete and I love our village, despite what everybody says about me. I just like to piss 'em off, keep Papa Michali and the other men guessing about me. But I am serious about the English. They are not our friends.'

Yianni shook his head and smiled at his friend. 'It's a good job I like you. You should have at least one friend in Ayios Stefanos.'

Christo refilled their glasses and together they toasted their eternal friendship.

The first traces of dawn were appearing when Yianni left Christo. In the village a cock crowed as if beckoning the young Cretan back home. The raki had kept his mind sharp, and he walked slowly, pondering what Christo and he had talked about. He knew a fight was coming; he just hoped he would not disgrace himself or his family.

Chapter 6

The celebration of the Resurrection of the Son of God was the start of the village's seasonal resurrection. The bright yellow oxalis and clover no longer blanketed the village's fields, and the rocky soil began again to dominate the landscape. To the south the last of the mountain snow reminded the villagers of how harsh the winter had been, but in only a few short weeks even the highest slopes would regain their customary brownness. Women sat outside to do their chores, enjoying the spring sun; men repaired the winter damage, whitewashing a wall here, fixing a broken shutter there, and readied their flock for the annual migration into their summer upland pastures.

Early one morning, together with their young helper, Alexi Doukakis, Antoni and Yianni loaded up a donkey with lumber, tools and enough food for a week and set out into the mountains, their destination the family mitata or cheese hut. The journey took two days, crossing from the lowland lushness of late spring to the harsh barrenness of the mountains. As Antoni had feared, the powerful winter winds had blown in the hut's wooden door, and even though a door would scarcely be necessary in a month's time, early summer storms could still bring torrential rains. The three men worked for two days until Antoni was satisfied with the repairs. In past years Yianni had been the one to stay on the high mountain pastures with the sheep and goats, living in the small hut alone where he would milk the ewes and make the cheese, and guarding the flock against the wild dogs and vultures that would try to carry off the lambs. But this year, Antoni had ordered Yianni to stay with the family and Alexi serve in his place, living in the upland pastures all summer, relieved only by Yianni who would occasionally bring him food and news of the village. Alexi Doukakis liked the solitude of the high mountains and the responsibility of shepherding the flock. He was proud that he knew all the village's best summer pastures, as well as the huts with the best cheeses in them. He was especially grateful that he would be alone, as he suffered from a stammer when he got excited, and sometimes the teasing of the villagers, especially from the small children whose taunts could be particularly harsh, was too much.

While the Manoulakis men had labored in the mountains, Anastasia and Elpida had been busy too. Each morning they tended to the garden as the young shoots grew ever taller. Yet the weeds always grew faster than their vegetables, and even Elpida complained that her back was throbbing with pain. Besides the weeding, Elpida had to water the apricot, plum and medlar trees that would provide rich and succulent fruit as the heat of summer turned its full force on the island.

One evening, soon after the men had returned from the mountains, Anastasia and Elpida, tired from another hard day of work, sat on the low stone bench, revelling in the shade. Anastasia mopped sweat from her brow, and Elpida sipped on a cup of water while Wawa curled contentedly on the little girl's lap. Five of Anastasia's orphans lay curled up at the old woman's feet.

'Yiayiaka,' Elpida said. 'I heard Baba and Papouka speak last night. Are we?' She hesitated. 'Are we going to be all right? You know, when the Germans come.'

Anastasia turned her head away and looked up and down the street as though she might find the right words lying on the ground, waiting to be picked up and spoken. After a long pause, she gently said, 'Yes, little girl, everything will be all right.' She kissed her granddaughter. 'Men like to talk. And sometimes,' she chuckled, 'they don't think before they talk.' Elpida gasped. 'Yes, little girl, even your Baba and Papouka. But don't you ever tell them I said that. We'll be fine, little one. Anyway I'm not sure the Germans will even come. Why should our poor little island be of interest to them? But if they do come, the English will certainly help us, for they are good people. The English love the Greeks, even you, Elpida.' The little girl's eyes opened wide. 'Do not worry, my love, the English will keep us safe. Papa Michali told Papouka that just the other day. They'll protect us. So, we'll be fine. And anyway, do you really think Baba and Papouka would let any harm come to you? Now, little girl, you are too serious for one so young. And on a beautiful day like this.'

Anastasia looked into her granddaughter's face, wiped away a speck of dirt from the corner of the girl's eye, and kissed her forehead.

'Now, little one, let's talk about happier things. Did I tell you that Uncle Spiro sent me a letter all the way from America? I got it just this morning and was saving it for a time like this. Come inside and I'll read it to you.'

'Yiayiaka,' Elpida squealed, for tales about Spiro were her favorite stories. They were even better than the stories from the Bible Papa Michali read to her and the other village children every Sunday, although she hadn't told anybody that, especially her yiayia.

'Yiayiaka, Please tell me. Is he as handsome as ever, and Aunt Maria is she still beautiful? Oh, I do want to see them. Do you think we can, Yiayiaka? Or perhaps they can come here and stay with us. I'd make them cheese pies and Baba could roast a lamb and...'

'Slow down, Elpida. Really you are worse than an old woman. You're worse than me.' Anastasia cackled at her own joke. 'Come inside and we'll have a little talk while the men are away. Yes?'

'Yiayiaka, tell me again about Uncle Spiro. And don't leave anything out.' Elpida tossed Wawa onto the floor, and the cat sulked off into a corner. Elpida cuddled into her grandmother and felt the old woman stroke her hair. Absent-mindedly the little girl picked out a little ball of snot and rolled it between her fingers before she flicked it away, hoping her yiayia had not seen her.

Anastasia looked at the photograph of her older brother that sat on the small table next to the fireplace. Spiro's hair was grey and he had a slight stoop. Still, it did not take away from the handsomeness she remembered, or the strength of his shoulders as he carried her around the village when she was a little girl. Behind the frame she had collected the letters he had sent her over the years.

'Well, little girl,' Anastasia began, 'Uncle Spiro says in the letter that everybody in the family is well, and their business is making lots of money. He has been reading all about the war in Europe in American newspapers and he says he and Aunt Maria pray every day that it will be over soon. Uncle Spiro also says he is glad that cousin Alex is in America and won't have to fight. Also—'

Elpida interrupted her grandmother. 'One day I'm going there, to Uncle Spiro's house. I'm sure he'd like to see me. Tell me about him again.'

'Okay, little girl,' Anastasia relented, for she never tired of talking about her brother. 'He was a very brave man to leave our village. He didn't want to go, but times were bad then, just like they are now, and he didn't have a choice. I was too young to go with him, I was even younger than you are now, and our parents were too,' she searched for the right word—*afraid* was correct but unspeakable—'too old to leave their village.

'Well, he took a boat all the way across the ocean to America and he got married to Aunt Maria and they have a daughter, Anastasia, named after me—that was nice of Uncle Spiro wasn't it—and a son, Alex, Alexander after his grandfather, my baba. And Alex works with Uncle Spiro in their business. Well, at first when Uncle Spiro and Aunt Maria went to America it was hard. Uncle Spiro used to be a miner, you know, someone who digs rocks for people to use. And it was really hard for them because they were very young, and the people who owned the mines were bad, and...' Anastasia stopped. There was no point for Elpida to know any more, although many times she had wanted to tell her granddaughter how Spiro had nearly been killed fighting the bosses in America.

'Anyway, now Uncle Spiro and Alex bring in olive oil from Greece and Italy and sell it to rich Americans. And they live in a big house by the sea.'

Elpida looked with longing at the picture of the house that sat next to her uncle's photo. It was bigger than anything in their village, bigger than anything she had ever seen.

Elpida laid her head on Anastasia's chest and slowly drifted into sleep. The old woman, lulled by the regularity of Elpida's breathing, let her memories take her back to that horrible day forty years ago when Spiro had left. She had awoken from a broken night, looking at the ceiling stones, blurred through the sleep in her eyes. She had rubbed her eyes and turned to see Spiro's empty bed, unwilling to believe what had happened. But when she saw his bag was no longer next to his bed, where he always kept it, she knew as though for the first time, like a clap of thunder waking her from a dream, that her older brother had really left her. She had known for many weeks that this morning would come but, young though she was, she had been able to explain it away as what Spiro had always told her it would be; the start of a big adventure for him and then his return to their family home, full of American riches and stories that would keep them all entertained over the long winter months in front of their little fireplace. But as the weeks of his absence turned into months and then into years, Anastasia knew Spiro was never coming home.

Anastasia gazed around at her little room, full of love but still threadbare and shabby, until her eyes fixed on the photograph of her brother's house in America. When she had first seen the three-storey house, with its sweeping lawn and swimming pool, she had felt anger, not just anger at her own lot in life but also anger—and envy—at his success. For many years she had silently blamed her parents for not allowing her to join her brother on his great adventure. But as she grew older, the anger crystallized into a self-contempt for being a female incapable of acting on her own, of being a female who had to do her duty and comply with whatever her family expected of her, regardless of her own wishes. As many times before, she wondered what she could have done with her life had she been given the chance. Her marriage to Antoni had assuaged, if only a little, that anger, for it had brought her own family and its own responsibilities. But the feeling that she would never do anything of consequence—that being a loving wife and mother was sometimes not enough— never quite left her. The anger was a constant niggling, like a callused foot stuffed into a new leather shoe. And now, as Elpida and she talked of Spiro all those miles away, safe in America and a long way from this latest war, those calluses pushed hard into her soul, into her very being.

Elpida yawned and her grandmother told her it was time for bed. The little girl nodded, her eyes barely open, and she tucked herself in. As Elpida drifted into sleep, Yianni came into the house and saw the pile of photos and letters lying open. 'Daydreaming about California again, are we?' He grinned at his mother and knelt down to pat his daughter's hair.

'Yiayia was telling me,' Elpida said through yawns, 'about Uncle Spiro and what a brave man he was.'

'He probably still is, little girl. Yes, he was very brave to fight the bad men in America. He is a palikari, a real warrior. I hope I can be like him.'

Elpida raised her head at her father's words. 'Why, Baba, is something bad going to happen?'

'No, little girl,' he said quickly. 'Everything is good. So, don't worry. Go to sleep now, little one.' He turned to his own mother.

'Mama, I'm going to meet Baba at the kafeneio. Perhaps we shall hear some news.'

Anastasia waited until Yianni had left and then she climbed the stairs to bed to toss restlessly for another night, hopeful yet fearful of what was to come.

The next day Anastasia and Elpida were occupied, as usual, with weeding. The ground was stony, and the weeds seemed to delight in wrapping themselves around each little rock, frustrating both of them. The sweat ran into their eyes, and Anastasia was wiping her forehead for the second time in as many minutes when she heard the deep rumblings of large vehicles and a strange metallic clanking as though the village blacksmith was in the middle of a particularly big and especially loud job. The noises, which seemed to originate in the plateia, suddenly subsided, and Anastasia could now clearly hear the shouts and cries of men speaking in a language she did not recognise. Throwing down their trowels, Anastasia and Elpida rushed to the square where they saw three army lorries disgorging heavily armed soldiers. Strange contraptions that Anastasia guessed had been the source of the clanking were parked in front of the church, their engines puffing out clouds of blue smoke. Antoni and Yianni joined the two women, as the whole village looked at the scene in front of them. Antoni told Anastasia they were English soldiers from New Zealand, from the other side of the world, and they were their friends and had come here to fight the Germans. She pointed at the big metal things and Yianni told her they were called tanks. She looked at the heavy armour plating and the large gun barrel sticking out of the top of the vehicle and nodded in awe. But what impressed her most was their lack of wheels, which had been replaced by, so far she could tell, by a continuous reel of joined metal plates, one on each side of the vehicle.

Almost inaudibly, Anastasia spoke to her husband. 'So, our worst fears are coming true, aren't they? There will be a war on our little island, after all.'

Her husband nodded, remaining silent as he and the other villagers continued to watch the spectacle in front of them.

The soldiers had been ordered to form up in three lines. They all were dressed alike, even down to the large, wide-brimmed hats that most of them wore pulled down low over their faces. They all carried rifles, and long bayonets dangled from their belts. Most of the soldiers were fair-skinned, but one group was lined up separately from the others. These men had very dark, almost black, skins, and each one of them seemed to be a giant, even bigger than the other soldiers, who themselves towered over the village men. Anastasia crossed herself and prayed that these men would always be on her side.

A soldier with a luxuriant, ginger-haired moustache detached himself from the rest of the men and in very halting Greek asked to talk to the mayor. Papa Michali pushed himself though the crowd.

'Sir, we have no mayor in this little village,' Michali used the little English he knew.' But I am the priest and I can speak for them.'

'Thank you. I am Major John Durrant of the New Zealand Expeditionary Force.' He tossed a half smile at the priest. 'My orders are to occupy this village. Please tell your people that we mean them no harm. We are here only to help them in any way we can.'

Papa Michali translated the young officer's words to the crowd and a buzz of excitement echoed around the square.

Durrant continued, his tone hardening. 'We will disturb you as little as possible, although I would appreciate your help in finding houses for my men.'

The priest did not follow every word but he understood enough to know that this was an order not a request.

'Of course, sir,' Papa Michali nodded. 'We will be pleased to help in any way we can. Perhaps, however, we can do this tomorrow as it is late? We must ready our houses for you and your men.'

'Tomorrow will be fine,' Durrant agreed. He saluted the priest and moved away to give orders for patrols to be placed around the village and for the men to bivouac in the square for the night.

Back in their house, the three Manoulakis adults sat by the fireplace and looked at each other.

'Despite all the talk from the Papa, I really did not think this would happen, you know, that we'd actually go to war. Or that the war could come to us.' Antoni broke the silence.

'And so quickly, and so unexpectedly,' his wife added.

Elpida, who refused to lie still while all this hubbub went on round her, climbed onto her baba's knee. He stroked her hair and kissed the top of her head.

'Baba,' Elpida said through a yawn, 'tell me about Mama, I love hearing about her.'

Yianni smiled. 'Pethi mou, we are all tired, perhaps tomorrow?'

'Please, Baba, tell me what Mama looked like and how you fell in love with her, please?'

'All right, little girl, I will. Mama was beautiful. She had long black hair, just like yours and when she smiled the sun hid behind a cloud because she was too dazzling.'

Elpida giggled. 'Tell me about how you tripped over Papouka. The first time you saw Mama, it is so funny.'

'Well, you know this story, but I'll tell you if you promise to go to bed and sleep. Okay?' The little girl nodded.

'Well, I saw her in the street, I was with Papouka, and she was pulling her donkey, and you know donkeys and the thing wouldn't move, and so I thought I'd be a big man and I went over to help her, but as I pulled on the rope, the stupid thing decided to move anyway, and I flew backward and I banged into

Papouka, and he flew backwards and both of us landed on our backsides, and the whole village was laughing and Papouka was yelling at me and your Mama was laughing so hard that she had to sit down.'

Elpida burst out laughing, and even Anastasia and Antoni grinned along with her.

'Well,' Yianni continued, 'I was so embarrassed that I just stood up and ran away and for the next month I prayed I wouldn't run into Mama. But I did, finally, and we talked and she laughed and she smiled and that is when I knew I loved her.'

'Baba,' Elpida said. 'Why did she leave us?'

Yianni was silent. 'I don't know for sure, my love,' he finally said, ' but I think that she was so beautiful and so kind and gentle that God decided that she needed to be with the angels. But she's waiting for us, you know that, don't you, and she looks over us. And every time you see the stars in the sky, remember that one of them is Mama, looking down at you.'

The little girl's eyes filled with tears and she snuggled into her baba's chest. Soon her breathing became shallow, and Yianni gently lowered her onto her bed and pulled over a sheet.

'Thank you, my son,' Anastasia said. 'The little girl needed to hear that.'

Yianni smiled and looked off into the distance while he smoked a cigarette. He remained quiet and Anastasia stole a glance at her husband, knowing what was going to happen. Yianni did not fail her. Without saying a word he abruptly stood up and left.

'Well, no need to ask where he is going,' Anastasia commented, almost to herself.

'What happens now, husband? Now that the English are here.' she asked.

Antoni pursed his eyebrows and gazed at the ashes in the fireplace as if trying to find some guidance.

'We wait, my love, we wait. And then pray that all will be

well. What else can we do?'

He lit the butt of a straggly cigarette and together with his wife sat in silence and waited for the new day.

May 1941

Chapter 7

The dawn was still a vague hint in a dark sky when the ship's engines throttled down. The bellows of sergeants rousing the men from the bunks echoed through the decks, and, startled, Paul Cuthbertson sat up and—not for the first time during the voyage—bashed his head on the bed frame above him. His stomach rumbled in time with the throbs of his headache, and he scratched at the mixture of sweat and dirt that seemed to cover every inch of his body. He'd hated the passage from Gibraltar to Crete, cramped in a hold for most of the day, sick from engine fumes and fearful, always fearful, of enemy attacks from the air or, worse, U-boats. Pulling on his boots, he shouldered his small pack and rifle and followed the rest of the men up onto the deck. He sauntered over to the ship's rail. The salt smell helped refresh him after the stench of the decks below, and the slight breeze chilled the thick layer of sweat. To his surprise he found himself shivering.

'Stop your bleedin' daydreamin', you Scouse git. Get over here,' his bombardier yelled.

'What now, Bomb?' Paul inquired.

The man drew on a cigarette and snarled. 'Well, we do what we always do in this bloody army. We wait while the bleedin' officers figure out what to do. And then while they're standing there with their thumbs up their arses, the sergeants and us'll organize the whole bloody thing. Just stay here, by this vent thingy, or whatever the Hell they call it, where I know how to find you.' He stalked away in search of the sergeant.

As soon as the bombardier had disappeared Paul went back to the rail. Terry Hendricks joined him. He was the same age and, like Paul, small in stature, the product of a working-class life in the industrial heart of England. Terry hailed from Birmingham, and because of their accents Terry and Paul had been ribbed by the rest of the battery, all of whom came from the East End of London. For this reason the two had struck up as close a friendship as Paul could imagine.

'Christ, Cuthy. You look awful, even worse than normal,' he said cheerily.

'Yeah, mate, not much sleep last night. It's so bloody noisy down there, plus, that swine in the bunk on top of me. Groanin' all night, he was. Dunno' know what's gonna' drop off first, his hand or his dick.'

'He should be so lucky. Christ, they're puttin' too much of that stuff in our tea. I swear to God I dunno know what I'd do with a bird, even if she sat on me and whispered sweet nuthins' in me shell like.'

'Well, chance'd be a fine thing,' Paul said. The young men laughed and watched the seagulls wheeling overhead.

You know, Cuthy.' Hendricks gagged on the last shreds of his cigarette, sniffed, and spat a deep brown glob into the Aegean where it dissipated in ever increasing circles. 'I think we're pretty lucky, all in all.'

Paul snorted. 'Yer wot? Lucky. How'd you figure that?'

'Well. The sarge there, that's right, Sergeant Drake,' and he pointed to a stocky man in his early thirties. 'He looks like a soldier, a real soldier. An' you know why? Because he is, he's a right old sweat. He's not like us or the Bomb even. Fred Drake has been in the army since he left school, when he was fourteen. Without him we're all in very deep shit. In fact, royally fucked, as me old man would say.'

Paul shot him a quizzical look. 'You're a little ray of sunshine, this morning, ain't you? Anyway what about Drake?'

'Well,' Terry explained, 'me and the Bomb got drunk that last night in Chester and he tells me all about the Sarge. You know he served in India? He said if we stuck by 'im, the Sarge that is, we'll be all right. He knows his stuff, that's what the Bomb said anyway. He also told me to stay away from the officers. Most of 'em are useless, but we know that already, don't we, Cuthy my boy. He lit up another cigarette. 'Fag?'

Paul shook his head. He had never told anybody this but he couldn't even touch a cigarette. When his Ma told him to go to the corner shop to pick up a couple he'd always have the shopkeeper wrap them in a little paper bag. He was, he had realized long ago, quite strange.

The two young men stood in silence, their elbows on the wooden rail as the sun appeared over the horizon. Paul had never seen such beauty or the speed with which the morning chill was dissipated. The sun rose rapidly, and as it got higher it chased shadows down the mountains and turned the dirty grey of the sea into a shimmering translucent blue, even lending the oil slicks on the water's surface a peacock iridescence. For an instant the ship itself turned a shimmering hue before regaining its matte grey. The men on deck, cramped belowdecks for too long, turned as one to the east, as though involved in some prehistoric solar ritual. They raised their faces and felt the warmth creep through their bodies.

The morning light showed Paul where they were; a huge bay flanked to the north by a steep headland and to the south by gentle slopes that gradually gave way to towering peaks, some of them still spotted with snow. Floating in the bay, or so it appeared to Paul, was the whole Mediterranean fleet, frigates, destroyers and countless supply ships all waiting to spill their cargo of men and equipment onto the docks. For the first time since he had embarked in Gibraltar Paul felt a little confident about what the future might bring.

But Paul's newfound faith in the Army and his euphoria at the dazzling natural beauty around him did not last, for the sun brought not just warmth but a wave of Stuka dive bombers. Paul instantly recognized the planes, with their distinct angled wings, from his training back in England but he was not prepared for how they attacked. A mixture of awe and fear kept him glued to the spot, unable to tear his eyes away, and it was only Terry's roughly grabbing him by the arm and pulling him away that broke the spell. Coming in high from the east and then dropping almost vertically onto their targets, their sirens caterwauling, the first three Stukas unloaded their bombs. Two of the planes missed, but a third hit one of the destroyers. There was a large explosion and black smoke bellowed high into the air fanned by the flames below. The ship and shore batteries had by now opened up, light naval *ack-ack*, pom-poms chattering away, and then the heavy shore-based artillery, all of them intent on breaking up the attack before the rest of the squadron could descend. But the slow-moving Stukas were still too fast for the artillery and none of them was hit. Six more planes dived down although they made only three hits, and as suddenly as the attack had started it stopped. The whines of the aircraft faded into the distance, and the last of the artillery shells traced their way across the sky.

Paul and Terry, crouched low behind a capstan along with the rest of the British Army, slowly emerged from cover as it became clear that the Stukas were not coming back. They looked up to see a bunch of sailors staring at them. 'Bloody Pongoes, and they're gonna' defeat Jerry?' one shouted, and the other sailors sniggered. Hendricks gave them the V-for-Victory sign.

'Christ, Hendo, they were bloody fast,' Paul gabbled. 'Did you see 'em? How the hell are we gonna' hit them?'

'Like they told us in trainin'. We'll be all right.' Hendricks's voice sounded steady, his Adam's apple was moving up and down his throat and Paul knew that beneath the calm exterior Terry Hendricks was a frightened man.

An hour more of waiting, each soldier in fear of the next Stuka attack, and then the longed-for orders to disembark. The transport ship pulled into what seemed an impossibly small space on the quayside, and soon Greek and army dockers were swinging over cranes to pick up the artillery pieces, ammunition, supplies and vehicles, each load swinging wildly from the cranes but all of them somehow arriving undamaged on the quayside. Paul looked at Hendricks and gestured in the direction of the equipment and stores stacked on the quayside. 'What do you think, la', don't look like a lot to me, considerin' what we're gettin' into.'

'Not me either. Still what the fuck do we know? Hey, come on, the Sarge is givin' us that look.'

Shunted forward by the press of men behind him, each one of them gazing around to try to orient themselves to this new world, Paul barely took notice of the smell of petrol, the burning ships or the heat that bounced off the concrete. His woollen uniform chafed him and he wanted to scratch himself, but it was impossible to reach the small of his back where most of his sweat had accumulated. He swung his pack over his shoulder, almost taking out Hendricks in the process, and walked down the gangplank. On the quayside, the men stood and waited for orders from the NCOs, doing their best to avoid the dockers swinging equipment off the ships, or the staff cars careening wildly around as the officers tried to impose some degree of organisation. Terry was starting his second cigarette when a sergeant wearing large blancoed gauntlets—looking to Paul like a traffic policeman back home—ordered the soldiers away from the ship's side and towards the back of the quay out of the way of the dockers.

Some of the men pulled out cards and started impromptu games. One group soon had a pile of money heaped up in its centre and their constant swearing, both for winning and losing hands, soon attracted some onlookers. Others played Patience. But most of the soldiers just slumped against the wall and waited.

Paul let his mind wander to what might lie ahead and to whether he would cope with it. He had preferred his own company for as long as he could remember. Through school Paul had remained aloof, as though exposing himself to his classmates on an intimate daily basis might in some indefinable way corrupt him. And so while he might participate in the everyday physical activities of school life—indeed, he could rightly call some of his classmates friends—still he remained apart from his peers in every essential meaning. He lived not in their shadows, so much as he stood apart from them, as though he was alone in the wings of a theatre, watching them act out a play in which he had no role. Paul was not unhappy with this situation. Indeed, he drew a large degree of solace from not having to depend on those around him. However, if he had considered this in more depth, he might have realized that his aloofness was made possible by his own selfishness, in that he was perfectly capable of turning to others, especially his family, when it was necessary, only to eschew them once the immediate crisis had reached a successful conclusion. Also, Paul felt that he was in some way superior to his peers, that he was strong enough not to have to seek the visceral comfort of the crowd. Yet in his frequent moments of self-doubt he became convinced that this arrogance, deeply embedded though it may have appeared to others, was, so to say, on the contrary merely skin-deep. For what gave his arrogance purpose was that very self-doubt; that whilst he might be inexplicably destined for something better than those around him (or so he thought), at root he did not deserve it and that he would one day be exposed for what he really was. This self-doubt provided him the necessary shield against both himself and the rest of the world. But now he was entering uncharted waters, for he had been forced into a company of men, most of whom were still strangers. He had been taught by the instructors to rely on them and have them rely on him. It was the novelty of the latter that scared Paul more than anything, even as much as the physical danger that awaited him.

Hendricks sat down next to Paul and drew deeply on his

cigarette. 'This is all we bleedin' do in this army, you know. Bleedin' wait. Christ, talk about Fred Karno's army. An' I tell yer something else, Cuthy. It's only May and it's already bloody hot. Christ knows what'll be like in a month or two. We're royally fucked. We really are. Hang on, here's something.' Hendricks gestured towards their sergeant, Fred Drake, striding towards them.

'Right, you lot,' he said, pointing at Terry's battery, 'follow me. At the double. Now.' The sergeant went off in search of stragglers.

'See what I mean, Cuthy, my boy. Sittin' here for hours doin' sweet F.A., and then we have to bleedin' run because we should have been there yesterday. What an army. Bloody hilarious.'

Paul's battery followed the sergeant off the quay into the small village of Souda to join other batteries, like Paul's waiting expectantly for orders. It was difficult for Paul to square what he now saw with the fact that just a few hundred yards away a whole army was being unloaded under the bombs of the Luftwaffe. An old woman, all in black, led a donkey, its cumbersome wooden saddle loaded down with bamboo poles, down the narrow street that bisected the village. Some of the houses and shops lay in smoking ruins, but the villagers acted as though nothing unusual had happened. Men sat outside coffee shops, smoking and talking, and women chatted with each other as they shopped for their next meal. And everywhere there was a wealth of smells Paul had rarely experienced: the deep yeasty smell of freshly baked bread, the earthy aromas of freshly harvested vegetables, and the sweet tanginess of fresh fruit. As the gunners marched down the street, the Greeks stopped talking and clapped. Some of the men even gave the soldiers three cheers and military salutes. One old lady crossed the street and offered Paul a peach. He smiled at her and sank his teeth into it, letting the sweet juice run down his chin before wiping it away with the back of his hand and licking his fingers. Ten more minutes of marching brought the men to a small army canteen where they helped themselves to hot, sweet tea and the rounds of bread and bully beef the cooks were offering. Two more hours passed with three more Stuka attacks on the ships, and then an officer told the sergeants to march the men back to the quay. Waiting for them was a small convoy of lorries and ordnance. Paul could only hope that his great pack was among the pile of kitbags still waiting to be loaded.

Nobody seemed in charge of the mass of men crowded onto the port's maiden, and so the men settled down for another long wait. The heat burnt into Paul's body, and even the shelter of the dock wall could not provide any comfort. His water canteen was empty and he was beginning to feel light-headed when finally the gunners were ushered onto the lorries to follow the guns and the officers' cars out of the port and along the edge of the bay. Slight though it was, the breeze from his lorry as it slowly grumbled its way down the street cooled Paul and he began to think he might actually survive the day. After countless stops while the officers consulted their maps, the convoy split up into smaller fighting units. Paul's section turned north and began to climb, passing through neighbourhoods of large houses, double-storied and balconied, and all freshly painted with carefully manicured flower gardens shaded by expansive bougainvillea bushes.

'We're getting to the outskirts of Chania proper, lads,' Drake explained. 'Looks like this is where the la-di-da live. And look at the size of that fuckin' church, for Christ's sake, and the colours. Whoever heard of a church painted blue and red?'

'Bloody rich, Hendo,' Paul said. 'Some of those houses are huge. And did you see the cars outside them? Christ, I thought everybody here was a peasant.'

Their route took them out of the town to a large terrace overlooking the west end of the bay. From there the ships looked like bathtub miniatures, the soldiers, sailors and dockers like so many ants.

'Cuthbertson.' Paul looked down from the lorry to see his bombardier glaring at him. 'You and Hendricks. Take these binoculars, get your arses over to that ridge, and see what the land looks like. And be sharp about it.'

The two of them picked up their rifles and ran to the edge of the terrace which gradually sloped northwards down to the sea. Through the binoculars Paul saw the coastal quarter of Chania, spread out before him like a picture of some magical Arabian Nights land, shimmering in a heat haze. The small harbour was filled with sailing boats, from small oared fishing boats to two- and three-masted schooners. At the end of the mole stood a tall stone lighthouse that dominated the harbour. Immediately to the south, elegant houses, even bigger than the ones Paul had just driven past, straddled a steep hill. But what stirred Paul's imagination most were the tall minarets and domed mosques. Paul knew the Arabs had once controlled the Mediterranean, and here in front of him was visible proof that the Germans were just the latest in the line of invaders that wanted to control this part of the world.

Paul lay on the stony ground and chewed on a piece of dry grass, while Hendricks, on his back, luxuriated in another cigarette. He coughed up a gobbet of phlegm and, rolling over, spat it down the slope.

'Hendo,' Paul grimaced as the phlegm splattered on the rock in front of him, 'if the Germans don't get you, those cigarettes will. That cough of yours is getting worse.'

'Christ, Scouser, you ain't my ma. Anyways, my old gran' smokes forty a day and she's still goin' strong, so don't worry about me, thank you very much. I'm just fine.'

Paul shrugged. 'Suit yourself. Your funeral.'

'Cuthy,' Hendricks said. 'You think you're a clever bastard, what are those birds?' He pointed to a flock of about thirty small birds that flew over them like a cloud.

'How the hell should I know? Look, in Liverpool there were just three birds, right? Seagulls, pigeons and sparrers. One was white, one was grey and the other was neither. An' I ain't a clever bastard, so shut yer gob.' Paul smiled at his friend.

'Charmin',' Hendricks retorted. 'A man tries to educate himself and gets shot down. Excuse me for living.'

After a while, Paul nodded in the direction of the harbour. 'Don't you think it wrong that only a war could bring us to such a spot and that this beautiful, magical town is likely to be destroyed?'

Hendricks said, 'Never thought about it, mate. I'm here 'cos I have no choice. Just like you. Got better things to worry about.'

Paul opened his mouth to respond, but at that moment a squadron of German bombers, coming from the west, flew in low over Chania. They moved slowly, almost languidly, for there was no anti-aircraft fire to harass them, and then their bays opened and racks of bombs were released to smash into the harbour and the surrounding buildings. Huge clouds of smoke erupted from the rooftops. Wooden boats in the harbour disintegrated into matchsticks. And then just as quickly as they had arrived the planes disappeared and again all was calm.

Paul and Terry picked up their rifles and slithered down the hill to the bombardier. 'It's amazin', Bomb,' Paul blathered. 'Like a fairy story, there's mosques and...'

'Christ all fuckin' mighty, Cuthy. I wasn't lookin' for no travel guide,' he shouted. 'Does that ridge drop right down into the town? Would it make a good observation post? Do you get a 360-degree field of vision? How defensible is it? You know, all the things you look for, when you're in the bloody army.'

'Sorry, Bomb. It's the top alright and the ground slopes away gradually. It's pretty open. We also saw a battery of our heavy guns to the northeast of us.'

'Right, lad. I'll tell the Sarge. He'll wanna have a shufty himself, anyway.'

The terrace they had occupied was more than big enough for their four 40mm Bofors, and Paul and the section spent the rest of the day setting up the guns, storing the ammunition and establishing their own bivvies. Paul had been put in charge of the radio; why he had no idea. He unpacked the set, a double dial and morse key combination.

'Sarge, what the hell do we do now? No batteries,' Paul shouted.

'You're kiddin' right?' Drake slapped his forehead as though he was in a cheap melodrama.

Paul showed him the empty box. Drake snatched it out of Paul's hands and hurled it at a rock. The case smashed in two, and for good measure he kicked the pieces over the side of the hill.

'It don't matter, Sarge, anyway. When I got the set from the truck I couldn't see any telephone cable either.'

'Well, this is fuckin' turnin' out to be a right bleedin' picnic, ain't it? Go over and give Hendricks a hand with the shells. And don't drop any. An' after that you and Hendricks'll have to be runners between us and the OP.'

'So, Cuthy,' Terry said, grunting as he stacked a shell at the base of a small rock face, 'we don't have no batteries or cable for the radio. Is that what I heard?'

Paul nodded.

'It seems to me,' Terry said, 'it seems to me, young Cuthbertson, that we are well and truly, how should I put it, facked.'

'That's the worst toff accent I've ever heard, Hendo,' Paul chuckled.

A shout from the bombardier made him look towards Souda Bay where Stukas were once more falling on the shipping. And once more the pom-poms on the destroyers and cruisers and the heavy artillery opened up to fill the sky with ugly black and grey splotches of exploding shells. The Stukas dropped their payload and carried on over Paul's position. Now Paul knew why they had been stationed there. He had the novel thought that perhaps the officers weren't so stupid after all. Maybe not today but tomorrow Paul could start paying the Germans back. For Mary McGinley, for the Blitz, for everything.

Chapter 8

The *son et lumière* of impending victory: officers giving commands and sergeants passing them on; ground crews loading ammunition and equipment canisters: mechanics making last-minute adjustments to engines; paratroopers, their equipment checked and checked again, with nothing to do but wait and pray; the banks of lights, their harsh brilliance etching the men and their machines against the darkness of the Athenian night.

Dieter Lehmann finally stopped checking his chute — every thirty minutes for the past three hours — afraid that in his nervousness he might make a mistake and doom himself to the worst of deaths. He stowed the chute in his locker and walked over to a small shaded beer stand that an enterprising Athenian had set up just off the airfield. The beer stand was ramshackle and fly-blown, but the beer was reasonably cool, even if it was only Greek. A gentle breeze — not enough to cool the sultry warmth of the evening — whispered in off the Aegean, and Dieter imagined just a short time ago that same wind may have blown over Crete, his destination. He put down his diary, searching for something new to write. He tried to make an entry every day, but the tedium of rehearsing the same manoeuvres until he could do it in his sleep left little new to record. In any case, on the threshold of his young life's greatest adventure, he struggled to put any of his thoughts into words, the magnitude of what was to come proving too much for his skills. He took another sip of beer and let his mind wander back to the day he had decided to join the Parachute Regiment. Had he joined this elite and dangerous regiment simply because he knew it would infuriate his father, or was it to prove to himself that he really did believe that the Führer and Nazism were worth serving even if it placed his own life in danger? Dieter recalled that last argument with his father — on the very night he had told them he was to be deployed—and how his mother had tried to calm them both down, until little Liesl had stepped in, as she always did, and quelled her brother's anger with just her smile. He rolled the warm beer around his mouth, wondering if he should spit it out and get something else to drink. A quip from some famous writer—he couldn't remember his name—slipped into his consciousness, something about how death concentrates the mind. Whoever said that was right, Dieter acknowledged. Tomorrow would be the biggest day of his young life, and now all that mattered were his comrades and the tasks they together had to accomplish. The answer to why he had become a paratrooper was quite inconsequential.

Dieter's thoughts were interrupted by a heavy shove in his back. Hans Becker, a twenty-one-year-old from Munich, who had gone through jump school with him, sat down at his table. He was puffing on a cigarette and handed one to Dieter. Dieter had to hold his friend's hands steady when Hans lit the cigarette for him.

'Nervous?' Dieter asked.

'Dieter,' Hans said. He vigorously scratched his head and picked his fingernails free of the hair cream that had turned his sandy hair to a greasy brown. 'Dieter, I like you and I know you went to fancy schools and all, but by God you do ask the stupidest questions. No, I'm not nervous. I'm shit scared. But nobody will ever know it, trust me. I swear to God, the sergeant would kill me if he knew, and then who'd protect your scrawny little ass.' He nodded at Dieter's diary. 'Still writing I see. I don't know why you bother. I mean what's so important about your life you have to write it all down. Christ, you'll probably be dead this time next week anyway.'

Dieter looked up sharply, and his face hardened for a moment, but his friend's grinning face relaxed him. 'Sorry, Hans,' Dieter said, 'a bit edgy, that's all.'

'I know. I know. Don't worry, you'll have to do a lot better than that to upset me. Anyway, you can't help being a crazy boy wonder, with your big words and everything. I'm just surprised the general hasn't called you in yet for advice. Or maybe he has, and you're not telling us poor slobs.' Hans drew on his cigarette. 'By the way, talking of the general,' he continued, 'did you see the notice he had put up? It's on the bulletin board.'

Dieter shook his head.

'Well, the General has said that we follow the rules of war, we show soldiers all the proper respect. You know, when we capture them, there's to be no bad treatment, we treat them with honour, they go straight to a prisoner camp, like we'd want to be treated.' Hans hesitated and looked into the Athenian night. 'But, if we come across civilians who oppose us,' he continued, 'we're supposed to show them no mercy.'

Dieter jerked his head up. 'No, I didn't see that, Hans. And frankly, it doesn't seem right. They're just defending their land. Wouldn't you do that?'

Hans shrugged his shoulders. 'If they shoot at me, I'll shoot back and do whatever I have to. And to hell with the Geneva Convention.'

Dieter broke the silence. 'You know,' Dieter said. 'I think we'll both be all right. I know, it sounds crazy, but I think that if there are only two men to come to out of this alive, it'll be us two.'

Hans frowned.

'You don't think so?' Dieter asked.

'I don't know what to think, Dieter,' Hans said slowly. 'They say we're the best of the best, like there's never been a force like us, but I don't understand why that'll protect us when the bullets fly.'

'Well, it won't, Hans. At least not like you think,' Dieter replied. 'What'll protect us is our training and, what's that French phrase, esprit de corps. We look after each other. Right? And we are the best at what we do, we all know that.'

'Well, you never really answered my question,' Hans said,

inhaling the cigarette smoke deep into his lungs and slowly letting it out through his nostrils. 'But that's all right. I probably wouldn't have understood it anyway. And the regiment did kick their asses in Belgium. I mean, the regiment was unstoppable. Lieutenant Maier was in on the Belgium drop. I heard he was a real bastard, but without him his company wouldn't have survived. So, I'm glad he's making the jump with us.' He took another drag on his cigarette. 'Are you frightened, Dieter?' He spoke gently.

'Of course.' Dieter spoke slowly, making sure he chose the right words. 'I'm just like you. Remember what the sergeant said; only idiots aren't frightened? Look, I believe in what we're doing. It's for the good of Germany, for National Socialism.'

'Well, there I agree with you, schoolboy,' Hans interrupted. 'The Führer has done nothing but good for Germany. My father was unemployed before he came to power. He couldn't remember the last time he had a decent job, one that paid enough to look after his family. Do you know how that feels, when a man can't put food on his family's table? Well, all that's changed. Because of one man. And if we have to go off and fight wherever he sends us, then that's all right with me.'

'Hans, you make it sound like I disagree with you. I totally agree. I'm always arguing with my...' Dieter paused, worried in case prying ears might be listening. 'All I am saying,' he carried on, 'is that I believe what happens to us is out of our hands. And I don't just mean that it's up to the British whether we live or die. No, and bear with me. I need to get this off my chest. I am frightened. God, I'm frightened, but everything will happen the way it is supposed to. I believe in something called predestination. Or something close to that, I'm still trying to get through the book I've got on it. I think everything is all worked out for us. I'm not saying that God has already figured out the particularities of our life. By the way, I'm not even sure God exists, at least the way they tell it in the Bible. No, God can't be involved in every little last thing of our lives. To me that's impractical. Or that he had nothing better to do with his time, and I don't believe that either. No, what I mean is very simple. Our essence, our nature if you like, is determined by our birth and how we were brought up, how we were trained. Once we've reached that point, everything we do is determined by those simple facts. If we were clever enough we could probably predict exactly what was going to happen to us, or at least how we would react, which to my mind is the same thing. So, all I'm saying is that what happens in the next few days is out of our hands; we'll react to it but we have no free will in how we react even though we think otherwise. Our bodies, our minds, are simply the vehicles that carry us to wherever we're supposed to go.'

Hans yawned and tried — unsuccessfully —to light a match on his belt buckle as Dieter spoke. He finally threw it away in disgust.

'I'm sorry, Hans,' Dieter continued. 'I know I talk too much. But let me finish. And try not to roll your eyes out of their sockets, if you don't mind. I'm frightened, Hans. Yeah, I'm frightened. I am terrified of pain, of being maimed, of letting my friends down. Of letting you down, even though you really are a sorry excuse for a paratrooper. But I don't see myself having any control over what happens. What happens to us is gonna happen. It's actually very simple and also very liberating.'

Hans took a very large swig of Dieter's beer, his brow pursed. 'You know, Dieter Lehmann,' he said in a deep voice. 'You don't half talk a load of shit.'

'Well, my friend,' Dieter said with a smile. 'With that I totally agree. Here, we'd better get back before the sergeant misses us.'

The sun was still below the horizon, but already Dieter was

awash in sweat. The heavy jumpsuit and life vest weighed him down, the straps of the parachute cut into his body, and the knee pads pinched his legs. He was shaking with nervousness, and he hoped that nobody would notice. Dieter was frightened, but he consoled himself with being a German paratrooper, the best of the best, and that he could deal with anything thrown at him. Still, he had not believed the general—in fact, nobody in the battalion had, so far as Dieter could tell —when he told them they would be welcomed by the Cretans like saviours. No, he knew a tough fight awaited all of them, and not just with the English. He rubbed the scar on his right cheek as he had done since childhood when nervous. It reminded him of Otto, who'd given him the scar in the first place, and he wondered where his friend was. Last Dieter had heard, Otto was serving in a U-boat in the North Atlantic. He was afraid for Otto and wanted him home safely, but he was also honest enough to admit that he was glad that their positions were not switched.

The propellers of the waiting Junkers 52s threw up huge dust clouds, and Dieter gagged as they stood in line for their sticks of twelve paratroopers each to be loaded onto the planes, each of them deep in his own thoughts. Dieter finally reached the plane door and he put the parachute release cord into his mouth to stop it getting entangled when he climbed into the transporter. Now it was his turn to board. Standing on a small wooden step he hoisted himself into the fuselage, helped by a judicious push from Hans directly behind him, and he settled onto the hard bench. Hans offered him a cigarette but Dieter shook his head.

One of the paratroopers started to sing the regimental song and the men joined in, but they fell silent as the pilot revved his engines. 'Thank God.' Hans laughed. 'We never could hold a tune. Christ, it's hot in here. I'll be glad to get in the air if only to get cool again.'

But then the plane engines throttled down and the sweating men sighed with impatience. Someone in the aft of the plane shouted to the pilot to get a move on, and slowly, as if in obedience to the command, the engines revved higher and higher, and Dieter felt a judder as the plane began to creep forward. It picked up speed, jostling the men as it sped down the grass runway. The paratroopers looked at each other with smiles on their faces, happy at last to be on their way. Dieter felt his fear wash away in the exhilaration of the moment as the plane rose. The plane circled the airfield, all the time gaining altitude as it waited to join formation with the other planes.

Twenty minutes later, the circling stopped and the plane leveled into straight flight. Dieter pushed himself against Hans to get some space, and he was able to get a glimpse out of the window. Below him lay the Aegean, glistening blue and silver as the rising sun caught the waves, so unutterably peaceful that it seemed impossible to imagine what horrors might be awaiting them. Dieter went over, for the hundredth time, the instructions his unit had been given in Athens. The paratroopers, along with glider battalions, were to concentrate on taking the coastline west of Chania, one of the three large towns on the north coast of the island. The gliders were to land by a small village called Tavronitis and capture the landing strip at Maleme a few kilometers to the east. Its capture was top priority in order to allow reinforcements to be flown in from Athens. The colonel in charge of the briefing had stressed that if the paratroopers failed the whole invasion of the island would collapse. Dieter's own unit was to drop slightly more inland than the gliders and take a hill-top village called Ayios Stefanos that commanded the main road along the coast. They had been told to expect heavy resistance from the New Zealanders who, according to German intelligence, were dug in there.

The plane bucked as rising thermals caught its wings, and after what Dieter thought was too short a time, he saw Crete, dominated by the high mountains that formed the east-west spine of the island. The jump lights went on, and at the same time puffs of black smoke wafted across the windows of the planes as the first shells of the artillery barrage sought their range. One airburst rocked their plane, but the pilot struggled with the controls and managed to keep it on course. The laughter and chatter of the paratroopers were replaced by quiet. The dispatcher at the fuselage door ordered them to stand up. The men hooked their release cords onto the overhead wire and prepared to jump. Dieter was fourth in his stick and he patted Hans on the shoulder. 'See you on the ground, my friend.' Dieter hoped he sounded confident. Through the doorway he was able to see the island close-up for the first time. Green fields and wine or olive groves blanketed the low-lying hills. Small houses were scattered across the landscape, and small villages as well. To the east lay the port city of Chania, already becoming a mere smudge in the hot humid air.

A Junkers behind Dieter's plane took a direct hit and exploded, burning bodies tumbling out of the wreckage. Dieter prayed to get out of his plane alive. At the door, Dieter let his training take over and concentrated on the complicated task of getting out of the plane. The dispatcher nodded to him, and Dieter grabbed the sides of the doorway and launched himself out of the plane, immediately stretching out his arms and legs, crucifix-style. His body was buffeted and he momentarily lost orientation, but then the release cord went tight and pulled hard at his harness, and his body was jerked upwards as the canopy filled with air. In the jump school the instructors had told the cadets that getting out of the plane was the worst part. They'd said it in jest as though to make light of what would await them on the ground, but Dieter had already witnessed enough jump accidents to know the instructors were serious. Of course, they weren't being shot out of the sky during their training jumps. The paratrooper who had jumped at the head of the stick was blown by the slipstream straight into the leading edge of the following plane's wing. His body folded over the wing and then was pulled away as the chute opened up.

Dieter's luck held. He dropped out of the planes' slipstreams, and now all was quiet except for the wind whistling around him. He tried to spot Hans but the number of parachutes around him made it impossible. For a brief moment he was able to enjoy the delight of defying gravity as he floated gently down, but the pleasure lasted only a moment. Heavy ground fire cut into the paratroopers. Already some of them were hanging limply from their cords, blood snatched from their bodies as they plummeted to the ground. Parachutes closed up like flowers at night as bullets ripped through the silk and the paratroopers plunged to the ground. A bullet ripped through Dieter's sleeve, but he felt nothing. Below him three paratroopers were jack-knifed on a cane break, each body neatly impaled on a spindly stalk of the plant. Dieter took out his pistol, the only weapon he had until he could get to the weapons canisters on the ground, and fired indiscriminately, without any target to aim for but hoping he might hit something or somebody.

Dieter hit the ground hard. The land was rocky and his ankle took a sharp twist, but the adrenalin had kicked in and he felt virtually nothing. Bullets ricocheted off the rocks and thumped into the trees, shredding the thick foliage until only the thicker branches stayed attached. Hans landed close behind him and the two of them struggled out of their harnesses. Neither of them was hit, and they rushed to the cover of a low stone wall to take stock of the situation. Looming in front of them and dominating the whole of their universe was the village of Ayios Stefanos, their immediate objective. A solid stone stockade sat in the valley at the base of the hill. Dieter nodded to Hans. 'Looks like a castle back home.' Hans followed his gaze. 'It's the prison the Lieutenant told us about. He said the gliders were going to take it.'

'Well, I hope for our sake he's right, otherwise we're trapped,' Dieter said.

The two paratroopers found themselves on the edge of a small terrace cut from the hillside. Around them other paratroopers were unbuckling their canopies and harnesses. One trooper was hit by multiple shots and crumpled to the ground. In front of them a dead paratrooper swung by his chute from the top limbs of a large olive tree, his head slumped forward as though in prayer. A paratrooper to their right raised his head above the top of the wall and immediately it dissolved in a wash of red as a bullet caught him between the eyes. Another, who had come down in the pasture, tried to crawl to the safety of a wall and was immediately riddled with bullets, the body twitching from round after round. Dieter spotted a sergeant kneeling behind a wall and they crawled as quickly as they could to him. He was still, and when Hans pulled at his body it flopped lifelessly, a large red stain still spreading over his tunic. The two young men looked at each other, uncertain of what to do, for although the paratroopers had expected resistance they were not prepared for the barrage of controlled and accurate fire from the New Zealanders they had landed among.

A mortar shell exploded behind them, sending a cloud of olives into the air, and tossing a paratrooper to the ground like a rag doll. The smell of blood, the sweet odour of olives, the screams of the wounded, the toll of a distant church bell, the chatter of rifles all created a sensual kaleidoscope that threatened to unhinge Dieter. He lay behind the wall, too frightened to move. Hans elbowed him. 'We've got to get into this fight,' he shouted, 'we're getting massacred. Look over there.' Hans pointed to a clump of trees. Hanging from them were coloured parachutes attached to canisters carrying equipment and supplies, guns and ammunition.

'Ready?' Hans asked.

Dieter nodded and running low to the ground they zigzagged their way to the ammo canister. They took shelter behind it and pulled out two MP40 submachine guns and as much ammunition as they could carry.

'Thanks, Hans. I almost gave up back there,' Dieter said. 'It's funny,' he continued. 'I'm not afraid anymore, now we can fight back. I know, it's strange, but now we're gonna fight, I'm almost enjoying myself.'

"I don't know about enjoyin' myself, but yeah, I feel good too,' said Hans. 'Come on, let's get to work.'

Together with the other paratroopers who had located guns and ammunition, the two men began to take the fight to the enemy. At first it appeared to Dieter as a series of uncoordinated uphill firefights, but the paratroopers had begun forming themselves into organized combat units to start pushing the New Zealanders back up the hill towards the village. Hans pointed out Lieutenant Maier to Dieter. Kurt Maier was a small man who exuded an animal fierceness as he barked orders at the troopers and chivvied them to attack. Dieter heard the *whomps* of mortar shells landing amongst them, but the Germans had spread out in a loose formation and only one trooper was hit. Dieter edged forward. Twenty yards in front of him and slightly to his left he saw two New Zealanders hidden in the trees, manning a heavy machine gun. They were intent on firing well-aimed bursts and did not see him. Dieter dropped to his knees, took aim and fired his Schmeisser. The bullets hit the two men in their sides and they slid over their gun to the ground. Dieter had not breathed during his attack on the machine gunners and he gratefully sucked in lungfuls of the moist air. His heart was racing and he looked around almost like a schoolboy scared of being found out in a terrible crime. But all he got was a thumbs-up from Hans and a huge grin. He waved back, amazed that he had killed another human being, two of them to be precise.

The firing from in front of them slackened, and the paratroopers increased their pace, half crouching, half walking, to another stone wall. Maier ordered them to rest for a few minutes and reload. Dieter swallowed a mouthful of warm water from his canteen and suddenly felt very tired. He popped a tablet the paratroopers had been given to ward off tiredness and took in his wider surroundings. The olive grove they were in stretched north to the sea, shimmering in the morning sun. To the south, behind the village, stood the White Mountains, still snow-covered.

On Maier's command, the squad renewed their advance with the other Germans. An NCO, somewhere to Dieter's left, barked out an order, but immediately was drowned out by rifle shots, recognizably lighter, Dieter noticed, than the guns of the New Zealanders. A paratrooper brought a cigarette to his lips and then fell to his knees as a blood gushed out of his nose and from under his helmet. Dieter hit the ground and began searching again for the enemy.

Chapter 9

Papa Michali, devoted follower of the Prince of Peace, waited patiently for his war to begin. Awakened by the low-flying waves of German planes sweeping in over the island like eagles searching for their prey, he ran, with shirt tail flapping out of his trousers, to the church and pulled on the heavy bell rope. The sweat ran down his face in sheets, but he kept to his task until the monotone peals had reverberated throughout the village and the villagers had scurried into the plateia, some of them pulling braces over their shoulders or buttoning up their trousers, all of them bearing rifles or shotguns. Their women were close behind, some armed only with pitchforks or spades.

The priest greeted them on the church steps. 'I have always taught you, my children,' he roared, 'to turn the other cheek, just as our Saviour taught us. But not today.' He held aloft a huge double-edged axe. 'See,' he roared, 'I am come to kill the Minotaur. This is God's work we do. Now, no talk. Let us do it.'

The men held their weapons aloft and shouted their approval. They kissed their wives and mothers, told them everything would be fine; fathers hugged their children and kissed their foreheads. Anastasia held Elpida to her waist as Yianni knelt down to his daughter. 'Little Elpida,' he whispered, 'Papouka and I will be back soon. You and Yiayia will be safe here. Don't worry, little girl, we'll all be home soon, and safe.' Yianni waited for his father to embrace his wife, then kissed his mother on her cheeks and moved out with his father and the rest of the men.

The throng, swelled by women who would not leave their men to fight alone, followed Papa Michali down the hill to where the heaviest concentrations of parachutes were opening up. Some of the villagers prayed aloud as they marched, others shouted encouragement to each other and threats to the Germans, so that from a distance they sounded like a swarm of bees fending off a threat to their hive. Halfway down the hill, Papa Michali ordered the men and women to take cover behind the stone walls that crisscrossed the slope. Yianni and Antoni leaned their rifles against a wall and carefully raised their heads over its top. They could see no movement in front of them but the sound of gunfire indicated that heavy fighting was in progress and coming their way.

'Maybe they won't come any closer, Baba,' Yianni sounded hopeful.

The older man shook his head. 'No, my son, they will. They will have to take our village. You can see the whole island from our little hill.' He smiled. 'Or at least most of it. No, they're coming.'

A scuffle made them look behind. Running across the terrace towards them was Christo, a pistol shoved into his leather belt next to a curved bone-handled knife, a rifle in his arms, and the beads of his kerchief bouncing up and down on his forehead.

'Ha,' Yianni shouted. 'You're ready to fight the Turks, my friend. Sorry, it's only the Germans this time.'

'I don't care who they are,' Christo said through a grin. 'I'll kill them all.'

'So, you have finally seen the light,' Antoni teased the young communist as he settled in next to the two of them.

Christo nodded at the older man. 'Kyrie Manoulakis'–he looked directly at Antoni–'I still think you are all fools to trust the English, but I am Cretan and show me a Cretan who can resist a good fight.' He nodded towards the sky, still filled with men slowly drifting to earth. 'This will be the best dove hunt the island has ever seen.' His laugh could not disguise his nervousness, and Yianni and Antoni laughed with him to hide their own fear. The gunfire below them was getting louder, and the olive groves in front seemed almost to throb with anticipation. The three men looked at each other, and Christo crossed himself. Antoni raised his eyebrows but kept to himself his opinion of the young man's sudden conversion.

Now the villagers could clearly hear the screams of the wounded, sometimes a low moan, other times a high-pitched scream of terror, German and New Zealander alike crying out for help. Some of the villagers started to run towards the noise of battle, eager to join in. But Papa Michali ordered them to stand fast. He was wise enough to know that if they were to have any chance they had to hit the Germans hard but only after the professional soldiers had taken the brunt of the German attack. Then they could attack the Germans while they were still recovering.

As the villagers waited, soldiers emerged from the groves, inching their way back up the slope. Yianni and Christo, right alongside their priest, raised their guns, but Michali immediately ordered them to lower their weapons. 'Don't you see, you young fools,' he barked. 'They are English. They are retreating in order, and that is why we see only their backs. Look they are still firing at the Germans.' The New Zealanders were retreating in orderly formation, and they held their lines in good order. They barely looked at the men and women huddled behind the stone walls as they moved back up the hill to the village.

Now it was the villagers' turn to fight. The blacksmith, standing next to Yianni, threw up, his vomit splashing on Yianni's boots. He mumbled an apology but Yianni was too nervous to acknowledge. Yianni moved away from the smell of bile and he and Christo piled loose rocks on top of the wall for extra protection. Through a gap in the rocks Yianni saw movement. The first German paratroopers slowly emerged from the olive grove into the small field in front of the villagers, their camouflaged jackets and trousers making them seem like ghosts appearing from the shadows of night. The Germans crouched low, peering to the right and left, searching for the enemy they knew awaited them. Yianni's hands trembled and his sweat made the rifle slippery in his grasp. He placed a hand on his left cheek to try to stop an uncontrollable twitching. These were the men, he told himself, who smashed everything before them. He felt his father's hand on his to stop him cracking his knuckles. 'Your daughter is right. That is a very irritating habit.' He smiled. 'My son, do not worry. All is in God's hands now.'

Now the Germans were close enough for Yianni to identify them as individuals. One paratrooper walked with a slight limp, another had a small flower stuck in his chest pocket, its purple petals clashing with the green mottling of his jacket. Another had a scarred cheek. Finally, when Yianni thought it too late, Papa Michali gave the order to open fire. A paratrooper entered Yianni's line of sight and the Cretan fired. The bullet hit the paratrooper's helmet, and Yianni thought he heard a distinct metallic clang before blood oozed out of the hole. There was no coordination to the Cretans' fire, just indiscriminate firing that by its very intensity carved gaps in the ranks of the Germans. Hidden in the olive grove a German heavy machine gun opened up, but almost instantly fell silent as the German gunners realized that they were likely to hit their comrades as they retreated to the cover of the trees. Yianni and the villagers cheered, and Papa Michali snarled in vain at them to shut up and stay behind the walls. An old woman, all in black, rushed into the grove and attacked a wounded paratrooper with a pitchfork, driving one of the tines straight into the German's eye. Her husband swung a hand axe into the soldier's chest. Blood splashed onto the old man's leggings. Other villagers followed her lead and began to dispatch the wounded Germans, striking them with their rifle butts or the rocks that lay all over the field. One paratrooper was hit in the leg and tried to crawl to safety, but a villager ran over to him and smashed his rifle butt onto the man's head. The helmet rolled off his head and the Cretan clubbed him one more time. Too many villagers had ignored Papa Michali's warnings to stay covered and now they were caught in the open. All the paratroopers still alive were back in the olive grove and they returned fire. The old woman with the pitchfork was thrown to the ground as a burst hit her midriff. Her husband ran to her, but he too was hit and fell lifeless onto his wife. Five more villagers collapsed in quick succession, their bodies flung apart by the heavy machine gun rounds that sprayed into them. A youth came down the slope from Ayios Stefanos and shouted in Papa Michali's ear. The priest nodded to him and then waved for the villagers to retreat.

As Yianni withdrew with the others he took a quick look back at the battlefield and saw Christo still firing. He ran back, grabbed his friend by the collar and dragged him to safety behind a wall. 'You're a fool, Christo, and I'm not getting killed because you're an idiot.' Christo struggled to get free, but his friend's grip was too tight and he soon realized that he could do no further good. He nodded to Yianni and the two of them hotfooted up the hill, backs bent, hearts pounding. A splatter of stone chips cascaded around them as a machine-gun burst traversed the top of the wall, but slowly the fire subsided into the distance as the villagers retreated out of range towards Ayios Stefanos. Now that they were safe, Yianni was able to get a good look at the killing field. German and Cretan bodies were scattered haphazardly in the last of the winter clover. Paratroopers stalked through the field, kicking the bodies of the villagers. The body of a woman twitched in response to a heavy boot to the head, and the German fired two bullets into her. Bile rose in Yianni's gullet, but he swallowed it down, its acridity making him cough and spit.

After the din of the firefight the terrace was unnaturally quiet, and the paratroopers took stock of their position. Lying behind a gnarled olive tree, Dieter drained the last of the water from his canteen, even turning it upside down to get the last drops, before placing a small pebble in his mouth to work up some spittle. It didn't help; the acrid taste of smoke and cordite was too deeply etched into his throat. Hans lit up a cigarette, slowly inhaling and letting the nicotine bite deep into his lungs before exhaling smoke rings that hung listlessly in the still air. Dieter shook his head when Hans held out a cigarette. 'I don't know how you smoke the damned things,' he croaked. 'Aren't you dry enough already? God, I could drink a stream dry.'

Hans lay back and smoked in silence, his eyes fixed on a bug that was trying to eat a leaf twice its size.

'Do you think we're winning?' Dieter asked.

Hans slowly turned his head. 'How the hell do I know,' he said. 'If the rest of the island fights like this lot, it's gonna be a long time before you and I can have a beer in peace. Now shut up and let me sleep.'

'But'—Dieter was talking more to himself than to Hans—'they told us back in Athens we'd be welcomed as liberators. And, now, thirty minutes of battle and we've lost as many men to Cretans as New Zealanders. They didn't even let us land and form into proper fighting units. Did you see that old woman with the pitchfork, Hans? God in Heaven, everyone was there, young men, old men, women. It was unbelievable.'

Hans finally lifted his head and threw his stub on the ground. 'Look, Lehmann,' his voice was harsh. 'Look, stop your fuckin' daydreamin' about white knights and chivalry. I'm sick of it. Don't you remember what the General told us before we took off? It was on the bulletin board. Christ, I told you about it. We could fight with, what was the word, gallantry against soldiers, but he'd have no problem with us killing civilians if they were stupid enough to turn on us. They're savages, you saw what they did with the axes and pitchforks. They're savages, and that's all they are. This is a war, and they're savages, and we're gonna have to kill the whole lot of them. Okay? You'd better get used to it. You're gonna get your hands a lot filthier than what they are now. So, grow up, for God's sake.' By this time Hans was screaming at Dieter, as his fear finally found an outlet. 'You see these men in the field? They're dead, and you can get killed just like them. A Cretan bullet will kill you as easily as an English one. So grow up, just grow up.'

Dieter's face drained of colour. He did not know what to say and turned away.

A sergeant—they did not recognize him for the units were all mixed up by the confusion on the ground—slithered over and looked at Hans. 'Any chance you can shout louder, they didn't hear you in Athens. Haven't you heard of battle discipline?' Hans mumbled an apology. 'Anyway,' the sergeant continued, 'Maier says we go in again in fifteen minutes. We have to take the village at all costs. Get as much ammo as you can. He says we either take it or we can all die on this shitty island.' The man scooted away to inform the other paratroopers.

Dieter nodded towards Hans and motioned towards a busted ammo container. Hans grabbed his friend's arm. 'Battle discipline, my arse. That bastard's been reading too many manuals. Like I'm the only one making a noise around here? We're in the middle of a damned battle.' Hans hesitated and placed his hand on Dieter's arm. 'Dieter,' he said, 'I'm sorry for what I said just then. I'm just tired, that's all. And scared.' He smiled and rescued a piece of tobacco off his tongue.

'I deserved it,' Dieter said. 'You're right. They're trying to kill us, and we need to kill them first.'

'All right, then,' Hans said. 'Let's forget about it.'

The two men crawled over to the canister, grabbed more ammo, and waited for the orders to advance.

Behind them, down the hill they had just fought their way up, two paratroopers held a man between them, a civilian. One of the Germans pulled a Luger from his belt and shot the man at pointblank range. A pink cloud erupted from the side of his head, and he dropped to the ground. The two paratroopers lit cigarettes and walked back up the slope to rejoin the rest of the company.

Dieter shouted. 'Did you see that? They just shot a Greek. In cold blood.'

Hans looked at him, pulling his head back in surprise.

'Christ, Lehmann, you're too sensitive. That's what we need to do with all of 'em.'

'Hey, I wasn't complaining, just telling you what I saw.' Dieter said.

'Hey, look smart,' Hans said, 'I think we're off.'

Ammo belts over their shoulders, Dieter and Hans followed the NCOs up the slope through more olive groves.

Suddenly, breaking the quiet, bullets shredded the olive trees. A paratrooper crumpled to the ground, and the men scrambled for what little cover they could find. Cries of "Kamata, Kamata" — deep, rumbling guttural cries that grew louder and louder — rolled down the slope as waves of huge, brown-skinned soldiers, all wielding long knives or bayonets, smashed into the German lines. There was no time to fire back as the horde sliced through the paratroopers, time only to avoid the slashing blades. The sergeant who had given orders to Dieter and Hans just fifteen minutes ago looked in disbelief as a Maori knife took off his arm just below the elbow. Hans went down on his knees as a bayonet thrust caught him in his thigh, a knife flashed in the summer sun, and Hans's head, still helmeted with the strap neatly positioned under his chin, was rolling down the slope until it lodged at the base of an olive tree. Dieter stood paralysed, battling in vain to tear his eyes away from the headless body that still pumped blood, until a paratrooper running back down the slope banged into him. A whistle blew from up the slope and the Maoris disappeared as fast as they had arrived. Suddenly all was quiet again. That Dieter had seen a man decapitated was incomprehensible; that it was Hans was too much to contemplate. A corporal ran over to Dieter and punched him hard on the shoulder. 'That's right, Lehmann, look at your pal. Get angry, get really angry. Kill every last one of the motherfuckers. Got it?'

Chapter 10

Through the fog that clogged his brain, Dieter vaguely heard Maier's order to advance. Around him only ten men were fit enough to continue the fight. He caught glimpses of other units, depleted like his own but in well-ordered skirmish lines, moving up the slope and assumed that his own corner of the battle had not been so different than the others; vicious fighting with heavy losses, but ultimate victory, and that slowly but surely they were tightening the noose around the village. Trying to force the image of Hans out of his head, Dieter concentrated on the task at hand.

The Germans came to the last open field, partly covered with cracked yellow maize stubble, before the outskirts of Ayios Stefanos, and for the first time got a really good look at their objective. An advance party had run into a rearguard of New Zealanders, and the field was still shrouded by gun smoke and the cloying odour of blood and cordite. German and New Zealand bodies lay where they had fallen, some of them twisted together in their own private embrace of the dead. A sergeant ordered Dieter to take point, and he edged forward cautiously. A clang sounded in the village, and Dieter dived for cover into a circular stone-lined depression. Dry wheat chaff forced itself into his nostrils, and he sneezed. A shout from the sergeant, and Dieter continued towards the village, pausing to check out the body of a dead New Zealander, officer's insignia on his shoulders. Dieter looked in admiration at the heavy ginger-coloured moustache. There was a bullet hole neatly drilled into the man's forehead, but Dieter still prodded the New Zealander's face with his rifle barrel, although why he did not know.

'Shit, Lehmann, get the hell on forward.'

Dieter continued across the field. At the edge of the village, Dieter knelt down at the corner of a small stone house. A rough track ran from the field up into the village itself. He looked back at the sergeant and waved that all was clear. The sergeant signaled for him to check out the track. Expecting to have his head exploded into a million pieces from a million Cretan rifles, Dieter tentatively stuck his head around the corner. Nothing. He signaled again that all was clear and the rest of the unit joined him behind the house.

'Well, Lehmann, what you waiting for? Get up that road.'

'Hell, Sarge. Why me?' Dieter's voice rose an octave.

'Cos you're good at it. Or maybe I don't like you. Either way, get up there.'

Dieter inched forward up the road, checking the roofs and balconies, the doorways and windows for any sign of life. Sweat ran down his brow and stung his eyes, but he did not bother to wipe them dry. His every sense seemed enlarged: colours were brighter, and the slightest noise echoed like a thunderclap. A small cat screeched and ran across his path and he stumbled in surprise. His outreached hand smashed through a window pane, but he ignored the blood dripping from his hand and kept moving slowly up the street. Something clattered, its noise amplified by the high walls around him, and he immediately pointed his Schmeisser in its direction, but it was just a woman closing an upstairs window screen. He arrived at the end of the road, where it opened onto a square. He dropped to one knee and scouted the plateia. Satisfied, he motioned the others to join him. Now that they were coming up behind him he felt a little safer.

The square looked peaceful—a whitewashed church, a grocer's shop, and a small coffee shop with rickety tables. Maybe too peaceful, Dieter decided, and he tensed in expectation of one final attack from the villagers. But all remained quiet. His unit joined him, all of the paratroopers covered in grime and blood, their faces drawn and grey. Lieutenant Maier knelt beside Dieter and scanned the plateia. 'Thank God,' he shouted and pointed to where paratroopers were coming in from all directions. The men looked at each other, the tension drained from their faces, some even smiled, though only a little, and pride began to overtake their fear as they realized that they had taken their objective.

It was evening of the first day of the invasion and the German curfew held Ayios Stefanos in its grip. Squads of heavily armed paratroopers patrolled the streets forcing the villagers into their homes, sometimes politely, sometimes not so much. A large red and black swastika flag hung languidly from the flagpole in front of the church. Tension filled the streets and houses as though the village itself was a living entity waiting for the next crisis.

Yianni and Antoni sat at the kitchen table drawing on their cigarettes, drinking the water that Anastasia kept pouring into their cups and visiting the raki flask frequently. Elpida, with Wawa on her lap, sat on her bed, eyes wide open as the adults spoke.

'I thought they would have put us all in prison by now,' Antoni whispered, as much to himself as to anybody. 'The Germans are tough bastards, but we did well too. We sent a lot of them to their maker, if that's who the Devil is, but we also lost men, and women too. But it's like today never happened. I just don't know what they're going to do next.'

'By the way, Mama,' Yianni said. 'That was quick of you to send that boy to warn us about the Germans encircling the village. Papa Michali is a good man, but he's no soldier and we almost got cut off from the village after the English left. I suppose we all should have guessed the Germans would try to surround us. Not that I'd have done any better than the Papa, of course.'

He let the tobacco smoke linger in his lungs before exhaling lowly. 'Still, Baba, you're right. What will happen now? We killed a lot of them. They're not done with us.'

Yianni took another swig of raki and began to list the names of the villagers he had seen fall. But his father saw Anastasia's face turn pale and he gently placed a hand on his son's hand to silence him.

Antoni looked at his wife. 'What was it like here, Ana?' he gently probed.

She spoke quietly. 'We locked ourselves in our houses, like you told us, so all we knew were the sounds. First, it was the Englishmen with their tanks and guns. Lots of shouting. And those big brown men, we heard them singing. Elpida was very brave, Baba. She and Wawa kept in the corner, and she didn't say a word. We heard the guns firing and the sounds got closer, and then everything was quiet. So I went out to the square. Don't look at me like that, Husband, I am not a girl, and I climbed the bell tower. And I saw the English leaving and there were Germans around the village, but they were a long way away. I didn't know what to do but when I ran into little Yiorgo, I told him to see if he could find you, but only if it was safe and then...'

Anastasia's words began to break and Antoni gently hushed her.

'You did well, Woman, you did well.'

Anastasia asked, 'What happens now?'

Antoni slumped into his chair. 'I don't know. The Germans beat us here, and I think they're winning everywhere, I don't know why, just know it, I've just got a feeling. But I suppose we go on here like normal.' He hesitated. 'I think not knowing is worse than knowing what they're going to do.'

Yianni took another swig of raki and slammed the cup down hard on the table. 'Baba,' Yianni said, his voice rising. 'I don't care if they hold all of Crete, all of Greece, I'm not stopping until every last one of those bastards is off my island.' Yianni smashed his fist on the table, and Elpida ran over to her grandmother.

'That's enough, Yianni, you're frightening your daughter.'

'I'm sorry, pedhi mou, I'm sorry,' Yianni's voice was gentle.

'Come here. Baba's tired. That's all.' The little girl climbed onto her father's lap. But even though he now spoke gently, like he always did, the harshness of that scene made the little girl wonder what was happening to her and her family.

Two days after the Germans had captured Ayios Stefanos, a staff car roared into the square and screeched to a halt outside the church, leaving in its wake a trail of dust and exhaust. A Wehrmacht sergeant, his uniform torn and dusty, stepped down from its back seat and flicked away a half-smoked cigarette which a village urchin dived onto. The sergeant walked over to a paratrooper who pointed to the kafeneio and then the newcomer strode to where Lieutenant Maier, who had taken temporary command of the Ayios Stefanos garrison, was drinking a coffee. The two men saluted Nazi-style, clicked their heels and simultaneously shouted, 'Heil Hitler.' The sergeant handed the lieutenant a piece of paper. The officer read it, and then smiled and saluted as the sergeant scurried back to his car.

Maier turned to the paratroopers in the kafeneio. 'Well, lads, we've done our job here,' he grinned. 'We're being replaced. We're going back to the coast for a quick rest. I don't think you deserve it, but the General Staff always were suckers for you lot. But then we've got more work to do.' The men thumped each other on their backs, revelling in the prospects of a well-earned rest with lots of beer and maybe even some girls as well.

The paratroopers took little time to collect their belongings, and their Wehrmacht replacements arrived one hour later. Maier had argued with the new garrison commander for some lorries but had been summarily turned down, and so the paratroopers walked. The soles of Dieter's boots caught on the ruts and stones of the track and he constantly stumbled. His feet ached and he smelt like a pig. He missed Hans more than he'd imagined, but he knew his friend would have been proud of how he and the others had stormed through the hail of fire to take their objective.

The soldiers came to the field where the Maoris had beheaded Hans. The trooper on point suddenly held up his hand and dropped to the ground. The men followed suit, their red-rimmed eyes searching for the source of the danger, adrenaline pumping them up to instant alertness. They looked around but saw nothing. The man on point slowly stood, and instantly his head was jerked back as a bullet hit it. The paratroopers returned a heavy covering fire, but they could see no targets, only the olive grove whose green depths melted into nothingness. Another paratrooper was hit and then another, but suddenly the firing ceased and again all was still. The paratroopers crawled towards the source of their firing and found two lifeless women, both of them hit in the chest.

The sergeant kicked the bodies. 'Fuckin' animals. They'll be sorry they did this. They must be from the village, and even after we were nice to 'em. No, that village is gonna catch hell.'

Maier strode over to the corpses. 'The sergeant's right, men. They're all animals.' The officer was screaming now. 'They're not soldiers, they're not supposed to be fighting. I don't care if they knew of the surrender or not. Animals, the lot of 'em. They'll pay for this, every last one of them. I'll make sure of that.' He kicked the bodies in their faces and spat on them, then ordered his men to move on.

Chapter 11

Two weeks on Crete and already the war had fallen into a routine for Paul Cuthbertson. Wait for the morning attacks on the ships at anchor in the bay, fire at the German planes, hopefully hit one or two of them, watch them leave and then repeat the process. Even Terry Hendricks's cigarettes were always lit up on schedule. The morning sun burnt through the thin canvas of Paul's pup tent. He rubbed his eyes, took a dirty crumpled vest from a pile of clothes in the corner of the tent, and wiped away the night sweat.

'Bloody hell, Hendo, it's hot in here,' Paul shouted.

Terry Hendricks sat up in the tent next to Paul's, and scratched his stomach.

'What?' Terry yawned and scratched himself again.

'I said it's bloody hot already, yer deaf Brummagen git. Hot.'

'All right, all right, don't get your knickers in a twist. I know, mate. It's not even six o'clock. Christ, you hear that? They're havin' a right go at one another in the bay. Jerry's early this morning. Bloody wake the dead.' Hendricks rolled onto his side to retrieve a cigarette and crawled through the tent flap to light up his first smoke of the day.

Hendricks struck a match but immediately dropped it and stuck his head in Paul's tent. 'Jesus, Cuthy, get out now,' he screamed, bits of tobacco spraying from his mouth. 'It's bleedin' happenin', get up.'

Paul jumped out of the tent, squinting his eyes against the sun, and saw that the sky was filled with planes. German DFS230 gliders were swooping down to their landing zones on either side of Souda Bay, heavy formations of Messerschmitt 109s and 110s were tearing into the ships, and to the west, dozens of Junkers 52 were disgorging paratroopers along the coast.

Sergeant Drake rolled out of his tent, muttering about where the bloody sentries were and were they all fuckin' blind? Still only in vest and underpants, the old soldier took charge and ordered his men to their guns, but by the time he had finished the order the first guns were already firing. Drake shouted at Paul, 'Get in contact with the OP and find out what the hell's happenin'. And hurry yourself.'

Paul hauled himself up the slope and slid to a halt beside the bombardier in charge of the observation post. 'Christ, they caught us with our pants down again. The Sarge wants to know what's up.'

'Look, lad, you can see as well as I can. Christ, they came in fast,' the bombardier said. 'The Germans are dropping gliders and parachutes all over Chania and right up the coast. We've got Jerry gliders coming in to the north on the headland. And it looks like they'll be coming our way sooner rather than later.'

Paul scrambled down the hill and told Drake what the bombardier had said. The sergeant looked at Paul. 'Don't worry, son.' His voice was unhurried. 'It's not as bad as it looks. We'll be all right. We've got the Hampshires between us and them. They're good lads. They'll stop 'em. Don't you worry. Now, get back to your gun.'

'I see what you mean about Drake, Hendo.' Paul panted as he loaded shells into the gun cradle. 'He's a real cool 'un all right. And the Bomb at the OP is like a block of ice.'

'Good,' Hendricks grinned. 'I'll be bleedin' scared for the both of 'em then.'

Working the Bofers like an automaton, Paul's line of vision was limited to Souda Bay. Enemy planes jammed the skies in an incessant attack, and the artillery barrage from the harbour was more intense than anything he'd seen. Large dark grey puffs of smoke exploded around the German planes. Some of the planes exploded in mid-air or looped crazily in the sky, black smoke trailing behind them before they crashed into the sea. One glider plane broke in two as an orange flash erupted out of its side and its human cargo was flung into the air. Not one of their parachutes opened.

At noon, Drake ordered the guns to rotate in standing down for a break, and Paul and Terry flopped down under a tree.

'Christ, Hendo, how long can we keep this up?' Paul asked. 'There's bleedin' thousands of 'em. I mean they're droppin' like flies, but there's just too many of them. And you know we're runnin' low on ammo, don't you? And where's the RAF when you need 'em. Bloody Brylcreem Boys. Useless, the lot of 'em. I've seen one Hurricane since we've been 'ere and all he did was wiggle his wings and bugger off. Twats, the lot of 'em.'

Terry lay on his back with his eyes closed and nodded in response, his only movement being to draw on his cigarette in lung-filling ecstasy. 'Now, now, young Cuthbertson,' he said between drags on his Woodbine. 'Your mother will not want you swearing like that. She wrote me a letter just the other day, in fact. Terence, my boy, she said, please tell young Paul to remember his manners, especially if the big, bad Germans are trying to kill him.' He smiled, lips unparted. 'Seriously, Cuthy, I've told you time and time again, we're all in Fred Karno's Army, but somehow it just ain't funny no more. By the way, Cuthy, you do realise it's my birthday in a couple of days. Yes, twenty-third of May when Mrs Hendricks's little boy first shone his beauty on the world. Right bloody birthday present this is, an' no mistake. Ah well, beggars can't be choosers, or buggers can't be boozers as me old man likes to say. Come on, mate. Break's over. Let's get back to work.' Terry rolled onto his side and pulled himself up.

'Fuck me.' Drake's yell made the two of them look up to see an ME 109 coming in low from the west and raking one of the Bofers. The rounds clanged off the metal and shrapnel slashed into three of the gunners as the German plane soared untouched over the bay. Two of the gunners took flesh wounds that the medical orderly patched up, but the third gunner had been hit in the head by a red hot piece of metal, killing him instantly. All Paul knew about him was that he had a Cockney accent and supported Arsenal. The orderly and a gunner carried the corpse into the grove and threw a dirty cloth over his face. Blood had spewed all over the dead gunner's shirt from what was left of his head, and Terry and Paul had to choke down vomit as they passed the corpse on the way back to their gun, the flies already trying to burrow their way under the bloody shroud.

'Hang on, Terry,' Paul said. He ran to his tent and came out with a blanket that he threw over the dead man's torso. 'It's the least we could do, right?' Terry nodded, and the two of them went back to their gun.

The battery received two more ME 109 attacks that day, but as the sun began to drop out of the sky their intensity slackened. Dusk fell and the fighting ceased altogether. The gunners flopped onto the ground, ignoring the hard rocks that stuck into their bodies, each of them trying to avoid looking at the dead body under the olive tree, but without much success. Someone brewed up tea laced with condensed milk and sugar, and the gunners threw it down their throats despite the heat. The men made themselves thick corned beef sandwiches and cracked open cans of fruit.

'You know, Cuthy,' Hendricks spoke, as he drank the last of the pineapple syrup from a can. 'All today, have you even seen an officer?' Without waiting for a response, he continued, 'No, of course we haven't. Christ, if it hadn't been for old Drakey sortin' us out, we've had been fucked. Between you and me I don't think much of our commanders. I mean, I think they'd be better off chasin' foxes and swiggin' sherry. Eh, look up, Scouser, I rest my case.' Hendricks nodded towards a staff car that had laboriously climbed the hill. A thin, almost emaciated, subaltern in his early twenties stepped down. His red collar tabs were bright, trousers were creased, his mustache clipped cavalry-style. A clean white handkerchief peeked out from his shirt cuff. The subaltern repeatedly slapped his thigh with a swagger stick. Only the bristles on his unshaven chin — and a nervous tic that lifted his left cheek slightly — prevented him from being the caricature of a proper English officer and gentleman.

The gunners started to rise slowly as he approached, but he waved them down. 'It's all right, men, as you were. Now, who's in charge here?' Drake stood up and saluted.

'So, young fellow, me lad,' the officer said, his back becoming even straighter with every word, 'what's the bag so far?'

Drake, a professional soldier at least fifteen years older than the lieutenant, spoke slowly. 'Well, sir, them 109s are bloody fast and they're flyin' right down the middle of the bay. The predictors can't keep up with 'em, sir. We're even having trouble with the Stukas and you know how slow they are. We're bringin' 'em down simply because there's so bloody many of 'em. Sorry, sir, excuse the language. We've had one gunner killed and a few got minor injuries.' Drake looked round to make sure his men could hear him. 'But, all in all we're doin' fine, sir, we'll see this lot off no trouble. We've been engaging the enemy all day, sir, and I can't believe Jerry can stand the losses we've dished out. We just need more shells.'

'I see, Sergeant, I see,' the officer replied, a blank look on his face. 'Well, Sergeant, we'll just keep plugging away, yes?'

'Sir.' Paul stood up and saluted. He spoke almost in a whisper. 'Sir, we don't have no radios, so we're kinda' in the dark here. Do you know what's happening? All we see, like, is our ships gettin' blown up. I mean, are we winnin'?'

'Of course we are, young man, of course we are,' the subaltern spoke with a mix of acerbity and contempt. 'I heard Jerry got pretty badly mangled west of here, so keep your chin up. Sergeant, the General is still expecting the main attack to come by sea. He believes this is just the overture. I agree with him.'

Hendricks looked at Paul and rolled his eyes. 'So,' he continued, 'we'll just keep on doing what we're doing, right?'

The young officer slapped his thigh once more and strode back to his car. He stopped and turned back to look at Drake. 'Oh, Sergeant,' he said, nodding towards the dead gunner, 'sorry to see your fellow. Damned bad luck. Damned bad war.' Drake nodded, and the gunners watched the car slew away down the hill.

'I betcha' old Freyberg's feeling good about Lieutenant Hoity-Toity agreein' with him,' Paul said. 'Our good general can sleep well tonight.' Paul's tone was light, but for once his friend from Birmingham could not respond with a comeback.

Paul slept deeply that night. Only once was he awakened — when a solitary plane droned overhead and Drake ordered the battery to stand to. But the noise of its engine receded quickly to the west, and Paul slipped back into sleep. Just before dawn, the nightmares arrived: Stukas bearing down on him, then flying amongst the men, so close that Terry swatted one with his hand and sent it spinning into the sea, Terry's body ripped by shrapnel, his arm hanging loosely from a smashed shoulder, Drake, dripping with blood, jumping into a slit trench that turned into a grave with a priest intoning over his body. Paul awoke drenched in sweat, confused if it was nightmare or reality.

It had been six days since the Germans had landed and the battle had passed Paul by. Still, they were harassed by German planes and even though the attacks were less frequent, the drain on the battery's ordnance had become serious. During one attack from a Messerschmitt 109, Paul loaded the last shell into his gun's breech. As the German pilot veered away for richer pickings in the bay, Paul shouted to his friend. 'I suppose you should tell him, Hendo. But he probably knows anyway.'

'Yeah, but why me? How come I always get to tell 'im the bad news.'

'Look, I'm already in the shit with him over yesterday, you know when I kicked his mug of tea over, you'd think it was a single malt, the way he acted. So I'm keepin' out of his way. You're on your own.'

'Well, bugger you, Scouse. You owe me.'

Hendricks walked over to Drake who was resting against a rock on a quick cigarette break.

'We're just about out of shells, Sarge.'

The old soldier simply shrugged his shoulders. 'Not surprised, son, not surprised. Had to run out sometime.'

They turned towards a lance bombardier who was yelling to himself. 'This is bloody useless.' He cried and he kicked a wheel of his gun. 'Christ, this soddin' Army is fuckin' useless. What are we supposed to do, throw fuckin' rocks at them? I'm out of fuckin' everythin'.'

The Messerschmitt had taken one turn over the bay and now returned. It banked lazily towards the battery and then swooped in, its shells ricocheting off the rocks and slicing through the bushes. The men by now were used to the attacks and they almost nonchalantly jumped for cover and waited until they heard its engine fade into the distance. Paul looked over at the bay full of British and Australian ships, some of them aground where the crew had made a race for land before they sank, some half-submerged with smoke curling up from their superstructures. And on the quay he saw lorries, half-tracks, even a few light tanks, and stores seemingly unwanted by the army and waiting for a more efficient organization—like the German army, Paul sourly concluded—to come and put them to use.

The gunners looked at Drake.

'Lads, I don't know what to do,' he replied. 'Stayin' here is pointless, I know, we're just about out of ammo, but, well, look, we just can't bugger off, can we?'

Hendricks spoke up. 'Why the bloody hell can't we just sod off? Look I'm not sayin' we desert, I'm not that stupid, but there's gotta be better things than sittin' here with our thumbs up our bums.'

'I agree, Sarge,' Paul chimed in. 'I mean, we're supposed to fight, right?'

Paul was surprised to hear himself say this. He had always accepted that this war had to be fought, and that it was to be done by men like him. But like most of the men around him, he did not eagerly go to the fray. Like most Englishmen, he supposed, he'd do his duty when called on, but he was not going to be a hero unless he had to. And he remembered his father's parting words: Don't volunteer, ever, for anything.

The sergeant looked at Paul and half-smiled. 'I know that, lad, it's just that, well, like I said, we just can't bugger off, can we now. Look, let's lie low for a while and see what happens. Forget the guns, we're not doing any good any more, we'll post lookouts and see what happens. Cuthbertson, you and Hendricks go back to the OP and tell 'em what we're doin'. And keep your eyes open. We should be okay but you never know with those bastards. They could be anywhere. See if the Bomb knows anything we don't.'

Paul and Terry lingered at the OP. They watched the German bombers continue their lazy loops over Chania, bombs falling onto what already seemed just a very large mound of rubble.

When they heard the repeated honks of a car horn, Paul and Terry grabbed their rifles and ran downhill to the battery. The officer who had visited them earlier had shown up again, and he was talking.

'Come on, Cuthy, hurry up.' Hendricks shouted. 'We gotta hear what he's sayin'.'

They were in time to catch the second half of the conversation and the gist of it was that things were going badly and the Germans had taken the airfield just to the west of them and were flying in more supplies and fresh troops.

'I am afraid, gentlemen,' the subaltern said, as Paul and Terry crashed into the backs of the men gathered around him, 'that General Freyberg has ordered outlying units like this one to consolidate.'

The gunners looked at each other in shock, not quite believing they were losing. Even in their small corner of the war they could see the enemy aircraft going down in flames, and hadn't the officer first told them that hundreds of Germans had already been killed or badly wounded. A bombardier started to ask the officer a question, but the Sergeant shushed him.

'Sir,' Drake said. 'If we could just get more ammo we can take them all down. Sir, we're winnin'.'

'I'm sorry, Sergeant, and I do understand your anger, but those are our orders. General Freyberg is most adamant. All Allied personnel are to abandon their posts. Destroy as much equipment as you can. We don't want to leave Jerry anything.'

So, sir,' Drake persisted. 'Where do we go?'

'Sergeant, the major rendezvous is a small village, Stylos, a few miles inland. From there you can expect fresh orders. The village is about twenty miles east of here. Men,' the young officer whispered as though afraid of unwanted ears, 'I have to tell you that this campaign is almost certainly lost. We have to expect a general evacuation order from General Freyberg. I hear on the QT it'll be tomorrow, the twenty-seventh. Sorry, but there it is.'

His last words were lost in the men's questions, but Drake ordered them all to shut up.

'Does that mean, sir? That we're just goin' to wait until Jerry puts us all in the bag?'

'Good God, man, no, of course not.' The subaltern's words tumbled out as though speed of delivery might hide the uncertainty they contained. 'No, no. I am reliably informed that from Stylos, if we are indeed ordered to abandon the island, well, from there you can march to the south coast for evacuation by the navy. If you can get to the south coast, I promise you'll be having a cold beer in Alexandria in twenty-four hours. And as I just mentioned,' the officer was now rushing his words, 'at Stylos you can expect new orders that will clarify everything.'

'But sir,' Drake insisted, 'we don't have no maps and this place Stylos, or whatever, where is it exactly?'

The young officer pursed his eyebrows. 'Well, it's over there, southeast of here.' He waved his arm in a general direction, its span taking in at least three hundred square miles of olive groves and mountains. 'Everything will be fine, Sergeant.' The man's voice again quivered. 'I hardly think you'll get lost. I have it on good authority that the Royal Navy is on the south coast in numbers and they are ready to take our men off safely to Egypt. I can't see the Germans being able to mount an effective chase.' He smiled. 'The foxes will be way ahead of them, eh? Look, I'd love to give you a lift, I really would, but I've got to get to other batteries, don't you know.' The lieutenant climbed into his car, perfunctorily returning Drake's salute as he gave the order to his driver to leave.

'Foxes will be way ahead. What a load of bollocks. Useless piece of shit, he is.' Hendricks's verdict was greeted with shouts of approval by the rest of the battery. Drake kept his mouth shut.

Paul watched the vehicle fishtail down the track. He felt alone, and for the first time since landing he harboured the thought that perhaps things might not be all right after all, despite the comforting presence of Drake. The sergeant ordered the men to back the guns over the hill, and they cheered as each of the guns smashed against the rocks below. A bombardier drained the truck of oil and then started the engine until it froze, before sending it to join the guns. Then, loaded down with rifles, and food and water in their small packs, the band set off. Moving south through the small holdings that fringed Chania, they at last joined a long line of men—British, New Zealand, and Australian—some still with their rifles and helmets, others with nothing but their uniforms to mark they had once been soldiers, RAF fitters, their blue uniforms standing out from the khaki of the infantry, cooks still in their white aprons, wondering perhaps what had brought them to a war for which they were not trained. The odds and sods, the human detritus of a lost battle, all mixed together in a tableau of defeat.

Chapter 12

The line of men stumbled on through the hot Cretan day. In Souda, Paul tried to identify what he remembered of the village. It was now a bomb-wrecked hulk, its destruction completed on the first day of the invasion. The greengrocer's shop, where the old woman had given him a peach, existed no more, and there curdled in his nostril the smell of charred wood and what he presumed was burnt human flesh. There was no sign of life, save a few dogs and cats helping themselves to whatever scraps of food they could find. The soldiers filed past the large church that still stood virtually undamaged. In front of the huge wooden doors there lay five corpses, all Greek. A priest was offering them a blessing. Sheets had been thrown over the corpses, but some were not big enough, and Paul recognized the old lady who had given him fruit. She looked untouched, and he wondered if she had she died of a bullet, or a heart attack or something else entirely. But to her it did not matter anymore; she was dead and she didn't deserve to be. Next to the old woman, lying close to her as though seeking protection for the journey ahead, was a teenage girl. A dark stain had spread over the front of her blouse. Her face still wore the grimace of recent death, as though she had not yet reconciled herself to her fate.

Out of the village, the soldiers entered open fields interspersed with olive groves and then they passed the remnants of the naval station, black smoke plumes still gyrating into the air from smouldering storage sheds and silos. Still on the alert for an attack, the men dropped to the ground when they heard machine gun fire. Paul looked around, searching for where it had come from. A unit of British soldiers, still fully armed — part of the rearguard, Paul guessed, set up to protect them — moved in formation into an olive grove. There was a burst of gunfire and a flock of birds soared into the air above the grove. Then the

British reemerged and gave them the thumbs-up. Paul silently thanked these unknown saviours for their courage, fighting to protect him and the others when they knew the battle was lost.

The track they were on now squeezed itself between the coast and a steep promontory and the progress of the men lessened to a very slow crawl. Paul nudged Hendricks and pointed out the anti-submarine net that still stretched unbroken at the mouth of the bay. All Hendricks could do was mutter that it hadn't done them a damned bit of good. A lethargy had enveloped all of the men and they kept their own counsel. Whether this was because of the heat and the monotony of the march, or shame, or simply because there was nothing left to say, Paul did not know. There was no noise except the scuffling of boots on dirt and the croaked coughs of men who had been without water too long. There was no movement except the men and the flies that buzzed around them. Even the cicadas seemed to keep silent.

Paul, deep in himself, barely heard it at first, a hum and then a growling that grew stronger by the second. Coming in low from the east and flying straight down the line of men was a Messerschmitt 109, its cannons flashing. The soldiers scattered off the track, flinging themselves behind olive trees and bushes as though leaves might offer some protection against bullets. But after one brief sortie down the line of men the plane flew off in search of new victims. Paul lay on his stomach, tasting the dirt in his mouth, listening to the screams of the wounded. He stood up and walked back to the track, marveling that he had covered so much ground to the safety of the olive grove in such a short time. In front of him, still on the track he had never had the time to leave, was Terry Hendricks, his back a shredded mess of blood, skin and clothing. He was not moving and Paul rolled him over. There was a hole where his friend's chest had been, blue and pink organs cascading out. Paul crawled away on hands and knees and threw up. He did not bother to check the bodies of his comrades. Drake lay on his face, one arm extended to the grove as if pointing to safety, and reminding Paul of the plaster casts of the victims of Pompeii, dimly remembered from a book in his beloved library.

Paul crawled away to the grove and wiped the vomit from his lips. It was cool under the trees and he could think of no reason to leave. He felt safe, as though the canopy was a shield against the world. He heard the shuffling of men's feet, the orders of sergeants to get back on the road, and he thought briefly of rejoining the march but could not find the energy or a reason to do so. Directly above his nose an insect hummed a lullaby, and he watched a bird trace intricate patterns through the sky in search of insects. He closed his eyes and slept.

When Paul awoke it was early evening, his face dappled by the shadows of the departing sun. He stood up and urinated, surprised that he had any liquid left in his body. His mouth was dry and his lips cracked as he licked them. The bodies of Terry Hendricks, Drake and the others had been placed at the side of the track. Paul tried to grieve for them, but he found real compassion only for Terry. Now that Terry was dead, Paul was alone again and as before in his life that loneliness somehow comforted him and urged him forward. Without looking further at his comrades, Paul joined the line of men, still snaking its way along the coast, and began walking eastwards. A small—very small—part of him simply did not care what happened to him, but another—much larger—part told him to continue, impelled by the absurd thought that he had been spared from Terry's fate for an—as yet—unknown purpose. Despite the heat, the thirst, the hunger, a cold and clinical logic formed in his brain, giving him a focus that superseded everything but his own survival. He knew that if he were to make it home the less time he spent on the coast with hundreds of other soldiers around to attract the

Luftwaffe the better. He decided to leave the line for as long as it followed the coastline.

Paul unbuttoned his fly and pretended to relieve himself. Waiting for a break in the line so as not to attract the attention of nosy sergeants still trying to exert some discipline, he slipped across to the south side of the road and went into the undergrowth at the base of the promontory. A steep path followed a wide defile that split off from the cliff face and Paul made for it. He felt exposed as he climbed up the path and expected to hear a sergeant ordering him back, but there was only silence broken by the wind whispering though the canyon. The path was broken by sharp stones and rocks, and Paul's boots pinched his toes. He threw away his equipment, first his rifle and ammunition pack, then his helmet and finally his empty canteen. Ahead of him were hills, rocky and covered with wild scrubby plants, a landscape quite different from the rich fields around Chania. His only companions were flocks of sheep and goats. He climbed steadily until he reached a small village close to an old stone fort that dominated the hill's crest. Below him to the east a large plain stretched to the sea, bisected by a long unbroken line of men weaving southward through a patchwork quilt of olive groves and fields.

It took Paul an hour of scrabbling down through the rocks along what seemed to be no more than a glorified sheep trail before he was able to rejoin the line of men, the very line he had abandoned hours ago. Perhaps, he realized, it had been reckless and pointless to leave the line in the first place, but at least, he had acted independently if only for a short time and his freedom from the army had tasted good. A dispatch rider on a motorcycle stopped and told them they were approaching the village of Stylos. Paul entered the village, passing a ruined church on his right. A crystal clear river, occasionally fringed by cane breaks, ran through the village, and Paul along with the other soldiers scattered to its banks and drank the cold spring water. There was no military organization in the village, so far as he could see, apart from a dressing station next to a church where, under the yellow glow of paraffin lamps, medical orderlies worked on the rows of wounded lined up either on stretchers or simply lying on the river bank. Hundreds of men sprawled under the olive trees or lounged outside the village's tavernas helping themselves to beer and wine. A fight between two drunks drew the men's attention but only for a moment. The few officers Paul could identify simply turned their backs on the fight as though nothing had happened. Military equipment of all sorts had been abandoned, guns, rifles, backpacks, helmets. Paul walked over to a chaplain and asked him for instructions. The man, who was not much older than Paul, drew on his cigarette and shrugged his shoulders. 'Go to the other end of the village, it's only a couple of hundred yards long, and you'll see what to do.' The village looked deserted of its inhabitants. There were two shops in the middle of the village, and Paul smiled when he saw that one of them was guarded by an old woman dressed in black. Her grey hair was pulled back in the obligatory style of Greek matrons. She held a pitchfork in her arms, as if daring any soldier stupid enough to try to steal from her. No one did. Then the road turned to the left and snaked out of the village.

Paul could not understand why his tiredness came in waves, interrupted by small bursts of energy where he thought he could run to the south coast, full pack and all. Now, taking advantage of a lull in his tiredness, he eagerly joined some of the men in picking oranges off the trees. Their skins were dry, but the juice tasted like the sweetest nectar. But as suddenly as his energy had appeared it fled his body. Legs aching, feet throbbing, he stumbled into an olive grove, and sank beneath a tree. When he awoke, he was enveloped in darkness. He closed his eyes and let himself drift away.

Chapter 13

The sand burnt through Dieter's boots as he and his squad followed a sweaty Wehrmacht corporal to the rest camp, a simple line of tents along a broad sweeping beach, with a row of large stoves shaded by a parachute canopy the cooks had attached to the wing of a downed Junkers. But for Dieter it was enough if he could find a comfortable place to sleep, get good food, lots of it and, most important of all, have the freedom to do whatever he wanted if only for a few days. Dieter threw his pack and machine pistol into one of the tents and, naked except for his underwear, launched himself into the sea. Too tired to swim, he floated on his back and let the luxuriant warm water wash away the physical and mental grime of battle. Sitting at the water's edge he became obsessed with the tiny fish that congregated around his toes, sometimes biting them, other times seeming to suck at his skin. Occasionally larger fish, perhaps all of four inches long, would dart in, but mostly they left Dieter's feet and toes to their smaller cousins. Dieter idly followed a fishing boat a few hundred meters out to sea, its sail flapping idly as it tried to catch a breeze. An elderly man threw out a net and sat down to finish his cigarette. It struck Dieter that the man had to be insane, with the fighting still going on in the hills, but he supposed that life had to continue and families fed.

A private, in solar hat and shorts, came towards him, and Dieter feared he was being sent back to the war. But the soldier only handed him a letter from his mother, which somehow, miraculously, had found its way to him. He tore it open, not caring that his damp fingers were smudging her writing, and read the familiar copperplate writing that made him gasp as memories of home flooded into him. The beginning of the letter was about the war, and the government censors had made sure that there was nothing in it that Dieter and the other troopers didn't already know. The battle in the North Atlantic was still going in Germany's favour (Well done, Otto, he congratulated his friend,) although the Americans were taking more than just an interest in helping Britain (who cares, they're soft and weak, Dieter told himself), and the Luftwaffe had severely damaged the British parliament building (Bravo, Reichsmarschall Göring). No, it was the news of his family that enveloped him: that Liesl's piano lessons were going well, that father was now a volunteer firefighter, and that mother was organizing clothing drives for the soldiers abroad. Everything in his family was as it should be. This is what he was fighting for, and the arguments with his father now seemed rather melodramatic and irrelevant. Lying in the gentle surf, he read and reread the letter until his eyes ached.

For the next two days Dieter swam, ate, and drank beer, letting the sun permeate his body, with sunglasses he had bought from an orderly shading his eyes from the worst of the glare. Yet as the sun pulled the tiredness from his mind and body, there returned the doubts he had tried to dispel since fighting the civilians at Ayios Stefanos, since the execution of the two women and Maier's comments. His mind was pulled back over and over again to the unavoidable truth that although the battle had taught him he could kill, it had taken something from him. He felt at some level betrayed, as though the killings of civilians had polluted him and made him less than what he had been. Yes, Dieter told himself, he would pull the trigger to take out an enemy, but was this all that was left for him to do? In indoctrination lessons during basic training, Nazism and the Third Reich had all seemed sensible, quintessentially right, not just for Germany but for mankind. German civilization and culture were destined to rule the world, and he was part of the military machine that would make this happen. But at what cost, whether to himself or others? He'd fought against as many Cretans as enemy soldiers. Did those Cretan peasants really deserve to die, despite the standing orders from his general to kill all partisans? Wouldn't he defend the Fatherland with the same ferocity? Could there not have been another way? This war, and how it was being conducted, was not what he had expected before he had made the fateful jump out of the Junkers several lifetimes ago. War was not clean, it was polluted and polluting, and he wondered why he had only now come to this conclusion. It was not what the Führer had promised. Also, war was…he sought for the right word. It was confusing. Not just in the sense of the actual fighting with the noise of battle, bullets and mortar shells, the cries of wounded and dying men, the orders coming in fast and sometimes contradictory. No, it was more than that, for although he still believed in the cause, he could find no moral clarity to what he had just taken part in. Did the ends always justify the means? Dieter pulled out his diary and tried to write. He searched for words to describe what he felt, but always came back to the two simple words, polluting and confusing. Perhaps, he had simply grown up and entered a world where nothing was black and white, that he had finally confronted what he had suspected during that last argument with his father. That finally his childish, almost utopian view of the great Teutonic past had been confronted by a harsh and authoritarian future called Nazism. But even as he wrote those words they seemed too simplistic. He rose and walked slowly to his tent, where the lapping of the waves lulled him back down into a troubled sleep.

The last vestiges of night cast a grey pall over Dieter's tent. He rubbed sleep from his eyes and heard a voice, distant at first but then louder and clearer as he regained consciousness. 'Lehmann. We've gotta move. Come on, paratrooper. Stop playin' with yourself and get up. Now.' A kick at the tent canvas outside, and Dieter looked out through the flap and saw the sergeant going up and down the line of tents. He threw on his uniform and retrieved his machine pistol and pack in time to jump into a waiting lorry, one of a large convoy, filled with over a hundred paratroopers. There was a solitary staff car at the head of the convoy. In it, sitting bolt upright as though on parade, was Lieutenant Maier.

'Where are we going, Corporal?' Dieter asked the man next to him, as the lorry rumbled off the beach.

The man rubbed his beard. 'To do some soldiering, boy, what we're trained for. Real soldiering, thank God, not this peasant shit. One of our spotter planes saw a bunch of British soldiers south of here. They were still armed, the pilot thinks, so we're gonna get 'em.'

The convoy moved south, weaving slowly through a patchwork of olive and orange groves until Maier halted them at a crashed Junkers, smoke still rising from its fuselage. The plane lay along the banks of a small river, one wing tipped into the water, causing eddies that spiralled slowly downstream. There was a large hole in its fuselage and the cockpit's windshield was blown out. A sergeant jumped down from the leading lorry and slowly inspected the plane. Taking the chance to stretch their legs, the other paratroopers joined in the inspection. The fuselage was empty. In the cockpit the pilot was slumped over his controls. Blood was spattered throughout the small compartment, and a sergeant pulled the aviator's head back to reveal that one side of his face had been shot off.

Maier ordered the troopers back onto the lorries. 'Men,' he shouted. 'Come on, we've got work to do. I will make sure this man's body is recovered and given proper treatment. He was a damned good man, a brave one too. It looks like he got everybody out of the plane, including his crew, but left it too late for himself. Remember this. Now, let's go hunting.'

It was a drive of thirty minutes before they left the coastal plain and climbed onto the slopes of the White Mountains. There were few trees, mainly open scrub and shrub, populated only by sheep and goats that dived for cover into the shallow gullies as the German convoy approached. Maier formed his command into squads, and they began a long sweep of the countryside, watchful for movement and mindful of where the nearest stone wall was. Hidden behind one wall they found the corpses of four New Zealanders, ripped open by heavy cannon rounds. A trooper prodded the bodies with his rifle but none of them twitched. Their khaki shorts were almost comically long, but sensible in this heat until you had to take up firing positions on the hard, stony ground, and then it seemed downright stupid. The stocking of one of the dead New Zealanders had fallen down his leg, and the whiteness of the calf stood out starkly and pathetically against the redness of the knee.

Dieter and the rest of the squad began to move forward when shots cracked in front of them. They dived behind the stone wall, rolling away the four corpses, and peered through cracks between the stones. More shots pinged off the top of the wall. Then silence. Dieter was at the extreme left of the line of paratroopers. Fifty yards to his left, a New Zealander ran diagonally across the Germans' line of fire and jumped over the stone wall before they could take aim. The man drew a knife — identical, Dieter saw, to the one that had sliced off Hans's head — and rushed down the wall towards the Germans, screaming at the top of his voice. Dieter swiveled and shot the man twice in the chest. But the New Zealander still came on and only a third shot from Dieter, this time in the head took him down. The giant slithered to a halt ten yards from Dieter.

'That was well done, Lehmann,' the corporal shouted, and the trooper next to him punched him on the arm. 'Of course, I could have got 'im, but I didn't want to spoil your fun,' he grinned. Dieter smiled back. His heart was about to pound through his chest and he wondered if he was the only one who saw his shaking but he had to admit it felt good. The sergeant had been right. This was real soldiering, and not, how had the corporal in the lorry put it, peasant shit.

The sergeant told Dieter to take the knife as a souvenir, but he shook his head. Despite the feeling of a job well done, the knife felt too much like a trophy, too much a reminder of Hans. It was sufficient to know that he had again done his duty for the Fatherland. Still, as the adrenalin surge settled down, Dieter looked back at the dead Maori and wondered if all this had been necessary. Could the war not have been avoided? Professional pride and self-contempt contested for the young German's conscience.

The paratroopers spent the rest of the day on patrol, swinging in a large arc towards their waiting convoy, but they came across no more resistance. The heat that splashed back from the rocks turned their clothes into sodden sponges, and Dieter's neck became red raw from his collar despite all his attempts to pull it away. His feet ached, as though a thousand red-hot needles were being pushed into their soles. The misery of the paratroopers – and their boredom – was relieved only when they came across a British Hurricane fighter plane. Its tail wing was shattered. Inside the open cockpit the pilot sat upright, still belted in. He showed no injuries, at least none that was visible. His buff-coloured canvas flying suit looked brand new, as though he had taken it out of his closet for the very first time. His goggles, still tight over his eyes, gave the impression he was staring fixedly at what lay in front of him. Perhaps he still was. To Dieter he looked like an iguana, and he wondered where on earth that particular image had come from. The paratroopers dutifully kicked the fuselage before hitching their weapons and continuing back to the lorries.

Chapter 14

The success of the mission against real soldiers, not untrained peasants, raised Dieter's spirits and somewhat to his surprise he found himself feeling proud of what he had accomplished. The revelation had hit him, and this also was a pleasant surprise, that while being in the Fallschirmjäger was worth every pain and indignity the instructors had heaped on him during training — the girls admiring him in his uniform as he strolled down the Berlin streets, the veterans of the Kaiser's war saluting him, and even his own father finally, albeit grudgingly, approving of his choice of regiment — it was clear that being a member of the Elite meant you also got the jobs nobody else wanted, or could accomplish. Paratrooper units were off in the hills clearing villages of resistance, the very same units who had taken the brunt of the fighting on that first day, while many of the Wehrmacht battalions, fresh off the transports from Athens, were allowed to take their time settling into their new billets. And now his own unit, strengthened by about one hundred and fifty Wehrmacht regulars, had been loaded into lorries for what the sergeants were calling a special mission.

Dieter lit a cigarette as he reflected on his newfound attitude to life and turned to a trooper next to him. 'Do you know where we're off to? And why's it always us anyway?'

'I don't know why it's always us. Maybe we're good, maybe that bastard Maier just likes volunteering us. How the hell do I know?'

'But where are we going?' Dieter persisted.

The man sighed. 'I don't know, for Christ's sake. Do I look like General Student?'

Dieter decided to shut up.

It was still night as the lorries moved slowly up into the hills, but in the far distance a pale blue was beginning to wash the eastern sky. The exhaust fumes and dust burnt Dieter's eyes as they approached Ayios Stefanos. He wondered why they had returned, but his fears grew when the vehicles carrying the Wehrmacht split into two smaller fleets and took off to the main column's flanks to form a pincer around the village. The paratroopers' lorries, following Maier in his staff car, rumbled into a grove about two hundred yards from the edge of the village. The sergeants told them to debus, threatening that there'd be hell to pay for the man who made any noise. Except for the faint rasping of matches, for not even the NCOs could stop the men from smoking, and the whispered commands of the officers, the troopers stretched to get the kinks out of their bodies and waited in silence. As dawn truly broke, small groups of paratroopers, on their officers' commands, moved quickly to the village and then dispersed through its narrow streets, banging on doors and, like well-trained sheepdogs, herding the villagers from their houses and into the plateia. There was no time for the villagers to do anything but throw on some clothing and obey. A dirty puppy, barely weaned, bit at the leggings of one of the soldiers as he hustled the villagers to the square. He kicked it away, and when it persisted he clubbed its head with the butt of his rifle until it dropped lifeless to the ground, blood seeping out of its ears. Once the villagers were in the square, the Germans separated them into two groups, men, and women and children. The soldiers jostled the women and children away from the men, and two sergeants immediately went down the lines of women roughly pulling the tops of their blouses down to bare their shoulders. Two of the women had heavy bruises on their right shoulders and they were pushed into the crowd of men.

The edge of the square was lined by a ring of Wehrmacht soldiers. Maier ordered a squad of paratroopers to detach from the main body and march out of the square, to where, none of the villagers could tell. Dieter, along with the remaining paratroopers, found himself next to the church, guarding the villagers who had unconsciously sidled to their usual place of refuge. The men talked to themselves, their voices carrying to the watching women like the murmurings of waves on a shingle beach, while the women wailed and the children cried and clung to their mothers' dresses. Elpida cried out when she saw her father and grandfather among the crowd of men. Yianni looked over and smiled at his daughter. Elpida tried to smile back. Anastasia put her arms around her granddaughter's shoulders and held her tight.

Sensing trouble as the crowd grew more agitated, Maier pulled out his Luger and shot a round into the air to shut the crowd up. Maier was wearing his combat fatigues, still stained with blood and dirt, and Dieter guessed that he had worn them deliberately. The Lieutenant drew on a cigarette and then pulled a piece of paper from his tunic. He looked around as he shouted out the words on the paper. The Greeks were surprised at his heavily accented Greek, but they were still not able to follow what the German was saying.

Papa Michali, who had taken his place at the front of the crowd, interrupted the German with a wave of his hand. 'Sir,' the priest said in halting German, 'as you can tell, I know a little of your language, from my studies in Athens. Can I read the letter to my parishioners? And if they have questions, then perhaps you will allow me to ask you for answers.' The lieutenant nodded his approval. 'Men of Ayios Stefanos,' Papa Michali began, 'you have been condemned as illegal belligerents and your sentence is to be taken to the prison in Ayia Valley for incarceration. There you will be well fed and cared for. No harm will come to your families if you obey all our orders.' As the priest intoned the edict as though reading the liturgy, the crowd began to grow restless and the murmurings grew louder. Some of the Germans ostentatiously drew back the bolts of their weapons, but Maier waved them down. Papa Michali spoke up again. 'My children, they are simply going to put us in prison. Who knows? Perhaps we will have some decent food for once.' He attempted a laugh but it was forced, and the villagers knew it.

Maier spoke to Michali, and the priest translated for the crowd that the men were to be marched to a field on the edge of the village where they would be given water before boarding lorries for the journey to prison. The crowd surged forward in protest, but the raised machine pistols of the guards halted them and they fell back to await the Germans' next move. One villager did manage to break through the ring of Germans and took off down the street, but a single shot from a Luger caught him in the middle of his spine and he flopped to the ground. The man's wife tried to run over to him, but she was caught by a paratrooper and pushed back to the other women.

In the commotion of the shooting, Christo took his chance. He had already sidled to the back of the men, and while the villagers and soldiers looked at the man still squirming from the bullet in his back, he dodged into an open doorway. He climbed out through a window on the other side of the room. Twenty seconds later Christo was out of the village. Expecting a bullet to take him down, he ran until his lungs and calves were wracked with agonizing pains. At last, hiding behind a stone wall to catch his breath he looked back towards the village but he could not see the square. He took out a cigarette and allowed himself a smoke while he wondered what to do next.

At Maier's command, a sergeant ordered the village men to form into a line and then indicated to Papa Michali that they should follow him to a grove on the edge of the village. Dieter along with five other paratroopers were ordered to make sure nobody escaped. Despite being pushed and kicked by the Germans, the men at first stood their ground and refused to move.

The lieutenant turned to the priest. 'Tell your people,' he said very quietly, 'that unless they obey, I might order my men to...'

he nodded towards the women.

Papa Michali's face reddened. 'You are no soldier,' he said, but Maier turned away, pointed at the women and began to issue an order to a squad of soldiers. The priest grabbed his arm. 'You win,' he croaked, 'you win.' The priest raised his voice and looked at his parishioners. 'My friends, please, it is all right. Please, we must do this. Everything will be fine, I promise.'

Clinging to their priest's words, the men shuffled out of the square. Some of them looked around for an escape route, but others seemed resigned to whatever might happen to them and stared down at the ground as if in shame. Antoni and Yianni passed their house and saw their clothes—shirts, trousers, underpants—still hanging on the balcony where Anastasia had hung them the day before. There were no lorries waiting in the grove to transport the villagers, just a squad of twenty paratroopers, some wearing only boots, shorts and solar helmets, smoking cigarettes and enjoying the warmth of the sun as it began to flood the crystal-clear blue sky.

Antoni turned to his son. 'This is not right. I don't like this. Those bastards know what we did to them. They're here for revenge and nothing else.'

The Cretans were herded into the middle of the field and waited, clustering into family groups. On Lieutenant Maier's command, the Germans formed a line, guns at their shoulders. Dieter and the rest of his section were ordered to join the firing squad. To his right he saw a grinning Wehrmacht corporal set up a camera and tripod. At the same time, two paratroopers pulled down a heap of olive branches to reveal two heavy machine guns. Papa Michali and three other villagers ran over to Maier, but paratroopers grabbed their arms and pushed them back to the other men.

The village men now stood in the olive grove, together but each one of them alone. Antoni, head slightly bowed, fingered his komboloi beads. The old man scratched his rough grey beard and rearranged a dirty handkerchief in his breast pocket, and smiled at his son. 'Not a wedding, only a funeral,' he whispered. 'But still, I think I should look good for my Maker.'

Yianni half-smiled and looked through hooded eyes into his father's. He arranged his own brown serge jacket and made sure it was buttoned correctly. The two men kissed each other on the cheek, and then turned and looked into the faces of their executioners, their eyes squinting against the harshness of the sun. Yianni and Antoni held each other's hands, and the old man spoke a prayer not just for them but for all around him. Papa Michali blessed his villagers and promised them that eternal glory and paradise was awaiting them all, just over the horizon. He kissed his cross and then closed his eyes and let the sun play on his battered old face.

Maier nodded his head. The Germans opened fire and the bullets began to strike the Cretans. Dieter aimed high. The others did not. Papa Michali was amongst the first to be hit. Even after the bullets slammed into his body he continued to stand upright, his eyebrows arched, as though the conscious realization he had been shot had been temporarily overpowered by a more primitive denial that this was actually happening to him. The two women, betrayed by the tell-tale shoulder bruising of rifle recoils, died as bravely as any man, standing hand-in-hand and shouting defiance at their killers. Kosta Vlakakis, The Man-Who-Walked-Backwards, turned to face the Germans. He shouted out, 'Now I know my future, I can face it with God.' The guns flooded his body with bullets. The other men were cut down too. Some fell to their knees like marionettes whose strings had been cut. Others were flung backwards. One youth, not yet old enough to grow a beard, was hit in the shoulder and he crumpled at the base of an old gnarled olive tree. He cried out, but a round hit him in the chest and his tears stopped forever. A few, only a few, remained untouched. Some of them started to run but it was too late for them as the pizzicato of a second wave of machine-gun fire rattled through the olive grove, and single rifle and revolver shots punctuated the air like metronomes counting to an infernal beat.

A single bullet entered Antoni's upper abdomen and the old man's body twisted as two more hit his side. As he stumbled, Yianni reached out to him as a bullet cut through his own left arm. With his remaining strength, Antoni pulled on Yianni so hard that his son dropped to his knees.

'Trust me, my son,' Antoni stammered. 'Think of Elpida, she is all that matters now.' Crimson froth began to bubble from his mouth. He pushed Yianni down and rolled on top of him. The son at first resisted, but as he felt his father's body press on him, peace descended. No longer did he hear bullets, the cries of dying men, or the harsh commands and laughter of their executioners. He knew what his father intended, he knew that his father was right, he always was. Elpida is what mattered now. Yianni felt the harshness of the stones pressing into him and tasted the dirt of his homeland on his lips, and permeating all, like the first embrace of a girl, unexpected but somehow already known, the smell of tobacco, the sweat, the musty clothes, the unadulterated humanness of his father.

'Remember Elpida, my son,' Antoni whispered through the blood. 'Stay still. God Bless you. Stay still. Give your mother my love.' Antoni softly sang a love song, Anastasia's favourite, one he had sung to her on their wedding night.

Be on the plain a lemon tree, and I on the mountains snow, so I can melt and water you, and make your branches grow.

Be on the plain a lemon tree, and I on the mountains snow, so I can melt and water you, and make your branches grow.

Be on the plain a lemon tree, and I on the mountains snow, so I can melt and...

Antoni stopped singing as his breathing became too laboured to continue. His eyelids closed for the last time, and Yianni no longer felt any movement from the body on top of him.

Dieter surveyed the destruction spread before him. Thirty bodies at least, he counted. All civilians. All dressed in rough peasant clothing, brown or blue jackets, rough shirts, tattered trousers pulled tight with rough leather belts, scuffed and holed shoes. All dressed as peasants, except for one man, an old man with a full white beard who, somehow anticipating his death, had dressed as a Cretan warrior should; knee-length leather boots; black baggy pantaloons; a black waistcoat over a crisp white shirt, a small black turban, a curved bone-handled knife thrust into a cummerbund. He looked like a bigger version of a play doll of his little sister's. Then Dieter saw the bloody hole in the old man's cummerbund and the blood that was splashed carelessly and wantonly over the shirt, and the comparison turned obscene, a violation of childhood, a violation of innocence itself.

Dieter was knocked aside by three paratroopers who, unprompted by the NCOs, pulled out their Lugers and strolled through the carnage. Whether they were mercifully delivering *coups de grâce* or merely prolonging the excitement that bullies feel when they control the playground Dieter did not know. A sergeant ordered Dieter to join them. He wandered through the killing field, trying not to find someone obviously alive, one half of his brain telling him to follow his orders as he had been trained, the other remonstrating that this was not how German soldiers acted; these were not Jews or other Untermenschen, only nondescript sons and husbands whose women, guarded by a platoon of paratroopers, waited to reclaim their men.

The corpses were relatively untouched, not like in battle where bodies too often had been blown by mortar shells into chunks of meat: German, Greek, English, all blurred into an unrecognizable gore. Here, in this field, most of the villagers had been shot in their torsos. The blood oozed out of their wounds and disappeared into the parched soil, as though the earth herself was reclaiming her sons. To Dieter the men looked as though they had tired from working on the olives and simply lain down for a siesta. Some of the men still breathed. He knew they would all die eventually and that at least his bullet would bring an end to their suffering. Yet still, he was aware that such executions would scar him only further, and so he moved on.

Dieter stopped at one corpse, an old man's that lay on top of another body, the body of someone much younger. A blade of grass quivered at the young man's nostril. Was it simply the breeze? No, now Dieter saw the body move, almost imperceptibly. Dieter looked around at the other paratroopers still busy taking in the enormity of the massacre or just fulfilling their blood lust. He cocked his Luger and fired. The bullet hit the ground inches from the younger man's arm, and the body involuntarily flinched. Good, Dieter hoped, surprised at what he had done. It will look like I hit him. He walked away from the two bodies to join the rest of the soldiers, smoking cigarettes, laughing and boasting of their kills. He followed the other paratroopers back to the lorries in the plateia.

One old grandmother ran at the Germans with a knife, but she was clubbed to the ground and lay there blood streaming from a head wound until two younger women picked her up and propped her against the wall of a house. Another woman threw rocks at the soldiers and yelled they would have their revenge. But the paratroopers ignored her and left the village as quickly as they had arrived.

The killing field echoed with the moans of the dying, and limbs twitched, kicking out at the dirt as though preparing their own graves, but most of the bodies of the men of Ayios Stefanos lay still, their blood already clotting in the heat. Their women scoured the field, looking for a recognizable piece of clothing. a distinctive head of hair, a well-loved face, and as they stopped at a body they would cry out, 'He is here, God rest his soul,' or 'My dear, poor husband, look what they have done to you.' And so it went on until each man had been found by his wife or mother, and each woman had found her husband or son. Anastasia was glad that she had told Elpida to stay in the square with Sophia Theodorakis, the oldest woman in the village and whose husband and sons she long ago had laid to rest in the village cemetery. Anastasia picked her way slowly through the corpses. She passed the bodies of Papa Michali and The-Man-Who-Walked-Backwards. Farther on, there was sixteen-year-old Niko Orphanadakis, who now would never get the shotgun his father had promised him for his eighteenth birthday. The boy lay next to his father, both of them with torn and bloodied chests. Anastasia crossed herself and prayed that all the deaths had been quick and painless. She saw that the wounds on the corpses were all in the front; not one man of Ayios Stefanos had died with his back to the enemy, and she was proud of that. At last she came to her husband and son, lying together where they had fallen. As she knelt down to comfort them she knew it was too late, that both of them now were with their Heavenly Father. She cradled Antoni in her lap, and she rocked in pain as tears rolled down her cheek. She kissed her husband's forehead and softly rubbed away the blood on his face with her apron. Then she gently laid her husband down to tend to Yianni.

'Mama,' she heard the word. No, she told herself, this cannot be. 'Mama,' she heard it again. She saw her son's lips move, slowly but distinctly.

'Shhh, don't say anything,' she whispered. She looked around and saw nobody except the women tending to their men.

'Mama, I am alive. I have a bullet in my arm but I think I am all right. Is Baba? Is Baba still with us too?' Anastasia shook her head, and her tears fell over her son's face.

Yianni's words drove her to action. 'We must get you back home, my son. All the Germans have gone. Come on. Baba can wait for now.' Slowly Yianni stood up and rested on his mother's shoulder. Women saw them rise from the ground, and crossed themselves and gave thanks to God. Yianni was heavy and Anastasia stumbled as she tried to support him, but Katerina Petrakis came over and together the two of them, still looking around for Germans, got him back to the house.

Elpida and Sophia rushed in and the little girl went to hug her father, but Sophia held her back. 'Not now, little one, let Baba rest. I must help your Yiayia. Now sit over there with little Wawa. We have work to do.'

The two women laid Yianni as gently as they could on the hard sofa. Sophia looked him over and could find only the wound in the arm. She turned to Anastasia. 'He is lucky. The bullet has gone clean through. Lots of blood but no damage. I think we can fix him.'

'Elpida,' Sophia spoke softly, 'Elpida, bring me a cloth and some water. Ana mou, go to your husband. I can look after Yianni. Antoni needs you now. Your husband needs you now more than ever.'

Anastasia straightened her back and walked out into the glaring sunshine, surprised that for once she did not have to catch her breath. She did not know how to bring her husband home, but there were male voices coming from the square and she saw that men from the nearby villages were already laying out the dead of Ayios Stefanos in the shade of the church, including Antoni, the blood dry and stiff on his shirt. He looks peaceful, she thought, as though he was already in Heaven, meeting his own father and mother, sitting at the right hand of Our Lord Jesus. Anastasia Manoulakis dropped to her knees in front of her husband and wept.

She felt a gentle hand on her shoulder, and a young man — she did not recognize him — asked if he could help. She nodded. 'Help me get him home. He is tired. He needs to rest.' The man beckoned to another from his village, and the two of them carefully picked up Antoni's body and followed Anastasia to her home. The two men placed Antoni's body on the kitchen table, making sure that his head was safely cradled on a cushion.

'Thank you, for all you have done.'

The men nodded. 'Kyria,' one of them said. 'We will light a candle for his soul. He will never be forgotten. And now he dines with The Lord.'

The house was empty except for Yianni. His arm was bandaged and he was sitting upright. 'I sent Elpida away with Sophia, Mama.' He nodded to his father's corpse. 'She told me where you had gone. Little Elpida does not need to see her papouka like this.'

'Will you help me, my son? I know your arm hurts, but Baba needs...' Her voice trailed away and her son took her in his arms and held her tight.

Wife and son gently and lovingly undressed the body of the husband and father. Yianni wiped the blood away with a damp cloth while Anastasia went up the ladder to their bedroom. She returned with a cloth bag and from it she pulled a black woollen suit, white shirt and tie. She and Yianni dressed Antoni. Yianni knotted the tie around his father's neck, and Anastasia smoothed her husband's hair and kissed him on the forehead.

'He looks just like he did on our wedding. What a handsome man he was.'

'He still is, Mama.' Tears formed in his eyes and a slight smile passed across his face. 'He loved you so much, Mama. I know he never told you, just like Baba, but he did. When I was a little boy and tended the sheep with him he would tell me how he prayed every night that when I grew up I would have a wife just like his. And I can still see those little looks you would give each other when you thought no one was looking.'

Anastasia smiled and cupped her son's cheek in her hands. 'You are a good son. Your baba was so proud of you, as am I. Now, let us pray.' The two of them knelt at the body of Antoni

Manoulakis and prayed for his eternal salvation.

That evening, now that their men had been seen to, the women and children came to terms with the tragedy. All through that first night, screams and cries rent the village, as though Saint Stephen himself was crying out in an inconsolable agony. Women, finally able to find what passed for sleep, awoke, only to be brutally thrust back into their misery.

Chapter 15

'I will not leave until Baba is buried.' Yianni's voice was harsh—harsher than he had intended—and it reverberated around the Manoulakis's tiny living room. Anastasia flinched and Yianni stepped across the room to embrace his mother. 'I am sorry,' he said, 'I did not mean to sound so rough. But I am his son and it is my duty.'

Anastasia opened her mouth but decided to remain silent.

'Anyway, Mama,' he continued, 'the Germans are no longer here. It is safe for me to stay, if only a little longer.'

It was the evening of the second day since the massacre, and the women and children of Ayios Stefanos prepared to bury their loved ones, to create the unbreakable bond between themselves and their God. That evening, as the still of night descended like a shroud over the village, the remaining inhabitants of Ayios Stefanos, along with men and women from the surrounding villages, brought in the bodies from their homes. The church bells rang plaintively through the still air and the young priest—sent from Chania to conduct the services—censed each body as it was carried in. The nave soon filled and the congregants spread onto the steps and then onto the plateia beyond. Yianni too was present, mingling with the men who would stand with the bodies throughout the night.

Laid out on hastily constructed trestles were the men of Ayios Stefanos, patiently awaiting, as though asleep, their blessed journey to God. Some were in simple rough-hewn wooden coffins, others simply in burial shrouds. The sweet, cloying aroma of incense hung in the air and grey smoke languidly spiraled upwards from the candles. A hastily gathered choir from a nearby village repeated the Trisagion: *Holy God, Holy Mighty, Holy Immortal, have mercy on us.* The young priest prepared himself. He scratched his beard. He had officiated the burial of individuals many times but never before had he needed to lay to rest in one ceremony all the men of a village. He prayed that he would get it right and prayed, too, that he would never have to perform such a service again. He scratched his beard again.

The priest theatrically cleared his throat and as the congregants settled into silence, interrupted only by the sobs and cries of the mourners, he began the Trisagion. As he completed the chant for the third time, the ululations echoed around the church. The young priest then moved on to prayers and hymns, asking that the deceased find rest and be granted forgiveness of their sins. Then, as the service closed, the women sang the simple line that had carried the village through centuries of pain and hardship: *May your memory be eternal.* In that simple service of one hour duration, the village of Ayios Stefanos had started its men onto the next phase of their eternal life.

The women filed out, some to wakes of simple food and wine, others to the quiet solitude of a home that would never again ring with the gruff laughter of men or be filled with the clogging blue smoke of their cigarettes. Anastasia made her way back home. Elpida was sitting at the kitchen table, and Anastasia sat down next to her, her reddened eyes reflecting the grief her soul felt. She took her granddaughter's hand.

'Papouka is now with our Lord, little one. He is safe now from all of the world's strife. Little one, we were blessed to have Papouka, but now we must rejoice that all his sins are forgiven and that his memory will live forever.'

Elpida let out a cry and snuggled into her yiayia's arms. The two held each other tight as their sobs rent the air and the night turned to the washed-out blue of dawn.

Yianni, knowing he would never be betrayed, joined the men who would stay with the bodies and take turns to recite the psalter throughout the night. Each man took a one-hour vigil repeating the one hundred and fifty psalms that had carried the village through all its previous miseries and hardships. But now the sun's first rays streamed through the church windows, dappling the bodies and the men with their heads bowed. The door to the church creaked open, and the priest entered with a tray loaded with bread and small cups of hot coffee. The liquid felt good, and they nodded their thanks to the young man.

The villagers heard the knell of the church bell, and they met once again in the church. Yianni stepped back into the shadows of the chapel until his mother and daughter had squeezed their way to Antoni's body, and he joined them, hugging his mother and then swinging Elpida up into his arms. The little girl's tears fell on her baba's cheeks and he kissed her eyes.

The priest entered the church, his black robes stark against the whitewashed walls. He arranged the bun that covered the nape of his neck and walked to the altar. He began by repeating the Trisagion and then he and the congregation chanted the Amomos, Psalm 119: *Blessed are those whose way is blameless…* The young man's words towered over the women's, as he settled into his role of creating the necessary dialogue between the deceased and God, and the faithful and God. He led the congregation in the *Our Father*, and as they chanted the Kontakion—*With the Saints give rest, O Christ, to the soul of Your servant where there is no pain, nor sorrow, nor suffering, but life everlasting*—he censed the bodies, the altar and the icons that covered the walls, and as the service moved onto the prescribed readings from Scripture and the final prayers and dismissal, family members kissed their loved ones one last time. Anastasia drew back a lock of Antoni's rich black hair, and kissed him sweetly on the forehead, as though they were still courting. Yianni followed his mother, and even little Elpida was helped up to gently brush her papouka's brow with her lips. The priest anointed the deceased with oil and earth, intoning *You are dust and to dust you shall return.* Then the shrouds were pulled up and the coffin lids closed.

Anastasia, Yianni and Elpida joined the long funeral procession, led by the priest and the choir singing the Trisagion, and made their way to the cemetery for the final and most painful part of the service.

'It is strange, Yianni,' Anastasia said, 'but through the service, I kept wondering why Father Michali could not be here to lead us, but then, of course, he is.' She sniffled and wiped away a tear from the corner of her eye.

Yianni smiled. 'He was a good man. They all were, Mama. And you know that they must be avenged. You know that, don't you, Mama?'

'Not now, my son, not now. We will talk later.'

'I am sorry. Of course, Mama. Later.'

The graveside service was simple and brief. The priest again chanted the Trisagion and then the hymn of Toparia. As the bodies were laid into the ground, each one of them facing east, and blessed by the sacred incense as they enjoyed the long sleep of eternal life, the priest intoned the Litany, asking for God's mercy not just for the deceased but for everybody. Mothers, daughters and wives sprinkled earth into the graves and then in silence they turned away to their houses and a future that was as black and as dangerous as a winter storm.

That evening, as grief finally overwhelmed Elpida and she sank into a deep sleep, Anastasia and Yianni talked quietly outside, on the stone bench that had once been Anastasia and Antoni's special place.

'So, I take it from the packed sakkouli that you will leave tomorrow, my son?'

Yianni nodded. 'Yes. It is too dangerous for me to stay here permanently. You must understand that. I should be dead, look at the two crosses on our door, and if they captured me, the Germans would hold you to blame. No, I must go. I still think I should be honest with Elpida and tell her everything. Slinking away in the middle of night makes me feel like a coward, that I cannot face my own daughter.'

'No,' his mother interjected. 'Sometimes, pedhi mou, being a father means putting yourself second. Better that you leave while she sleeps. I will tell her you'll be back soon. She will understand, trust me. But remember, Yianni. Elpida is our future, she and all the other children on this island. What we do, we do for them, even if they, and sometimes their fathers, do not understand.' She squeezed her son's hand until he nodded.

Yianni kissed his mother on her cheeks, promised he would stay safe for little Elpida, and slinging his sakkouli onto his shoulders made his way down the little lane and out through the olive groves to the mountains.

Chapter 16

Moving carefully through the night, Yianni reached a small mountain cave as dawn was breaking. The remains of a fire smouldered at the cave's mouth. He put down his sakkouli stuffed with bread, cheese and wine, and then he sat down inside the cave's mouth and waited, gazing at the distant Aegean until sleep finally overcame him. Uncounted hours passed, but as the sun began to sink below the horizon there was the sound of steps crunching on the loose stone below awakened Yianni. He was instantly alert but relaxed when he saw Christo Papadakis climbing the slope.

'I thought you might come here to find me,' Christo said, slumping down next to his friend.

'Where else would you go?' Yianni smiled. 'Remember when we would come here tending the sheep and we would pretend we were palikaria, killing all the Turks.'

Christo smiled. 'Yes, now I do. You always did have a good memory.' He paused. 'Yianni, I am sorry for your father. Those bastards will pay.' He flicked a stone with his foot and watched it bounce down the slope until it disappeared from view. 'Forgive me, how is your mama and little Elpida? And how are you? I was told that you had survived, but I couldn't believe it.'

'They are both good, considering what they've gone through. Mama doesn't show her feelings too much, and Elpida is a little too young to really understand what happened. She knows her papouka is dead, of course, and the other men in the village too, but she doesn't know what it means. I am glad she is so young. But first her own mother, and now this? How much more can the little girl take? This island is cursed, I know it.' He paused. 'I'm okay. I only got hit in the arm, but it still hurts like hell. But I can still shoot and that's all that matters.'

He took a deep swig from the wine flask Christo handed him.

'You know, Christo, I envy you,' he said. His friend looked at him, his brow creased. 'Your parents died when you were still a child. We all remember that horrible summer of the plague. And I always felt a little sorry for you, although it never seemed to bother you.'

'I learnt to hide my feelings early on,' Christo said.

'But now I envy you, my friend,' Yianni whispered. 'To see my own father gunned down like a rabid dog by men who just laughed at us in our misery. The bones of my beautiful wife lie rotting in the village cemetery, and hasn't little Elpida, the spitting image of her mother, suffered enough already? And now she is in the middle of a war. Family is a blessing, Christo, but it can also be a terrible curse. You at least have been spared that, and right now I rejoice in that for you.'

'You are right, of course,' Christo gently chided him. 'But never think that my heart does not ache for my village. Because it does.'

The two men ate their bread and cheese, and sipped their wine.

'I know you don't understand my communism, Yianni.' Christo whispered, staring at the distant sea. 'But for me,' he continued, 'it somehow replaced something that was missing. Maybe it simply replaced my parents, you know, something to learn from, to respect, maybe even to love.' He paused. 'But I was foolish. I was wrong.' Yianni cocked his head and sat up straight. 'Not about my communist beliefs,' he said. 'No, that hasn't changed. No, I was wrong back in the church when the Papa told us the Germans were coming. I thought it was so simple. The English were as bad as the Germans and I said we needed to fight all of them. But I know what the Germans did to,' he hesitated, 'to your father, to all our men. For me now, life is simple. Kill the Germans and we'll worry about the English later.'

Yianni said nothing. He picked up some loose pebbles and

threw them aimlessly down the hill.

'You are with me, aren't you?' Christo asked hesitantly.

'A stupid question from a man who knows me like you do. Of course I am. Why did I come here if not to fight? Of course I will fight. And I have to kill the man who killed my father. I would know him if I saw him. He had a scar on his face.' Yianni ran his thumbnail along his cheek. 'Plus, there was something about his eyes.' He screwed his brow in thought. 'I was playing dead, so I couldn't get a really good look. Yes, I remember now. His eyes were different colours. It made him look inhuman. The bastard stood over us and shot my father even though he was already dying. One day I will kill him. I swear that on my father's bones.' The young Cretan let his words drift into space.

'But there is something else that troubles you, my friend, isn't there.' Christo spoke quietly. 'Come on, we have been best friends since we were children, I know when something is bothering you.'

Yianni took his time in replying. 'You always knew me, better than I know myself, I sometimes think. Well, I remember walking into our house a while ago, and Mama, again, was going on about the great Spiro, my uncle, her older brother. You know all about him, too, I suspect. God knows she told us his story often enough. That he had gone to America, had bravely defended his family when the army tried to kill them, how he had been shot, and how they had all escaped to California, where Spiro had become a rich man. Sometimes, God forgive me, Christo, I wish Spiro had never been born.

'I am afraid, Christo,' he continued. 'There I've said it. I'm not afraid of the Germans, I'm not afraid of death, and I will avenge my father's death. No, it is something else. In our family, Spiro is bravery in person. He has become perfect, especially in Mama's eyes, and I am afraid that whatever I do, it will never be enough.'

'Forgive me, my friend, but that sounds a little like, oh, what was that word the old Greeks used, hubris? Yes, that's it, hubris.

Surely, it is enough that we do what we must do, regardless of where that takes us. Let the future and what people think of you look after themselves. Okay?'

'Well, yes, but…'

Christo interrupted his friend, seeing that he was sliding into despair.

'Can I change the subject? We all want revenge, so I've been busy. I've gone to some of the villages around here and there are men who will come and fight with us. We can meet them tomorrow if you like, and then we can start killing Germans. But first, my friend, sleep.'

Yianni nodded, thankful that his friend had once again lifted him up from his misery.

Before the sun had fully broken over the island, Yianni and Christo set out for their rendezvous, a cheese hut high in the mountains. It took most of the day, keeping to goat tracks away from the ridge tops. The sun was low in the sky when Yianni and Christo climbed onto the terrace in front of the cave where a dozen men were lounging. A whole goat was slowly being turned on a spit over a large bed of embers. One man was drenching the carcass in olive oil, and the fire hissed as the oil splashed onto the coals. There was little talking, and the men pointedly ignored Yianni, although some of them nodded at Christo. A large man in his fifties, his face heavily bearded, stood up, grinned at Christo and shook his hand.

'I have watched you the last hour,' he said. 'My God, a herd of elephants could not be more conspicuous.'

Christo's face stiffened.

"I am only joking, my child. Come on, now, don't be so sullen.' He thumped Christo on the back, and the young man had to step forward to keep his balance. He muttered something under his breath.

The older man pulled Christo aside and continued. 'Everything is going to plan. The English fools are giving us everything we want, guns, ammunition, beautiful gold sovereigns, sometimes more than we need.' He scratched his arm and picked at a scab that oozed blood.

'Now, my question for you is this. Are you ready?'

'Yes, Kapitan, I am ready. The Germans are flush with victory. They know we're up here, but they haven't come after us. Still, we will need some more time to prepare. Is it the same for you over in Iraklion?'

'Yes, exactly the same. Up here in the mountains, it is as though the war has never happened. Still, that will change very soon, thank God.' He smiled. 'Once we go after them they'll have to come for us. And when we get them in the mountains we can kill them. The mountains are ours, after all. Now, let me meet your friend.'

The two of them walked back to Yianni.

'I am Kapitan Stathis.' His voice boomed in the still evening air. 'I control all the andartes from here to Iraklion. Well, most of the andartes at least. Some refuse to say I am their leader. But they are fools, and soon they will come around to me and together we will win. So you see, I am powerful. ' He chuckled.

Yianni looked askance at Christo, unsure of what to say.

Stathis, sensing Yianni's hesitancy, continued. 'I am glad you came. All of us know what happened to your village. I am sorry.' The man hesitated and pursed his brows. 'Yes, I am sorry but, forgive me. That was in the past. We must see to the future.'

Yianni held his tongue.

'Yes, we must plan for the future,' Stathis said. 'But first we must kill all the Germans and then,' he looked at Christo, 'we can remake Crete so no man ever goes hungry and all men are free. But now I must go. You children are not the only ones in my care. Christo, we talk soon, yes? And remember, my children, as long as we have life and a chicken, we'll be fine.' He roared with laughter at the old Cretan saying, and gathering up his bag bounded down the hill, accompanied by two heavily armed men. His booming laughter could still be heard even after they had dropped out of view.

Now that Stathis was gone, the air of tension hovering over the terrace quickly dissipated, and the men broke out flasks and started talking to one another again.

Yianni looked at Christo, his face hard and unyielding.

'Yes, I know,' Christo slowly said. 'I should have told you before. He is a communist. But he is a good man. And he will help us win. I know it.'

Yianni smiled. 'My friend, I don't care what he is. Since my father was killed everything is upside down in my world. So, if you think the Kapitan is the man to help me kill the Germans, then okay. Now then, I need to meet my new comrades.'

'Yianni, my friend, you're going to do a lot more with them than that.' Christo's laugh echoed around the hills. 'Now, let us try to celebrate.'

Christo introduced the men of the band to Yianni, and as the raki flowed and the goats were consumed, so did their inhibitions to the newcomer disappear. Yianni and Christo shared a hunk of meat that the cook hacked off the carcass with his knife and then picked at a portion of kokoretsi, goat meat wrapped in its own intestines. The raki was young and harsh and bit Yianni's throat, but it felt good for him to throw off the memories of the last week if only for a few hours. The two friends watched the men form a line, arms around each other's shoulders, and the lyre player started a slow rhythmic pulse on his instrument. Gradually the tempo increased, and the men's feet weaved an intricate web of movement until exhausted they knelt down and clapped in rhythm with the lyre and let two young men take centre stage. The men competed, each one daring the other to throw himself higher and spin his body more recklessly. One of them kicked high in the air and slapped the sides of his boots. The other, not to be outdone, kicked even higher but on coming down his feet slipped on some pebbles and he crashed unceremoniously to the floor. His companion held out his hand and was pulled down to the ground where the two men began to wrestle each other. The wrestling became too boisterous, and finally one of the older men pulled them apart and made them shake hands. He handed them a flask of raki, and soon they joined the other men, lying on the floor, catching their breath and consuming more alcohol.

'You're not worried about the Germans seeing you? That bonfire's pretty big.' Yianni asked before a particularly strong mouthful of raki made him splutter.

'No, not yet anyway,' Christo said. 'Like I told Stathis, they're not interested in us up here, yet. But they will be as soon as we start on them.'

One of the andartes came over and pulled Christo up, and the two started to dance. Yianni was content to watch, but he too was pulled away from his raki, and the night turned to day, as the andartes danced into their future.

Chapter 17

Paul opened his eyes and looked around in confusion. It was still cool, despite the sun that peeked through the canopy of olive trees, and he lay still for a few moments, reluctant to leave his refuge as he tried to get his bearings. A strange sound entered his still fuzzy brain, a rustling sound that reminded him of leaves blowing down his street back home or—weirdly—of his mother pouring sugar into the jar on the kitchen table. Curious, he edged on his stomach towards the sound, and from the edge of the trees he spied men, hundreds of them, still tramping in single file along the rough dirt road. Of course, Paul chastised himself, I can be real stupid at times. Paul stood up and shouted at the top of his voice, 'I'm British, a gunner, I'm coming in.' The men barely looked up, and Paul rejoined the line. He spied a discarded canteen, grabbed it and filled it up at a small stream that ran with the same clear water as the river at Stylos. Then he started walking. Again. A solitary sheep in a vast flock.

As the sun rose higher, the heat burnt through the head cloth Paul had fashioned from his shirttail. His boots were full of burning embers and his body ached even after the night's rest. Soon, east of Stylos they came to another small village. Most of the houses were in ruins, and the smell of smoke and cordite shrouded the village. A woman knelt over the body of a man, her keening splitting the air. She swatted angrily at a dog that nosed up beside her, ready to help itself to some fresh meat. A man ran at the dog and smashed a heavy cane over its back. It scampered away and lay down on the road, its eyes still devouring the corpse. One group of old men were trying to pull apart the rubble of the buildings; others were recovering bits of broken furniture, but most of the villagers, many of them only children, sat in the street, heads in hands, as though incapable of making any more decisions.

At the village crossroads the line of soldiers turned south to face the first of the hills they had to cross. The incline was steep, and many flopped down at the side of the dirt road, but Paul persevered and reached a plateau. As the landscape opened up and the thick stands of cypress trees thinned out, he was able to gauge what lay ahead of him; fold upon fold of hills that climaxed in steep, treeless mountains, the higher ones still dusted with the last of the winter snow.

A rumbling in Paul's stomach moved through his intestines, and Paul tightened his anus as diarrhoea threatened. He hurried off the track and into a small vineyard until he was hidden from view. He pulled down his trousers just in time and heard the squirting liquid splatter onto the hard ground. He had hardly the energy to clean himself properly, but he found a page of the battery orders he had stuck in his pocket for just such an occasion and wiped his hands on the clover. He adjusted his trousers' belt and was about to rejoin the line when he heard a high-pitched moan that turned into a shriek. It was followed by a woman's voice, in Greek he reckoned, and in pain too.

He crept slowly towards the sound, unsure if Germans were waiting to ambush him. Just inside the olive grove that fringed the vineyard he stopped. The same voice, muffled this time, and he went further into the grove, curiosity overcoming his fear. At the bottom of a three foot high terrace he saw the source of the screams. A young girl was on her back, her skirt at her ankles. A soldier—Paul did not recognize the uniform, only that he was not German—lay on top of the girl, pinning her down as she struggled. The soldier leant back and punched the girl on the left cheek, drawing blood. As her head jerked to the side from the force of the blow, she saw Paul. The soldier followed her gaze.

'Get lost, boy, unless you want some later. Then take your turn.' Paul could not place the accent, maybe it was a Kiwi or an Aussie, but he didn't really know. The soldier laughed and, still pinning the girl down with his body, helped himself to a leather flask. He drank greedily and the red wine splashed from his mouth onto the girl. The girl no longer struggled and the soldier began to loosen his trouser belt.

Paul jumped off the ledge and kicked the soldier in the side of his head. The man rolled to his side, off the girl, who scrambled out of the way. The soldier fumbled at his sidearm holster, but Paul kicked out again, grateful that years of football had finally paid off, and caught the soldier on his shoulder. Paul was conscious of what he was doing, but somehow he seemed no longer to be an actual participant, merely a rather intimate witness to somebody else's action. He picked up a rock and swung it down on the top of the man's head. A sound like a coconut being hit with a hammer, and then the man rolled onto the ground. Paul looked around in vain for the girl. He turned to the soldier. Blood and a creamy white liquid oozed out of the wound. A fly settled into the gore and was soon followed by others. Paul, recalling what little he could remember of a Saint John ambulance course he'd taken in the Boy's Brigade, felt the man's pulse and then his neck. But Paul did not need to do this; the wound alone told him he had killed a man. Paul sat down hard and looked at the body and the eyes that stared into the sky. He found it curious that the first person he had killed had been a supposed ally rather than a German. Yet he felt no guilt, only a small sliver of pleasure, as though in his own little corner of this world he had been able to right a terrible wrong. It was as though the frustrations of the last weeks, the humiliation of defeat, the death of Hendricks and the rest of his unit, the squalid corpses lined up in the village, had at last found release. The young man scrambled back up the terrace face, crossed the vineyard and rejoined the line of men.

The landscape Paul now trekked through had turned harsh as the track climbed sharply and cut through the base of yellow-brown cliffs and massive scree slopes, some baked as hard as concrete. The dust from the tramp of hundreds of feet choked the marchers, sharp stones slashed their boot soles and cut their arms and legs as they stumbled. The heat bounced back off the rocks, burning the exposed arms and legs of the men. Some of the soldiers had placed knotted handkerchiefs on their heads against the sun, reminding Paul of his father on summer day trips to New Brighton. The sweet bitterness of the memory made the bile rise, and he spat as it burnt his throat. The sky was cloudless except for a few mares' tails, but at least it would make the German fighter planes easier to spot. He stopped and massaged his calves, and wanted to take off his boots to do the same, but he was frightened that he might never get them on again. All around him men were being dragged to their feet by comrades, while others lay on the stony ground, immobile, faces blank, red, dust-rimmed eyes staring at nothing. The sound of marching made him look down the trail and there he saw fifteen regular army soldiers. They carried their rifles smartly, and marched in step. They passed him, and Paul saw their shoulder flashes: Guardsmen, the best of the best and still soldiers, real soldiers, even in retreat. The men sitting by the side of the road even croaked a cheer as they passed, and Paul, heartened by their example, picked himself up and continued.

Yet as the regulars faded from his view, so did the lethargy of despair return. His thoughts did not come straight to him but bounced around in his skull. A blur of images appeared and disappeared, a woman's head, flies laying eggs on an oozing brain, burning villages, a library, Terry's incessant smoking, the bloody hole in Terry's chest. There was no logic to how these thoughts emerged or how long they stayed. They were like worms that birds pull from the earth, half-eaten, dying but still squirming. And though the sun was bright overhead, Paul walked as though in the dark, slow and stumbling. He felt blind, as though the only sense left to him was that of touch. He was back in his childhood bedroom groping in the dark for a wall, feeling the edge of his bed, hoping to find the door and the way out of the darkness. His only guidance was the men around him, occasional words of encouragement but mostly quiet as the men walked in their own private universes of pain and humiliation. Paul kept on with them, simply because he could think of no alternative.

Late afternoon, his body telling him he could not go much further, Paul—mercifully—came to the rim of a deep, basin-shaped depression about a mile across, its floor covered by green fields encircling a small village. To his left a stone castle of some sort sat on the crest of a high hill, dominating the whole area. A cheer arose from the men ahead of him as they met a detachment of Australians armed with rifles, machine guns and light artillery guarding the track that curved down into the basin. 'Welcome to the saucer, yer bleedin' Poms. Not far now. Go on, lads, we've got ya backs,' an Australian private shouted with a smile.

Paul could hardly stir to say anything but a mumbled 'Ta, mate.' He knew these men would probably die or be captured, and all to act as a rearguard so that he and hundreds of others could escape. Paul knew he was not worthy of their sacrifice and wondered what sort of man did that, what sort of soldier. But he already knew the answer: the best kind. And again Paul asked himself how men such as these and the guardsmen who'd marched past him on the ascent could have been led by officers so stupid as to lose a battle they should have won.

The track to the bottom of the bowl was steep and Paul kept slipping on loose pebbles. At the edge of the village, Paul slumped down in the shade of the houses, exhausted. The women and children of the village were offering the soldiers bread and water. Many of the men stretched out and awaited their fate, but as though heeding a silent command, most of them, as soon as they had eaten and drunk, stood up, figuratively and literally dusted themselves down, and continued their march, this time up the other side of the bowl. Paul joined them. Close to the rim he felt a breeze, cool and clean. He walked for another thirty minutes along flat rocky ground and then saw before him, glistening in the thin, clean air, the washed out blue of the sea. It was then that Paul began to feel really afraid, as though he might be denied at the very last moment the freedom that he had fought for. But the knowledge of being so close to escape soon overpowered his fears and with almost a spring in his step he began the final slog to the coast.

Paul arrived at a military roadblock. Two MPs were shouting to the men waiting to get through that they had two choices, either to continue down the mountains, in the open and vulnerable to enemy strafing, or take a gorge, harder and steeper but at least protected from air attacks. Paul decided to take the gorge route and gathered himself for the final push. He soon saw what the MPs had meant, for the defile was narrow and rocky and it would mean scrambling over large boulders and picking his way carefully through the stream bed to avoid twisting his ankles. Paul had just entered the gorge proper when he ran into a group of soldiers scrambling their way back up. One of them, a corporal, slumped down in front of Paul. 'Fuckin' navy,' he croaked. 'Fuckin' navy. They've gone. Deserted us. We're stuck on this bloody island. Senior bloody service.' An MP rushed over to the corporal and offered him a canteen of warm water, which he gulped down. 'Right, son, take your time, what happened?' The MP spoke softly, as he would to a child.

'Well, Sarge, like I said,' the corporal now spoke more calmly. 'I was halfway down when I saw this lot,' and he jerked his thumb over his shoulder, 'coming back up. They were bleedin' scared all right, and they said the navy had sailed away, gone back to Egg White. Jerry's strafin' the harbour down at the other end of the gorge, right, and a lot of our boys went west. The navy took off thousands, but now they're gone and we're stuck here.'

The news spread through the crowd of soldiers waiting to start their descent and the mass began to shred itself apart. Some soldiers, unwilling to believe the corporal, started down the gorge, others slumped to the ground, devoid finally of hope that someone in authority might have a new plan to get them out, and waited for the inevitable — capture, transport to a POW camp and then an end to a war none of them had wanted to fight in the first place.

Paul knew that he was, to use Terry Hendricks's favourite phrase, royally fucked. Every muscle in his body burnt, but with an effort and a determination that surprised him he forced himself to look for an escape route, although he was quite certain of its ultimate futility. He wondered why he just didn't give up and wait for the Germans, but he could find no decent answer, only that he had to go on. Perhaps he was simply drawn by the chance to be alone, to be his own master, if only for a few blessed hours, but his mind was too befuddled to think it through clearly. He just knew it was right to continue. He walked away from the road and the soldiers milling around in uncertainty and began to climb back into the hills, following a track that looked as though it skirted around the foothills of the highest peaks. Every step was an agony. The toe of his left boot was cracked, and blood from the blisters on his toes seeped through the hole. Paul's nose was red and peeling, and the burnt tips of his ears stung as though acid had dropped on them. How long Paul walked and in what direction he was not sure, but the sun was beginning to drop low into the sky when he thought he saw a glimpse of the sea far away in the distance. Acid bubbled up from his guts and sizzled in his throat like a thousand red-hot needles, and out of boredom — for even in a war boredom is an equal partner with fear — his mind wandered and finally in his daze he began talking to himself.

'I know they started it and the Blitz an' all, an' I'd like to get my hands on the pilots who dropped those bombs...But still they're only doin' their jobs, aren't they? I mean I bet regular Germans are okay, they probably hate this war as much as we do, but still they fuckin' started it...I dunno, we've got an empire, doesn't do me much good though, does it, and it's not like anybody asked my opinions about anythin'...But me dad was right and Uncle Arthur too...They said Hitler was a bastard and we'd have to sort Jerry out, just like last time...Some things are just plain wrong, Paul mate, like the Germans invading this island, like that bastard trying to rape that girl, like Terry getting killed...Christ, an' now I'm supposed to just give up and let the Germans, the bastards who'd blown up half me street, to just waltz in and take whatever they wanted. This is it? This is what it's come to? So, I just slink off like that dog Georgie Thompson in the next street was always kicking around? Sod it.'

Chapter 18

Paul staggered as his boot once again caught on a rock, and someone grabbed him from behind, stuck a hand over his mouth and pulled him down. Paul struggled but the man was too strong. Another man rolled on top of him, and lying on the ground next to them were five others, all in civilian clothes and all loaded down with pistols and rifles. One of the men put his finger to his mouth, and Paul knew enough to stay still and keep his mouth shut. The group slithered away behind a stone wall and one of them grabbed Paul by the shirt and pulled him along with them. The man who had pulled him down rolled over and spoke one word. 'Yianni.' The other stuck his thumb in his chest and said 'Christo.' A third man offered him a leather flask. Paul drank hard on it and choked as a fiery liquid burned its way to the ends of his toes. Paul wanted to cough his stomach up, but Yianni's look suggested that it would not be the best thing to do. The other men smiled broadly and the man with the flask offered Paul a piece of hard brown bread and a slab of very drippy cheese. It smelt like old socks to Paul, but he wolfed it down nonetheless. The men stood up, cradling their weapons like their own children, threw their sakkoulia over their shoulders and began to file away towards the hills. Paul gazed at their steepness and the harsh, treeless landscape that awaited him, but he did not know what to do except follow. They kept to no track and in his tiredness Paul kept tripping on the loose rocks. At one point he slipped and began to roll downhill until someone's rough hands grabbed him by the shoulders and heaved him back upright. The sky was black ink when the group arrived at a small cave. In the cave was a burnt-out fire in a small rock-lined pit and the debris of past meals, mostly animal bones and empty bully beef cans. The man called Yianni pointed to a corner. He placed his hands together as though in prayer and put them to the side of his head. Paul nodded, curled up like a baby and sank down into a deep sleep.

It was midmorning when Paul awoke. His face was to the cave wall and for a moment he could not remember where he was. He smelt something roasting, and he turned over and looked out. One of the Cretans was grilling a whole lamb on a spit and rubbing it with olive oil. The man grinned toothlessly at him, and Paul smiled back. He crawled outside to where the men were sitting, smoking and talking amongst themselves. The man called Christo gave him a ceramic jug and Paul tentatively sipped it. This time it was water, warm and brackish but drinkable. The cook offered him a hunk of meat and piece of hard bread, which Paul took. The Cretan smiled again. 'How do you do?' he said. His heavy accent and toothless grin combined with the splendid formality of his greeting charmed Paul, who tucked into the food until the olive oil and sheep fat ran down his chin. He hesitantly gestured for more and surreptitiously surveyed his new companions as he ate. They all looked the same to him—short in stature, dark hair, heavy bristles, shabby clothes. They constantly sipped at small earthenware flasks and ate prodigious quantities of meat. As Paul worked on his own food, their individualities began slowly to crystallise in front of him. One man had a broken nose and breathed heavily, another rocked as he spoke, another smoked constantly, lighting up a new cigarette from the butt of his old one. One of them was clearly the camp comedian because whenever he spoke the men laughed at the tops of their voices. Another was using a long, wicked-looking knife to delicately clean the dirt from his fingernails. The men liked to shout everything, and on a few occasions Paul was convinced they were going to come to blows, but they never did and soon someone would crack what Paul guessed was a joke and they'd all start roaring with laughter. For the first time since he had landed on Crete, Paul began to see its inhabitants as individuals, not just poor peasants who had to be rescued from the Germans. Paul smiled at the irony of that observation and helped himself to more meat and a slice of hard bread.

Yianni ordered one of the men to go over to Paul. In halting English he told Paul that they were andartes—Paul had never heard the word, but he guessed what it meant—and they were going back to a village later that day to learn more about what the Germans were doing and, with God's blessing, to kill some of them.

'What do I do?' Paul stammered.

'Why, come with us,' the man replied. 'We kill many Germans. Bang, bang, bang. Yes. What else you do? You need anything, you ask me. Me is Anesti, Anesti Mandrakis. Me your friend. Tomorrow, we kill Germans, yes, all good.'

Paul remained silent. The men took this for his agreement.

Yianni joined the two men and threw some very old and very smelly Greek clothes at Paul. He then pulled Paul's uniform off him and gestured that he put his new clothes on. The clothes barely fitted him, and within five minutes he was itching from the fleas he had just inherited. Yianni took a handful of dirt and rubbed it all over Paul's face, and then rubbed the burnt end of a cork into his eyebrows. He took a battered hat and pulled it down low so that most of Paul's hair was hidden, although the dirt and grease that covered every inch of his body almost made the hat unnecessary. Yianni stepped back, looked the Englishman over, made one more adjustment to his cap and nodded. He grabbed Paul's uniform and tossed it on the embers of the fire. Paul shouted at him to stop and went to retrieve them, but Anesti pulled him down. 'We do this, okay,' he said. 'You English, never here. All Greek. Kill German, bang, bang.'

Paul grudgingly agreed. 'Okay, for now. We kill Germans. Like you said, bang, bang.' He knew he had to start thinking like his new companions did, but why he had just talked that way he had no idea. He hoped that he had not insulted them.

Paul had nothing else to do but lay on the rough ground outside the cave for the rest of the day, moving every so often into the shade as the sun worked its way around the sky. The first time he needed to pee one of the men accompanied him, making sure that he did not break the skyline of the ridge above them. After that, he was allowed out on his own. Slumped in the shade of the cliff, Paul watched the Greeks interact and concluded that Yianni and Christo were their leaders. Although ignorant of what they said, Paul noticed by his body language that Christo often deferred to Yianni. Both men looked tired beyond help. Their eyes were bloodshot and Yianni's cheek twitched every minute or so. They both fumbled with the mechanisms of their rifles, as if afraid that inactivity would lure them into a sleep they could not afford.

Anesti, the interpreter, came over and joined Paul as the heat of the afternoon sun dissipated.

'You English, all rich, yes? All lords, I know this, I do.'

Paul smiled and shook his head. 'No, I'm not rich. I do not have a big house. I'm not a lord.'

Anesti raised his eyebrows. 'No, you English, you rich. How much do you have? Millions of drachmas, yes? And children. How many children? You big man, you have many. I go to England one day. Make money.' Anesti laughed. 'We go together. I meet your sister. She like me. I am good man. Make money.'

Paul had to laugh. If only he knew how rich I really was, he thought, he'd be offering me his sister, out of pity if nothing else.

Anesti winked and tapped the side of his nose. 'It is okay, my friend. I tell nobody. We friends. You keep your sister for me. I like you. We friends.' He lay back on the ground and lit a cigarette, a smile playing on his face.

As the day slipped into the numinous beauty of another Cretan summer evening, a newcomer arrived. He was in his teens and Yianni immediately came over and embraced him. 'Alexi Doukakis, it is so good to see you. We knew you were in the hills. I am glad you can join us.'

The young man nodded and helped himself to food. 'Kyrie Yianni, I mourn for your family,' he said after he had swallowed. 'Your father, Kyrie Antoni, was like a father to me. I pray for his soul.'

'Thank you, Alexi. Yes, he was a good man.'

'Kyrie, I am here to help fight the Germans. Will you let me?' The boy's plaintive tone moved Yianni.

'Alexi, you will fight with us whenever we have to. But for now, I want you to stay here and guard the camp. You are tired and you must rest.'

The young Cretan opened his mouth, but Yianni waved him down.

'If that is what you want, Kyrie, then so be it. But I will kill Germans one day.'

Yianni nodded. 'Indeed you, will, my child, indeed you will.'

As long shadows fell across the valley below, Yianni ordered his men to move out into the lowlands. They were a motley group, unshaven and dirty, cigarettes permanently, or so it seemed, stuck in their mouths, clothes tattered and darned, shoes often hanging off their feet, kept there only by the string or wire wrapped around them. But all of their weapons were cleaned and oiled. The men kept up a rapid and unchanging pace, and Paul had a hard time keeping up with them as he stumbled from one rock to another, sometimes slithering twenty or thirty feet down the scree and wondering if he would ever stop. But always there was someone with a smile to chase after him and pick him up.

The ground was now flat and the first signs of agriculture had appeared, olives, vines and fields awaiting the next planting. As they followed a trail that bisected a small olive grove, Yianni, who was on point, motioned the men to drop behind a stone wall. After ten minutes of waiting there was a murmur of voices that became louder and more distinct. Paul knew they were German. He crouched lower, his heart racing, his stomach turning.

The andartes waited until the Germans were in range and then opened fire. The six Germans were killed instantly in an encounter that took about fifteen seconds. The andartes ran to the bodies and stripped them of their guns, ammunition, food, first aid kits, and money. Then they dragged the bodies away from the track and dumped them into a fold in the ground. They hacked some branches off a nearby tree and covered the corpses until they could not be seen from the track. During the ambush and its aftermath, Paul had never moved from behind the stone wall. The andartes were, Paul realized, natural killers, and the Germans were simply inanimate objects to be disposed of as quickly as possible. He was still crouched at the wall when Anesti grabbed him by the collar and dragged him to his feet. He was smiling. 'It's okay, Tommy, next time you get 'em, yes?' It was a small victory but an important one for the andartes and they hugged and kissed each other. A word from Yianni instantly stilled them, and in silence they made their way back to their mountain lair.

June 1941

Chapter 19

June brought only frustration for Yianni's band. The Germans had retreated into the villages, and despite all the band's efforts they were not able to engage with the few German patrols that were sent out. Frustrated, Yianni and Christo ordered the men to disperse temporarily, either to their own villages or back to the hills. Yianni, Christo, Alexi and Anesti, with Paul in tow, set off for Ayios Stefanos as soon as the sun had set behind the hills. The five of them walked through the night before halting at a ridge that overlooked the village. Paul lay next to Anesti, who told him that it was safe to go there because now that all the men were dead the Germans had left the village for larger garrisons. Paul pursed his eyebrows. 'Ah, you do not know, German come, kill all men, bang, bang, bang.'

The five men slipped into the village as the sun was breaking over the eastern hills. The streets were deserted, and all was quiet except for the dogs as they awoke for another day of guard duty and a cock on the edge of the village that crowed atonally. Paul looked around; the houses seemed small and shabby, and he noticed that each door had painted on it one, two or sometimes even five crosses. Christo, Alexi and Anesti slipped down one street, while Yianni and Paul made for a small house off the plateia. Its door had two crosses on it. They opened the door and Yianni tiptoed to a small pile of sheets and gently gathered them into his arms. Paul saw that the pile of sheets contained a young girl. Rubbing her sleep from her eyes, the girl realized what was happening, and threw her arms around her father, at the same time kissing his cheeks. Paul, unsure of what to do, squatted against a wall, and silently observed the homecoming.

A voice came from the room above. 'So, you are back, my

son.' Anastasia, dressed in black and with red-rimmed eyes, came down the ladder. Yianni rushed to his mother and held her tightly.

'Are you all right, Mama? I worry about you all the time,' Yanni spoke quietly but his voice carried through the room.

'Yes, my son, we are all well as can be expected. Little Elpida misses you, of course, and her papouka as well. We lit a candle for you over his grave.'

'I pray for his soul, Mama, you know that, don't you?'

Anastasia nodded and looked away. She saw Paul for the first time.

'He is English?'

Yianni nodded. 'We found him lost. Don't worry. Mama, is Elpida coping?' He sat down at the table and let the little girl cuddle into him.

'She is very brave, my son. She cries over her pappous, of course, but she is brave and very strong. I think I need her more than she needs me.'

Paul knew he was intruding in their conversation, and Yianni folded his hands to his cheek and motioned him upstairs. Despite Paul's hand-signal protests that the downstairs floor was adequate, Anastasia insisted on giving him her room. This was for his own safety as much as due to Cretan hospitality. At the top of the ladder he looked back to the three Cretans at the table, holding each other's hands in a silent prayer.

For the next two weeks Paul spent most of his time in the loft although he was allowed down for meals when night fell. He mostly enjoyed the solitude of the loft—for some perverse reason he even enjoyed listening to the old couple in the next house. They must have been deaf for their voices carried across the alley and through the thick stone walls of the houses. But as the house settled into evening darkness, he would lie impatiently on the bed, his taste buds exploding at the cooking aromas that wafted up to the loft from downstairs; spicy sweet oregano, pungent lemon, acrid garlic, the faintly anise-like dill, and fruity olive oil. As soon as Anastasia called, he would rush down the ladder and wait at the table for Anastasia's latest culinary delight. These times with Anastasia and Elpida became special to him, and the young Englishman slowly came out of his shell. He even tried out a few words of Greek, laughing along with Elpida at what he supposed was his terrible pronunciation. Yianni was only a visitor to his family home during those days. Paul never knew where he went but presumed he was meeting with his band of fighters. He was, he admitted to himself, more than a little afraid of Yianni and was glad whenever he was absent.

Anastasia had just lit the oil lamp for the evening and Paul was wondering if he should retire for boredom had made him lethargic, when Yianni slipped into the house after several days' absence. He first swung Elpida into his arms and gave her a hug and a kiss. 'Now then, little one, I must go but I will be back soon.' He kissed his mother on her cheeks. Anastasia started to speak, but Yianni motioned for her to be silent, and she turned away abruptly. Paul noticed that Yianni's face twitched even more than normal, as though he was perpetually smiling and winking at somebody. He wanted to laugh but realized that would not be a good thing. Yianni stood still for a moment, but then, as if he had made his decision, nodded to Paul. 'Ela, come. Bring all you have.' Paul was surprised at Yianni's simple English and wondered where he had learnt it. He patted his coat to make sure he had everything he owned, and, pulling his cap low over his ears as he had been taught, followed Yianni out of the door and along a maze of streets. The Cretan deliberately backtracked and Paul soon became disoriented, knowing only that they were approaching the edge of the village. At last, they arrived at Christo's house. Christo was standing outside, and he motioned Yianni and Paul through the front door. It was dark inside and Paul felt fear.

'Ah, there you are, Private, I'm glad we could at last meet.'

Paul recognised the clipped nasal tones of the British upper class, but he was confused because, as his eyes became more accustomed to the dark, he could make out only a dirty-faced Greek dressed in a moth-eaten pair of trousers and a grey shirt that Paul supposed might once have been white. The man's boots were scuffed and falling apart. He looked to Paul to be only a few years older than himself. The man pointed a Webley pistol at Paul.

'Private, it is customary to salute an officer.' The voice became harsher.

Paul immediately stood to attention and automatically snapped a parade-ground salute. 'Paul Cuthbertson, Sir, Gunner Royal Artillery, One, Eight...'

'It's alright, Gunner. No need to stand on ceremony here. Just my little joke.' He sniffed and snorted the words out, and Paul wondered why the British upper class always seemed to have large, pointed noses. Inbreeding he supposed. 'And I assure you,' the officer continued, 'you'll come to love my sense of humour, such as it is.' The officer smiled and thrust his pistol into a broad leather belt. He motioned to a chair. Paul sat down.

'I am Captain Cranford. Lord Cranford, to be precise but that does not matter in the least,' which made Paul want to question why the hell he had said it, but he kept his mouth shut.

'Yianni here tells me you've joined his little band of merry men.'

'Well, Sir, I wouldn't go that far, you see I...'

Cranford cut him off. 'And he said you are a real palikari.'

Paul's eyebrows went up.

'A warrior,' Cranford explained, 'a young man, a warrior. It's a Cretan word, I suppose. Actually, I'm sure young Yianni here is exaggerating, but I have no doubt that in time, you'll fit the bill. And you will learn very quickly, by the way, that the Cretans make all sort of claims, some of which will actually have a passing acquaintance with the truth. But, and this is important so take note, you'll hear a lot of gossip, and like I said, a lot of it is rubbish. I call it the Cretan wireless by the way, and frankly I wish our lines of communication were as fast. But every now and then there'll be a real nugget of information about the Germans. I'm still learning to separate the two. Now, to business. How are you feeling?'

'A lot better than a month ago, sir,' Paul said.

Cranford chewed the inside of his cheek and continued looking Paul up and down.

'Good, I've heard from Yianni how they found you. Damned bad show all around, if you ask me. We had Jerry on the run, I'm sure of it, but...' He let his sentence trail into silence.

The officer's voice hardened. 'But that's all in the past. Let me tell you what's what and where you come into it.' Cranford leaned over to a small glass tumbler and took a swig of raki.

'Cuthbertson, I did hear correctly, did I not?' Paul nodded. 'I am one of a number of British officers and men who either have stayed behind after the evacuation or who will be coming in from Alexandria on a regular basis. We're posted all over the island, mostly at this end as we're not too worried about the Italians. As long as they have wine and women, they don't seem all that bothered about anything else. And good luck to them too, as far as I'm concerned. Now I have to tell you that we're still getting all this set up, so it's very rudimentary, er, basic. There was one of our chaps over in Iraklion who'd been working with the locals for years, a professor or something like that, but he got clobbered the same day as the invasion, so it's all still a bit of a pig's breakfast without him.'

Cranford helped himself to another swig of the raki. 'Anyway, he continued, 'over here, in our part of the island we have the Germans, God bless 'em, and our job, your job as well now,

Private, is to play merry hell with them, work with the local resistance'--he nodded towards Yianni and Christo--'both in harassing the German forces of occupation, as we like to call them, and also in providing intelligence to the grown-ups in Cairo. As you can see, we live with the Cretans and, as far as we can, look like them too, although I must admit that sometimes their clothing does leave much to be desired. Still, as they say back home, any port in a storm. Cuthbertson, these Cretans may look like a gang of tramps, but trust me, they are tough and they'll fight. And Yianni and Christo here are some of their best. They'll fight until every damned German is off this island. Not like the bloody French. Didn't last five bloody minutes.'

Cranford's jaw tightened and he looked away. It seemed to Paul that he had momentarily wandered to another place and time. The officer snapped back to the present. He spoke to Yianni in Greek, and then turned to Paul.

'Private, for now, I'm seconding you to Yianni's and Christo's little band of andartes. Yes, that's the name for irregulars like themselves. I want you to note all German activity. Planes, ships, convoys, regiments, foot patrols, anything. I will liaise with you and Yianni or Christo every week or two. Don't worry, Private, this'll be fun. Right, any questions so far?'

'Sir, 'Paul stammered. 'But I'm an artilleryman, sir, a private. I'm not trained for this. Why me?'

Cranford laughed. 'Christ Almighty, man, do you think any of us are. In civvy street, I was just a...' He stopped. 'Look, Cuthbertson, the simple truth of the matter is this. We need all the help we can get, here and everywhere. And Yianni, whose opinion I respected until you came along, tells me you are the bees' knees. Why, I have no idea. But there you are. That's life.'

Cranford's voice turned sour. 'So, stop your bloody bellyaching and do as you're damned well told.'

Paul sensed an animal ferocity in the man that not even his accent and the half smile could hide. 'Yes, sir, sorry, sir,' was all

Paul could manage.

The officer relaxed and took another swig from the glass. 'Don't worry, old son, you'll get the hang of this. We all have. And in any case, you're stuck here, so what else do you have to occupy your time? Any more questions?'

Paul felt like he had to say something even if it was the first thing that came into his head. 'Sir, what's happenin', you know, elsewhere. Are we winnin'?'

Cranford smiled. 'Actually, despite this mess, things could be worse. From what I can gather, North Africa is like a game of tennis, not sure who's winning there, but at least we haven't been run out yet. The Yanks haven't openly declared war on Jerry yet, you know the Yanks, when all else fails they'll do the right thing. Still they are stepping up their help with the Atlantic convoys.' Cranford hesitated and then a smile cracked his face. 'Of course, how could I forget, this is the big one, the Navy sank *Bismarck*.' In response to Paul's quizzical look, Cranford explained. '*Bismarck* was a huge battleship that was threatening our convoys. Now she's in Davy Jones's locker. But...' he grimaced, 'our own *Hood* got blown up. Terrible show, only three survivors, apparently.'

'Bloody Hell, sir, the *Hood*. I remember her docking at the Pier Head when I was a kid. And she's gone? Bloody Hell.'

'Quite, Private, quite. I know, hardly seems possible. But there you are. Anyway, any more questions, any at all?'

Encouraged by Cranford's attitude, Paul ventured another.

'Sir, I was told that when Jerry attacked, the women killed 'em with pitchforks when they were hangin' by their chutes in the trees. Is that true, sir?'

'Yes,' Cranford said quietly. 'You'll find this little island quite different from anything you're used to. By the way,' he continued, changing the conversation, 'how is your Greek?'

Paul's eyes widened. 'My Greek, sir? Don't have any apart from a few phrases.'

'Don't suppose at school you did Ancient...no, of course not, stupid of me to ask.' He hiccupped. 'Well, that can't be helped. Don't worry, Private. Before I came to Crete all I knew was a little Ancient Greek from prep school. You know, Herodotus, Themistocles, rosy-fingered dawn, think that was Homer, but I'm not sure. Sounds like him at any rate. Load of old tripe if you ask me, which no one ever did, mind you. That damned prep school seems like centuries ago now, and a fat lot of good it did me. Ha,' he roared. 'Try speaking that to a Cretan and he'll think you're completely mad. Which I sometimes think I am anyway, so that's all right then. Now, let's have that drink.'

'Yes, sir, thank you, sir.' Paul felt himself warming, against all his instincts, to this eccentric if not completely mad Englishman. Still, Paul had a horrible feeling that shit followed this man around and he was about to get a faceful.

Christo poured the four of them small tumblers of raki. It was only slightly less rough than the stuff Yianni had given him up in the hills but it still made him cough and he was glad that the three others could not see his face turn red. Paul noticed that they all downed their shots in one quick swig.

Cranford smiled. 'Don't worry, Private, we'll soon have you drinking like a Cretan, though God help your liver. Here, have another one.'

Dawn was beginning to light up the little house when Paul, still bleary from the effects of the raki, was awakened by a kick from Yianni. He and Christo were fully clothed, with their rifles and sakkoulia slung over their shoulders. Paul knew that something was wrong. No words were necessary, and he quickly followed the two Cretans out of the house. Cranford was nowhere to be seen. The three men slipped out of the house and into the fields. Keeping below the stone walls, they hurried back into the hills.

Chapter 20

Life in the village continued. It had to. The men might have been murdered, but the flocks still had to be pastured, the gardens watered and weeded, the children fed. And even though men and women came from the neighbouring villages to help as much as they could, the new workload for the women of Ayios Stefanos was almost impossible to bear. For Anastasia, and she surely was not alone, the extra work brought a small crumb of comfort for it kept her mind from returning too often to the massacre. And it was good as well to have Elpida's company, her granddaughter's constant chattering taking away the dark thoughts that plagued both of them. Even if sometimes she really wasn't listening too closely to the little girl, merely hearing her voice was enough. Yet Anastasia could never fully escape the memory of her husband, nor did she want to. They had grown old together, secure in the knowledge that the other would be there until the Lord took one of them when He wanted. She knew he was still with her, and Antoni's absence was a constant and strangely comforting presence in their little house.

The morning after her son and the Englishman had left so quickly, Anastasia sat outside her house in the shade of a plane tree, preparing greens. The sun was still not over the mountains, and she tried to enjoy the coolness and the quiet before the village fully awoke. She looked up at the tree and wiped a tear from her eye. The tree had been carefully trimmed so that its branches curved up onto the roof of the house to provide shelter from the summer sun. Antoni had started this soon after they were married when the tree was barely a sapling, and over the years, whenever he had a spare moment, he had unobtrusively worked on what he called Anastasia's little haven. She wiped away a tear, for the little haven—and how Antoni had built it for her—had been their marriage in a nutshell. No fuss, no drama, just a Greek man who had looked after his wife and family as best he could. She reminded herself to find some flowers for his grave. The ones there were already wilting and needed to be replaced.

Elpida came out and sat down next to her grandmother. She yawned and rubbed the sleep out of her eyes. Anastasia gave her a kiss on the forehead and, cheered up by her granddaughter's beauty, began to hum a tune.

'Yiayiaka,' Elpida asked. 'You hum that song a lot. I've never asked you, but what's it called. It's pretty.'

Anastasia put down the vegetables. 'Well, my little girl, I don't really know its name. But I heard it many years ago, when I was younger than you. My baba took me to a concert. Have I told you about it?' the old woman smiled, knowing the answer.

Elpida had been raised as a polite little girl and she still hadn't figured out how to get out of listening to her yiayia's story about the concert yet again for all she wanted was the name of the tune. Fortunately for her, their talk was interrupted by a commotion from the plateia as the sounds of lorries and shouting men reverberated through the village. Anastasia placed her vegetables on the bench next to her and with Elpida hurried into the square.

Many of the women had already beaten them there. They gathered outside the church and gazed at a large squad of German soldiers who were climbing down from their lorries. A slightly built officer climbed onto the bonnet of his staff car. His uniform was impeccable, every crease in its right place, every medal polished and carefully pinned to his chest. He motioned to his command to ring the square and then took the megaphone his sergeant had handed him. The officer removed a piece of paper from his front pocket and began to read. 'Women of Ayios Stefanos,' the speech had been hastily translated into simple Greek, 'I am Lieutenant Schneider.' He shouted. 'The battle for your island is over and the forces of Germany have defeated the enemy. By order of the new German governor of this island, all Cretans will give up their arms and return to their peacetime ways. If you disobey us, we will execute you. You already know this, don't you? If you give help to the English soldiers we will execute you. If you resist in any way, we will execute you. We are authorized to occupy your village and put down any resistance from anybody. But all of us, I am sure, want the occupation of your lovely village to be over as soon as possible.'

There was a murmur of discontent from the women but nothing more. None of the women moved except for Eleni Apostolakis who slowly sidled herself to the front of the women, directly in front of the officer. She ostentatiously pulled back her hair, a deep shiny black in colour. Yet the German officer barely looked at her and motioned to his men who began to scour through the village in groups of two and three in search of billets. The women scattered to their own houses to try to defend what little they had.

Anastasia and Elpida followed two soldiers into their home. They were big men, much bigger than any of the village men, and in their grey uniforms and heavy leather boots they seemed to fill the little room. Wawa was not afraid, however, and she went for one of the soldier's legs. The little cat was met in midair by a jackbooted kick and sent flying against the wall. Anastasia dropped to her knees and picked up Wawa, who was bloodied but still alive. The attack infuriated the two Germans. They threw the wooden furniture against the walls, and even ripped Anastasia's precious icons from the wall. One of them tore down a photograph of her father and then urinated on it. To Elpida's horror, they kicked apart the old spinning wheel that Anastasia has promised her as part of her dowry. But out of nowhere the doorway to the house was filled by a huge German, more massive and threatening than the two soldiers already inside. He looked the same age as Yianni and was dirty and unshaven. Anastasia heard him yell at the two men, and stepping inside he cuffed the nearer of the two around his head. And then, to Anastasia's surprise, he kicked both of them outside. Elpida started to laugh, but her grandmother immediately hushed her.

Then in very slow Greek the German spoke to them. 'I will make this all right,' and he carefully set the furniture upright again. He also placed the icons very delicately on the dresser by the fire and wiped down the photograph with his handkerchief. 'I stay here, okay? I make no trouble for you or your Liebchen. You are safe now. I promise.'

The two Greeks did not understand all he was saying because of his thick accent but his actions at least spoke of something they had not dared imagine, a kind German. Still, Anastasia did not know how to deal with him. She would not bring herself even to think of liking him or even to smile at him, but at least he was better than the other two. The German slung down his pack in the corner of the room and pointed to his chest. 'I am Manfred, Sergeant Manfred Schulz. And you?' He pointed at the two.

'Anastasia Manoulakis and this is my granddaughter Elpida. Her father and her grandfather, my husband, were killed. By you.'

'I know,' the sergeant replied gently in Greek. Although most of the woman's Greek was lost on him, he was sure he understood what she was saying. 'I know,' he continued in German. 'And I am sorry. But war makes us all do things we do not like. And, remember,' his voice hardened momentarily although he knew they did not understand what he was saying, 'they, you, tried to kill us. It was not your fight. They, you, should have stayed in your villages. Still, that is all behind us. I know we cannot be friends now but perhaps soon?' He offered them a brief smile. 'And now,' he asked in simple Greek, 'where do I sleep?' Anastasia pointed to the ladder and grabbing his kit Manfred climbed the ladder to his new billet. Anastasia thanked God that she had already checked that Paul had taken all his belongings before he left. She entertained the thought that the upstairs loft was simply becoming a hotel for passing soldiers.

Despite her continuing hatred of the Germans, Anastasia had to admit that this time their presence was not completely intolerable, though like the other women she could not fathom why they had even bothered to come back for surely they could make their patrols into the countryside anywhere they chose. Still, she forced herself to remember what they had done to Antoni and the rest of the village men. In the village itself the soldiers kept to themselves, confining themselves mostly to their billets or the kafeneio, and limiting their movement to patrols through its streets; her own lodger, Manfred Schulz, was a virtual gentleman.

One morning, Anastasia made her way to the village fountain. Sophia Theodorakis was already there and the two of them helped each other fill their pots.

'Well, I suppose he could be worse, Sophie,' Anastasia grunted, 'but I still don't like him.' She poured the last of the water into her jugs and sat down to wipe her brow.

Sophia replied through wheezy breaths, her habitually blue face turning a slight red as the exertion and the heat combined to take their toll. 'I have two young men in my house and neither of them is old enough to shave. They're almost too polite. One of them even bowed to me the other morning.' The two women giggled at the absurdity.

'I see Eleni Apostolakis got what she wanted, Sophie.' The old woman cocked her head towards her friend. 'Oh, you don't know, do you? I heard from Katerina Sotiraki that the German officer is staying in her house. Just him, nobody else. Now isn't that a cozy little nest.'

That doesn't surprise me,' Sophie replied, her face turning redder. 'I've said all along she was too pretty for her own good. And don't tell me her life has been hard and we should understand. Yes, I know she lost her family. That is terrible. But it doesn't give her the right to become a whore.'

'Well,' Anastasia said. 'Let's sit down for a while. I'm too old for this.'

The two women sat down on the small stone bench and closed their eyes to enjoy the morning sun before its fierceness overwhelmed them and drove everybody inside until evening. A cloud passed over Anastasia's eyes and opening them she saw her lodger, Manfred, standing over her.

'I thought you might like some help, they look heavy.' He pointed to the clay pots.

Anastasia could not help herself and she smiled at the German.

'Yes, thank you,' she heard herself stuttering. The German picked up the pots and immediately left for the house.

When Anastasia arrived a few minutes later, Manfred was sitting at the table.

'Kyria,' he spoke quietly. 'I want to ask you. Why does your door have two crosses on it?'

Anastasia crossed herself. Hesitating for a moment she spoke up. 'It is the number of dead. This house has two because my son was killed with his father.'

'I'm sorry. But some of the houses have five crosses on their doors. Does that mean...?'

'Yes, it does, all the men, grandfather, father, sons all dead, all gunned down in that cursed olive grove.'

Manfred looked away. 'I'm sorry. I did not mean to pry.' He stood up abruptly and rushed out of the house.

Anastasia tried not to look at the crosses painted on the door whenever she came in or out of the house but Manfred's clumsiness had brought up the familiar feeling of anger mixed with inconsolable sadness. She sat down at the table and watched the dust motes play in the sunbeam that sliced the darkness of the room.

Chapter 21

Eleni Apostolakis was not a bad woman. She told herself this every day. And it was not her fault — she told herself this every day too — if she was pretty. Sometimes she regretted not remarrying but all her suitors seemed second best, and the only man who really interested her, the only man who could make her love again, Yianni Manoulakis, had insulted her just this last Easter. And now even Yianni could no longer be in her life, although she was fairly sure she had spotted him at the funeral and he was not dead at all. Perhaps, he had survived the massacre and that he was somewhere up in the hills with his best friend, that crazy man, Christo Papadakis. Sometimes Eleni wondered if she had some sort of death wish, or at least some sort of wish that would incur the hatred of the villagers because she regularly found herself doing things that were simply not in her best interests. Take last week, for example, when the Germans came to occupy the village and she found herself almost involuntarily preening in front of the German officer. And now here she was with that same officer billeted in her house, alone, and the whole village scandalized, again, by her behaviour.

Her thoughts were interrupted by a man's gravelly cough. She turned away from the sink where she was washing vegetables. 'I am impressed, Eleni.' Lieutenant Gerhardt Schneider rocked back on his cane chair and luxuriantly drew on his cigarette. 'Here I am, not so bad-looking. I give you food and still you will not sleep with me.'

She did not fully understand the mixture of Greek and German her boarder was speaking, but it was enough for she had heard the same little speech almost from the day Schneider had installed himself in her house, even taking her own bed, in hopes, she supposed, that he would not be sleeping alone for long. She smiled at him, and she wondered how long he could maintain this veneer of chivalry before he took matters into his own hands. Eleni refilled his cup with real coffee, not the ersatz grounds most of the villagers were already drinking. She sometimes felt guilty that she was able to enjoy the young officer's largesse. But would anything have changed for the better had she refused, she asked herself. No, of course not, and she helped herself to another cup and a slice of the dark Belgian chocolate that Gerhardt always seemed to have in abundance. Absent-mindedly she stuffed the rest of the chocolate bar into her apron pocket for later.

'I go now for water.' Eleni said slowly. She smiled at how she would always speak Greek to Schneider this way, as though he was some sort of imbecile. The German smiled and unbuttoned his tunic to allow the summer sun streaming through the doorway to lull him to sleep. Eleni avoided going out in public as much as possible for she had already tired of the dark looks the village women gave her, but there was no avoiding her daily visit to the well. She hoped that there would be nobody else there at this time, but no, there was Anastasia and Elpida Manoulakis, plus that old witch Sophia Theodorakis. God, does that woman live here, Eleni asked herself. She always seems to be hanging around. Probably gossiping, and probably about me, Eleni continued her thoughts.

Eleni liked the little Manoulakis girl. She never seemed to smile anymore, what with her grandfather and perhaps even her father killed in the massacre, and even though the other children of the village had begun to play with each other again, little Elpida still liked her yiayia's company best. Eleni smiled at the little girl who held back, her eyes constantly flitting at her grandmother, and without thinking Eleni took out the last of the chocolate bar and handed it to Elpida. The little girl hesitated, not knowing what to do. But the lure of the bittersweet chocolate was too strong and she stretched out her hand, but squealed in pain when Anastasia slapped the little girl's wrist, knocking it away from the chocolate. Elpida started to cry and Anastasia screamed at Eleni. 'Get your filthy chocolate away from my granddaughter. We all know how you got that chocolate. Is that payment for services, you little whore? Is that all you get for bedding the men who killed my family?'

For a moment Eleni thought Anastasia was going to strike her, and so must have Sophia, for the old woman rushed over to the two of them and pulled her friend away.

'Go now, Eleni, go,' Sophia said in a low voice. 'Go now.'

Ignoring her water pot, Eleni ran out into the square, red-faced with embarrassment. At home, slamming the plates and cups on the table and cursing that she had left her pot, her embarrassment was replaced by anger. She stormed into the small back kitchen where Schneider was helping himself to coffee and slammed the door. He turned, startled by the commotion but relaxed when he saw who it was. 'Is everything, all right, Liebchen?'

She turned to leave but stopped in mid-turn. She pointed to the bed and loosened her blouse. Schneider's eyes jumped wide open, but he quickly recovered himself. He grabbed her hand, pulled her into the bedroom and threw her onto the bed, unbuckling his trouser belt at the same time. He entered her roughly, and she cried out in pain. His thrusts were hard. His lips searched her breasts and his tongue licked her nipples. It struck Eleni that she had finally become what the villagers had accused her of for too many years, but she no longer cared. The coupling took ten minutes, and the German remained on the bed as she threw on her clothes.

He lit a cigarette and pumped smoke rings towards the ceiling. 'Eleni. Why now?'

The young woman hesitated in adjusting her blouse. 'Nothing, nothing at all. Nothing happened,' she said.

The German came over to her, a bead of semen stuck on his flaccid penis, and stroked her cheek. He moved his hand to her breast. She pushed it away.

'Friends, yes?' Schneider said.

Eleni heard the menace in his voice. She raised her mouth to his and she tasted the acrid nicotine on his breath. She realized that this was the first time they had kissed.

Eleni flopped onto the side of the bed. 'I hate this village,' she eventually said. 'And everybody in it. I am sick of their stupid beliefs, that I am not good enough for them.'

Schneider could only look at her, not understanding what she was saying, but the set of her face and the harshness of her voice told him all he needed to know.

He cupped her face in his hands. 'You help me. I help you.' His Greek was just enough for her to understand.

Memories crowded into her brain; Anastasia's attack at the fountain, Yianni's rejection to her advances last Easter, all the slights and snubs she had endured over the years from the village women. She felt Schneider's sperm oozing down her thigh and made up her mind. Looking with eyes of ice at Schneider's face, she led him back to the bed and said, 'I am ready to help. In any way I can.'

Chapter 22

Yianni, Christo and Paul had barely escaped the Germans re-garrisoning Ayios Stefanos, and only because word of their advance had been rapidly passed up from the coast by Cretan mouth to Cretan mouth, an informal but highly efficient communication system. But now they were safe the two young Cretans scampered up the hills like sure-footed mountain goats, laughing as they competed with each other to be the first to make a particular ridge line or the bottom of a rocky slope. Paul kept up as best he could but kept tripping on rocks. Only when the two Cretans were sure they were completely safe did they stop and allow Paul a decent rest. But the respite was short-lived and after a cigarette break the two of them dragged Paul back onto his feet. His lungs were bursting when finally he dropped onto the terrace in front of the cave, where the band was awaiting them. Paul gladly took the flask of water one of the men handed him and took himself off to recover while the andartes conferred with Christo and Yianni. A murmur of agreement from the men made Paul look up and soon after he saw young Alexi Doukakis take off down the hill. The other andartes spent the rest of the day smoking cigarettes and cleaning their weapons. Paul continued to sit away from them, for he was tired from the climb and still not sure that he liked being part of the band despite, or especially because of, Cranford's orders.

Late that afternoon Alexi returned and reported back to the two leaders. The young man kept hopping from one foot to another, and Yianni had to place his hands on his shoulders to slow him down. After the young man had finished talking the two men dismissed him and broke into what appeared to be a heated discussion, but eventually the two of them settled down and broke out a raki flask. They called over the andartes and Yianni spoke. Interpreting, Anesti Mandrakis told Paul that they were going hunting again. Anesti laughed uproariously at his little joke, spittle sizzling between his blackened teeth like fat in a frying pan. But Paul could find nothing to laugh at. He just wasn't cut out for this sort of action, he knew, especially killing men in cold blood from behind stone walls.

So began days of flitting over the countryside, searching for patrolling Germans, knowing that to attack the Germans at Ayios Stefanos itself would be a death sentence both for them and the women and children. Yet they were never able to engage with their enemy, and Paul on more than one occasion wondered if Yianni and Christo really knew what they were doing. The only relief to the monotony of the patrols was when a German spotter plane would be heard and the band would have to scramble for cover. After another day of pointless walking and searching, the men would spend the evening as they always did, smoking, drinking, talking, and singing romantic songs about Crete.

One evening, exhausted and frustrated, Paul lay on his back in front of the cave. Cottony white clouds filled the sky, their shapes constantly changing as unseen, powerful forces buffeted them. The clouds took him back to Liverpool and carefree days in the local park, looking at the clouds as they shape-shifted. He imagined that the clouds were in fact countries or even continents. A large billowy cumulus was Australia, which in the twinkle of a young boy's eye became New Zealand, then Japan, and then sometimes it miraculously disappeared altogether, leaving only empty blue ocean where once a whole continent had been. Now his boyhood dream of visiting a foreign country had been fulfilled. It was just a shame that he was not able to enjoy it.

The scuffle of feet on rock brought him to his senses. He grabbed his gun, along with the others, but relaxed when he heard Cranford's unmistakable accent. Accompanying him was a small, wiry young Cretan. The two visitors walked over to Yianni and Christo, and after hugs and cheek kisses the four of them sat down to talk. Every so often, Christo raised his voice, but always Yianni would place a hand on his knee and the talk would subside into an indistinguishable murmur. Yianni's tic was very pronounced that evening, a sign, Paul had quickly learnt, that the man was more than usually nervous.

Paul could hear nothing of what they said and after a while turned back to his daily chores. Since he had joined the band he had picked up many new skills, how to keep away from ridge tops, how to try to keep pace with the fast walking Cretans, how to keep his gun clean of the dust that constantly threatened to clog its firing mechanism, and even how to put cardboard inside his boots to make them last longer. But no skill was more valuable than the knack of tracking down and killing the fleas and lice that infested him, and it was to this task that he now turned. The lice—as always—were concentrated in his pubic hair, and he spent ten minutes each day checking that area, as well as his armpits, before tossing his captives into the lid of a cigarette tin where he would burn them, with great delight, with a match. He suspected his hair was full of them too, and his scalp itched badly to the point where in places he had scratched until it bled. But he felt uncomfortable asking the other andartes for help in delousing his hair. Too much like the chimps at the zoo, he told himself.

Paul had finished his ritual and was ready to turn in for the night when Cranford, seeing that his countryman had finished his toiletry, came across to him. 'Good evening, Private. Glad to see you're settling in. Little buggers aren't much fun, are they? Still, looks like you know how to deal with them. Thought we'd have a bit of a chin wag, eh? See what's cooking, eh. You know, that's a strange expression, isn't it, Private. See what's cooking. Think I heard that in some Yank film. Strange people the Yanks, talk oddly too.' Paul could see that Cranford's gabbling was the result of too many nights without sleep. His eyes were ringed and bloodshot and he kept stifling yawns. Cranford's companion joined them. 'Private, this is my good friend, Ari Hatzidakis.' Paul took a closer look at the newcomer as he shook his hand. He was a little more than five foot tall and his clothes hung loosely on a thin, almost visible skeletal frame. The man's trousers were held up by a piece of thin rope and his right shoe consisted of a piece of tyre rubber fastened with wire to ancient and very tattered leather uppers.

'He is,' Cranford nodded at the Cretan, 'what we call a runner, which means he takes messages from one of our groups to another, especially between us British. He's rather like our own private Pony Express. And he's bloody good at what he does. Yesterday he brought me a new wireless set. Damned thing must have weighed sixty pounds, yet he threw it on his shoulders like it was a box of feathers.' The young Cretan grinned sheepishly not understanding Cranford's words but sure it was complimentary. Paul, as when he had first met him, was slightly mesmerized by Cranford's polished accent, something he had never heard in England except on the radio. Listening to the captain brought back memories of a simpler time, of huddling around the radio on a winter's evening to listen to the BBC news or ITMA, a comedy programme that had recently become popular.

'Oh, Private, dear Private. Are you with us? Time for dreams of Betty Grable later.'

'Sorry, sir,' Paul said. 'Bit tired, that's all. Sorry, you were saying.'

'Well, actually, I wasn't. But I'm about to. Tell me your impressions. About anything, about anybody.'

Ari interrupted. 'I eat now, okay?' Cranford nodded and the Cretan joined the other men.

'Well, sir,' Paul said. 'I'm not sure I can help you much but here goes. They're all good men. They'll die if they have to so long as every German gets off the island. And after what Jerry has done here already I can't blame them. Oh, Yianni and Christo are the leaders, you know that, but they sometimes get into arguments and then everybody joins in and it becomes a free-for-all. I think it's about politics, that's the only word I can make out...'

'Well, let me stop you there, Cuthbertson. You are right, they do argue about politics a lot. In fact they talk about everything a lot. But unfortunately there's a lot of internal bickering as well amongst the different factions, and all of it has to do with their politics and who's going to rule Greece once we've booted the Germans into touch. I swear to God, they make Trollope's clergymen look like a choir of bloody angels.'

'Sorry, sir, who's Trollope, is he one of the padres? Never heard of him.'

Cranford chuckled. 'Sweet prince, you have no idea, do you? No, Trollope was... Oh, never mind. It's not important. Politics, that's what we were talking about just now, and it's bloody complicated. But in a nutshell, Christo there is a communist and he wants to join with other like-minded andartes. They'll fight with us while it's convenient. But trust me, we're next on their list after they've got rid of the Germans. The communists are not well organized yet, like they are on the mainland. And a lot of the Cretans are what we call Republicans, they don't even like their own king, but our high command tell me they can be brought round to our way of thinking. No, it's the communists we're worried about. They're our biggest threat and they'll only get worse as this bloody war drags on. Okay, Private, go on.'

Paul continued. 'Well, sir, when it comes to the Cretans having a go at the Germans, the biggest problem is, and I'm just a gunner so what the hell do I know, and you know all this better than me, the biggest problem is that the Germans are still frightened of the Cretans despite everything, and they seem to be concentrating themselves in the villages. If they do go out into the countryside, it's in big patrols. Yianni knows they're too big to take them on. Anyway, the chances of ambushing the Germans are getting smaller because they're sending out fewer patrols anyway, even if they're bigger, if that makes any sense. And I think Christo wants to take the risk of attacking some of the smaller village garrisons. He's just really frustrated. I think that's one of the reasons they argue so much. Yianni's not as crazy as Christo. I know we've already surrendered, but all the Cretans want to do is keep on fighting. They know the Germans are getting total control, not just in the towns but everywhere. There's nowt the Cretans can do about it and it's pissing everybody off. Sorry, sir. I'm frightened they'll go off half-cock and get everybody killed. Including me. Anesti'—and he nodded toward the Greek, who was smoking a cigarette and watching the two Englishmen from a makeshift perch on a rock—'Anesti tells me a lot. He's the only one with decent English, and that ain't really good, but it's better than mine, my Greek I mean, I learnt a few words back in the village, but it's really hard an'—' Paul stopped when he heard Cranford snore in mock sleep.

'Yes, well, quite, Private. But, I have to say that what you've given me is a pretty accurate appraisal. So, well done, my boy.' Cranford nodded vigorously, and Paul felt that he had successfully passed a test of some sort. 'But, we've got to bash on here despite the odds. London has decided that even though we've lost Crete we've still got to keep a presence here, to keep a lookout for troop buildups or reductions, shipping activity and so on, just like I told you when we met in Ayios Stefanos. Plus, any resistance from the Cretans that keeps German troops here and not somewhere else, like North Africa for instance, is all to the good. Jerry's got a new general out there, Rommel, and he's damned good from all accounts. That's why you and I are stuck here. It's still a bloody mess, of course, because, as I mentioned, the andartes are starting to split into political factions. What's going on between Yianni and Christo is happening all over the island. Still, it's the only war we've got so we might as well make the most of it, eh? Any other observations?'

Paul shook his head.

'Right then, Private.' Cranford stood up. 'For now, I suppose we just keep on doing what we're doing. Private, one more thing. It's to be expected I suppose, but we're hearing of increased collaboration between some of the civilians and Jerry. Just keep your eyes and ears open, and don't think every Cretan thinks like that lot.' He nodded in the direction of Yianni and Christo.

Cranford drank a mouthful of raki. 'Now then, Paul,' Cranford said with great gusto. Paul did not like this use of his first name; in his limited military experience it always meant he was about to get shit on from a great height. 'I want you to leave this lot for a day or two and come with me. I think it's about time you learnt a little more about what we're doing. We'll leave at first light tomorrow.'

Chapter 23

Paul spent most of the night awake, his mind turning over what Cranford might be leading him into. Above him, the stars seemed to crowd out the darkness of the night and a huge swath of shimmering dust in the sky he identified as the Milky Way. Paul had only ever read about it and he finally fell asleep trying to recall what little he knew.

He awoke to the smell of sizzling lamb's meat. Alexi Doukakis was kneeling at the spit and rubbing olive oil over the carcass. He sliced off a piece of lamb and gave it to Paul. The meat burnt his fingers and although he wasn't ready to eat this much so early on he forced it down, aware that later on he might regret refusing it. Cranford came over to Paul and started to say something but stopped when he saw Paul's look of amazement. For Paul had stopped eating and was staring at Ari who had just finished off a huge leg of lamb, which he had ripped in one piece from the carcass. Now he'd put a huge flask of raki to his lips and was guzzling it down.

'I know, Paul, prodigious, isn't it,' Cranford said. 'All the Cretans can drink and eat like pigs at parties and such, but little Ari, here, why, he has to have the island's record, Hell, the world record. I don't see how he does it, but I've seen him drink pints of the stuff and then go off and do a thirty-mile run through the mountains. If I drank a tenth of what he did I'd just fall down and never get up. Just take me to the graveyard and bury me as soon as you can.' He laughed.

Ari grinned at the two Englishmen and offered them a huge belch. He ripped off another piece of lamb and continued his meal.

'Sir, where are we off to?' Paul enquired.

'Well, if I told you that, it'd spoil the surprise, wouldn't it?' The officer smiled and told Paul to gather his belongings. 'We leave with Ari in ten minutes.'

Cranford was nothing if not punctual, and as soon as Ari had taken a last swig of raki, the three of them set off. Paul felt strange in Cranford's company. He had grown used to being the outsider in the little band of andartes, and felt strangely comforted that they treated him like a child to be looked after. But as he followed Cranford into the high mountains, he felt, despite their Cretan garb, that he had taken one step back into the army again and he did not like the feeling at all.

As the three of them climbed higher and higher into the gaunt treeless mountains, Ari and Cranford stopping regularly to allow Paul to catch up, Paul had the chance to look around him and it hit him—again—that this island was the most beautiful place he had ever seen. He stood on a carpet of wildflowers, of every hue and shade, as the fresh, clean breeze perfumed his face and blew away his fatigue and fear. The limestone massifs gleamed in the sunshine, row upon magnificent row. A line of windmills, turning languidly in the summer breeze, fringed a distant ridge. Huge eagles soared in the distance, catching the thermals in search of food. Paul even fancied he identified a vulture. And all around him lay the Mediterranean, washed-out blue and winking, or so it seemed, as the sun caught the tops of the waves that rolled to and from eternity.

The afternoon sun rose too high in the sky for comfort, and Cranford ordered them to rest. Ari pointed to a small cheese hut a few hundred yards away, and the three of them flopped into its cool interior, the aroma of centuries of cheese an almost palpable barrier at its threshold. Ari passed the two Englishmen a large leather flask of warm water. Paul gulped at it greedily, but Cranford pulled the flask away from his lips.

'Slowly, young man. Have you forgotten what you learnt from Yianni and Christo?'

'Sorry, it just tastes too good,' Paul said. 'And Ari here does keep up a pace. Not sure I've ever seen a man with so much energy. Or who smiled so much.'

'He is something, isn't he,' Cranford conceded. 'He seems truly happy helping us. The Cretans call high spirits like Ari's keph, or something like that. It sounds Turkish to me, but who knows. Ari is a hell of a man, Cuthbertson. I wish we had more like him. Anyway, for now, that's enough about our friend, Ari. We need to rest until the damned sun's a little kinder.' The officer stretched out and soon his snoring filled the hut. Paul followed his example, while Ari sat in the doorway slowly sipping from his flask.

Early evening and the sun's harsh brilliance was fading. As it slipped below the horizon, it lit up the western sky in vibrant pink and blue hues, reminding Paul of a bruise, like the ones he'd get playing football in the streets back home. And then, as quickly as the light show had appeared, it vanished, leaving only gray smudges that soon turned to the blackness of night. The three hitched their bags over their shoulders and started the last leg of their journey, grateful for the coolness of the sea breeze. A three-hour hike brought them to their destination. Cranford whistled a series of low notes. Paul heard an answering trill but he could not see anything, just the limestone slope and scattered bushes. Slowly one of the bushes moved and Paul tightened his grip on his rifle. Then, a head appeared from the middle of the bush and finally a whole body.

'Evening, Captain, glad you could make it.' Paul recognized the accent as either Australian or New Zealand. A man stood up. He was covered in dirt from head to foot. His hair was greasy and matted, and he scratched himself constantly. Every item of his clothing was holed. Even the darns had been re-darned.

Cranford grinned. 'Let me introduce Sergeant Bill Presley, late of his Majesty's Australian Expeditionary Force and one of the finest wireless operators on Crete. Probably in the Mediterranean.'

The Australian stuck out a hand, which Paul took, resisting

the urge to wipe his hand on his trousers afterwards.

'We've brought you some goodies.' Cranford motioned to Ari to bring over the large bag. 'Canned food, water and a small bottle of scotch. Oh, and some itching powder, though you know as well as me the damned stuff doesn't work. By the way, I think I've got my hands on the new valves you wanted. But I'm afraid you'll just have to do with what you've got until I can get them shipped over from Alex.'

'Thanks, Cap. Who's he by the way?' Presley pointed at Paul.

'Well, hopefully and in due course, your replacement.'

Paul jerked his head at the officer. Paul now knew why he was now addressed as Paul, and not private or soldier, or Cuthbertson. He was right, shit was coming his way. Paul blustered. 'I, what, me, I don't. Captain, I don't know nowt about radios and things.'

'Oh, but you do, young man. Do you think I wouldn't check up on you? You had training on radio communications during your basic. So, you see you can do this. We've got other plans for Sergeant Presley here.' Paul started to protest, but a sharp look from Cranford told him it would be a waste of time.

'Don't worry, Paul, it won't be for a few weeks. And in the meantime you'll be off to Cairo for a little bit more training. Until we can arrange a pickup you'll have to content yourself with playing cowboys and Indians with your little band of merry men. Damn me,' he chuckled, 'always did mix my metaphors.'

'Sir,' Paul asked, 'what exactly does Sergeant Presley do?'

Cranford motioned to Presley who spoke directly to Paul. 'Most of the time, you sit here bored to death. You can only play with yourself so many times a day, so the rest of the time you scratch yourself raw and try to see if anything is happening with the Germans. I'm talking about shipping movements along the coast, long-range patrols, that sort of thing. Plus, and this is what we're really here for, you'll get regular visits from Ari here, or someone like him. He'll bring you supplies or messages or both.

You then transmit the messages to Alex.' He saw Paul's brow furrow. 'Don't worry, son, it's pretty safe. The German patrols rarely come this high so you've only got the occasional spotter plane to worry about. You've been hanging out with one of the bands the captain tells me, so you've already got some knowhow about you. And when you get to Cairo, all they'll do, basically, is work you on the specifics of radio transmissions, times, codes, that sort of thing. Piece of cake, mate, piece of cake.'

'Well, I suppose...' Paul did not know how to finish the sentence.

'Now then, Sergeant, how about some of that whisky Ari gallantly lugged all the way up here?'

The four men sat down, and Ari pulled out the bottle from one of his bags and handed it to the captain. The three soldiers drank the scotch and nibbled on hard biscuits while Ari sipped on his raki and gnawed on a lint-flecked sheep's leg that still carried a few traces of meat. Cranford slipped into a deep sleep, but Paul was too agitated to join him, and he found company in Presley who was all too eager to talk about the war, the invasion and, most of all, cricket.

The next morning Paul awoke to an empty scotch bottle and a headache that started in his toes and ended somewhere above his head. Cranford had already left, and Presley told Paul that Ari would take him back to the andartes and he should expect his orders soon.

'You'd bleedin' get lost or took by Jerry if you didn't have old Ari 'ere,' the Australian smiled. 'Mind, from the looks of you, gettin' shot by Jerry might be the best thing for you.'

'Tell me, have you always been a git or did you have to work at it?' Paul tried to smile through the throbbing that seemed to be ripping his skull apart.

'Comes natural, Pom. Especially with you lot. Now sod off.' The Australian hesitated. 'You be careful, mate. See ya' soon. And Paul. Don't worry about Cranford. I know he sounds like an upper-class bastard, and he is, but he bloody well knows his stuff. He'll look after you. Trust me. Okay? Just keep your wits about you, mate, and you'll be fine.'

'Will do. And you be careful, too,' Paul replied, and he slid down the slope to catch up with Ari, hoping he wouldn't throw up too much.

July 1941

Chapter 24

Most of the paratroopers had been pulled off the island and sent, or so the rumour went, to the Eastern Front to join in the invasion of Russia that had begun a few weeks earlier, but Dieter and a couple of sections had been kept behind under the command of Lieutenant Maier. In early July, they had moved back into Ayios Stefanos. It made no sense, to Dieter at least, as there was already a sizeable Wehrmacht presence there, and this fed into Dieter's fear that the section was to be used for some special mission. Still, until that happened Dieter was stuck with nothing to do. He threw first his shirt and then himself onto the bed that took up most of his makeshift billet. The morning sun was already cruel, and the sweat trickled down his body making him itch all over. He was tempted to kill a spider that clung to the ceiling, but even that seemed too much effort. He jumped up, as though intent on doing something but immediately sat down on the edge of the bed as he realized there really was nothing to do. He pulled off his boots, which killed the best part of a minute.

He needed something to kill his boredom and his increasing depression, and so he pulled out his diary from his pack—there was a bloodstain on the front cover, though whose he had no idea—and reviewed all his actions since the invasion. This was not a pleasant task, and Dieter did not fully understand why he needed to punish himself—he visited his writings regularly— unless it might expiate, if only a little, the sins he and his comrades had committed. Dieter had killed men; that was his job and he would kill again if necessary. But the massacre had changed him in ways that he sought in vain to identify, and the treatment of the Cretans had forced him to question German strategy on the island. He had got sick of watching old women and men beaten up simply for not getting out of the way of a German soldier quickly enough. He'd seen a ten-year-old have his arm broken because he'd mimicked a salute to an officer. Since they'd taken the island, it seemed to him that the German authorities were going out of their way to be as cruel and vindictive as they could be to the local populace. And Dieter could not reason why because, so far as he could tell, all it did was to increase the islanders' resistance. Dieter read his diary entry from a few days ago. *There is surely a clear line between what is good and what is evil, but either we are too willfully stupid to see it or, because of self-delusion or moral weakness, we allow that line to be smudged beyond recognition. Only after we have crossed that line and looked back can we realize its existence, and know that we have transgressed it with no hope of ever redeeming ourselves.* He asked himself again whether he still wanted to be a good soldier if killing and torturing civilians were what it took. He packed away his diary and fell into a troubled sleep.

Lorries rumbling past his billet to the square roused Dieter, and at the same time his sergeant stuck his head through the doorway. 'Move it, son,' he yelled. 'We've got a job to do. Get to the square right away.' Dieter hopped off the bed struggling to get his boots on. He joined the other paratroopers and a squad of Wehrmacht assembling in the square. Sergeants ordered them to climb onto the lorries. Overseeing the operation from the back of his staff car was Maier.

'Don't ask. I don't know yet,' a sergeant snarled at Dieter's quizzical look as the lorries bumped along the stony track. 'I'm afraid High Command forgot to tell me when we were having drinks last night. I guess we'll all know when we get there. All I can tell you is this, I heard it last night in the mess. There's a small village up in the mountains, been actin' up so we're gonna check it out.'

Despite the jolting of the lorry and the fear of being involved, again, in something shameful, Dieter found himself dozing involuntarily. His sunglasses offered little respite to the sun that bored through his eyelids into the back of his skull. A long bumpy drive brought the convoy to a tiny hamlet of five or six small houses, at the base of a sixty-foot-high cliff. The rumbling of the lorries, as they pulled in front of the houses, drew women into the street. Two men, their gray beards streaked with years of tobacco stains, sat at what passed for the village taverna, a ramshackle structure with a cane roof. Maier stepped out of his car and spoke quietly to his sergeants. Dieter wondered where the rest of the men of the village were, but then it struck him that they probably were in the hills fighting, and this was why they had come to the village, to wreak punishment on whoever was left.

With another paratrooper whom he had never met before and who felt no inclination to be friendly, Dieter took up position at the entrance to the village. Maier took out a sheet of paper from his breast pocket and read something in Greek. As he spoke, the women began to mutter loudly amongst themselves. The oldest woman in the group, wearing a heavy black dress, stepped forward to confront the officer but was pushed back by one of the corporals who flanked their officer.

Maier spoke to the NCOs, who ordered troopers into each of the houses. At first nothing happened, but then smoke began to curl through the roofs and windows and pirouette into the sky. As the fire took hold of the ancient timbers the houses ignited in huge balls of flame. One old woman tried to get into her house but the flames drove her back. She sank to her knees and broke into sobs. A woman spoke up, surprising the soldiers with her fluent German. 'You bastards. Yes, I know your language. I lived in Germany once. When it was a good place. But now,' she spat on the ground in front of the officer. 'Do you know why the woman ran into her house? No, you don't know and you don't care. Her mother was there, lying in her bed. She is eighty-five years old. She cannot walk, but she is still alive and feels everything. You burnt her alive, in front of her own daughter. I hope by Saint Titus that all of you rot in Hell for what you have done. And you wonder why we hate you.'

Maier flicked his head at the two corporals, men who in the past had relished carrying out the most unpleasant orders for their officer, and then pointed to the burning house. They punched the woman who had spoken to them in the face, grabbed her by the arms and legs, and tossed her through the crumbling window into the flames. Dieter could hear her screams over the crackling of the flames and the explosions of jars of olive oil. Just for a moment a charred hand tried to grasp the edge of the window sill. But the hand disappeared, the screams ended, and the roof collapsed onto her.

The paratroopers climbed back into their lorries waiting to depart, but they were quiet. Normally after any operation they had relieved themselves of the tension with childish jokes, sometimes with exaggerated boasting, always with the conviction that the Cretans deserved what they had got. But not this time. They sat stone-faced, immobile. Only the lieutenant and the two troopers who had murdered the woman seemed unperturbed. Maier walked over to the villagers who were too numb to move. He lit a cigarette, drew on it four times and then flicked it into the group, smiling as he did so. Flicking cigarette ash from his jacket, he strolled back to his staff car, stretched, and ordered the convoy down the hill.

Dieter needed the drive back to the village to be over as quickly as possible, as though stepping off the lorry would allow him to escape the memory of what he had witnessed. The lorries rumbled to a stop in the plateia of Ayios Stefanos. On his way back to his billet, Dieter passed two soldiers roasting a chicken over an open fire. He smelt the burning flesh and heard the hissing of the olive oil, and he wondered if he would ever again be able to eat roast meat.

Dieter lay on his bed in the cool of the evening as inescapable thoughts began to crystallise, thoughts that would not disappear but grew only stronger and more nightmarish the more he tried to dispel them. From the very first day in the Hitler Youth, through the months of his basic training, to that glorious morning when he had been awarded his paratrooper's insignia, Dieter had drunk in Goebbels's propaganda and never needed to struggle with concepts like discipline and obedience. In that interlude of innocence the two words had meant the same, both needed to further the glories of the Reich and the Führer. Now, staring at the rough ceiling beams of his billet, he saw more clearly than ever that he been a naïve fool to confuse the two. In the simple, naïve time before Crete, *discipline* had always been a rather unconsidered and necessary proposition: saluting when he should; jumping from the plane when the green light flashed; moving into battle formation on his sergeant's orders. All these actions were done virtually without conscious thought; they were the result of discipline. It was easy to have discipline if one practiced enough. But true obedience required a man to make a conscious reaction, to commit himself to a cause higher than himself, to follow a command, fully aware of its consequences. As the pictures of that afternoon flickered through his brain — the shrieks of the burning woman, the image of the charred hand futilely grasping the burning window sill — he knew that the only obedience he had learnt was the wrong kind. For the obedience he thought he had willfully exercised had in fact been blind, and like discipline, the result of mindless unthinking repetition. For too long Dieter had been blind. Blind to everything his country had told him, blind to everything he had learnt in the Hitler Youth, and worst of all, blind to everything his own soul had tried to tell him. A quote from Nietzsche, half-remembered from school and not understood until today, entered his head: 'Whoever fights a monster should see to it that he does not become one.' Dieter Lehmann had stared into an abyss and realized the monster he was looking at was him and him alone.

Chapter 25

Paul shook his empty canteen, as if he might conjure up some water. His feet ached from a pair of boots that had virtually disintegrated. The sun burned through his head cloth and the back of his neck felt like crispy bacon. He was, in a word, miserable, and his misery was lessened only by the knowledge that the other andartes were miserable in their own way too.

'We need to rest, Yianni.' Christo pleaded. 'That damned spotter plane. The scramble into the gorge near killed them. Do you think they saw us, by the way?'

'How the hell do I know? I don't think so, but I don't know.' Yianni's voice was hoarse, and he put a small pebble into his mouth to get some spittle. For once, he refused Christo's offer of a cigarette.

'Let's head over to Apostoli,' Yianni continued. 'It can't be more than a couple of cigarettes away. Then we can rest up for the night, okay?'

Christo nodded, and the two of them ordered their men up.

The exhausted Cretans took their time making for the hamlet. As they got closer they smelt burnt wood, and saw a gray cloud hanging at the base of the cliff. They quickened their pace, but at the edge of the hamlet stopped, aghast at what they saw. Apostoli no longer existed. Women and two old men sifted through the embers trying to save what little they could but knowing they had lost everything. Yianni told the men to stay where they were and he walked up the lane to talk to one of the men. Yianni came back to the andartes, his face hard and his words bitter. Anesti translated for Paul as Yianni spoke. 'Two days ago, Germans come. Burn all. Burn two women alive. For nothing, for nothing.' The Cretan spat. Paul sat down hard, cradling his rifle like it was a baby.

A slight breeze stirred the air, and a thick, sweet smell wafted to Paul's nostrils from the burnt houses. He heard women wailing, while over the village circled a flock of large black birds, patiently waiting for food. Yianni knew that the villagers needed to be alone to deal with their grief privately and in their own way, and so after his men had filled their water flasks and received some food and wine from what little the women of the village could gather—for even in their torment hospitality to strangers had to be maintained—he moved his men into a small defile away from the village to bed down for the night. They unrolled their blankets and ate what the women had given them, but they spoke very little, silenced by the savagery of how the Germans had killed two defenceless women. The massacre of fighting men, as the Germans had done at Ayios Stefanos, was barbaric but perhaps understandable. But burning women alive was indefensible and inexplicable. The men slumped onto the hard ground of the defile and Christo posted sentries. Soon the men fell into light and disturbed sleep, their fatigue fighting with the nightmare of what they had witnessed. Yianni kicked the band awake even before the sun had risen. They did not complain. The village was cursed and they wanted to escape from it as soon as they could. Wordlessly, they picked their way across the scree slopes towards their cave.

The men kept their own counsel that day. Paul sat alone, and his mind went back to Liverpool, to the blitz, to Mary McGinley and her head covered in blood, obscenely lying there in the ruins of her home; to his wonderful little library, to the Prince Alfred, to home, to Mum and Dad. Paul surveyed his comrades, but he knew that their depression would soon lift, and the men would go back to war. But now he would go with them willingly.

Late that afternoon, young Alexi Doukakis scampered up the slope. As they always did, Christo and Yianni took him aside to a small rock outcrop where they sat and talked, and then the boy joined the rest of the andartes while Yianni and Christo continued their discussion, their voices low, their brows furrowed. Paul, who had followed their movements out of the corner of his eyes—there was something about their demeanour that frightened him and he did not want to catch their attention—watched the two men come back to the group. They shouted something he could not understand, but the men immediately stood up, hefted their weapons and shouldered their sakkoulia. Paul did the same, glad that the waiting was over.

The two leaders kept their men at a brisk pace, much quicker than usual, for two hours, and at times they half-slid, half-ran down the slopes, their speed almost causing them to tumble head first. Paul tripped regularly but he kept up with them for he sensed that no one would wait for him this time. They arrived at a copse of trees through which ran a small track that led to Ayios Stefanos a few kilometers away. Yianni had the men split into four small groups, each group hiding behind the trees and boulders and forming the corners of a rectangle that effectively boxed in the track. Then they waited. None of them smoked and they kept conversation to a whisper. Despite the shade of the trees the sun beat down on them and each man had to keep wiping the sweat from his eyes. Paul could feel the tension that gripped the men. Even Christo was playing with the bolt of his rifle. Fifteen minutes later the Cretans heard the tramp of boots.

'I don't like these patrols, Corporal, they stink like bad meat.' Manfred Schulz kicked hard at a rock on the side of the road. The young soldier looked at his sergeant. 'Look, son,' Manfred explained, 'how many of us are there? Twenty? Twenty. Think back over the last few weeks. We've only ever gone out in force, a lot more men than we have with us today. And you know as well as me that these hills are full of crazy Cretans and all they wanna do is kill us, as painful and slow as possible. The captain was right when he called them all men of darkness, that's what they are. Fuckin' men of darkness. But you know what, we've done ourselves no favours. Christ, we shot dead all the men in that village in cold blood, and then the generals wonder why they hate us. I'm even nervous around the women, but you don't tell anyone that or I'll kick your balls off. And then they send us out in these piss awful patrols to, now what's the word they use, pacify the region. Good luck with that one. And I don't know where this track goes. The lieutenant said check it out. Check what out? It's a track an' it goes fuckin' nowhere.'

'But, Sarge, the family you're with seems okay. I mean that little girl seems really sweet,' the corporal said. 'She likes you a lot.' He winked at Manfred.

'Yeah, I suppose so, and they've treated me well. And I've been nice to them. Still don't trust them until you really get to know them, and even then don't be so sure. Still, like you said, that family seems all right to me. Come on, let's get this over with and then we can head back. My feet are killin' me.'

A warm, sticky liquid sprayed over Manfred's face and it took him a moment to realise that only half of the corporal's face was still attached to his head. Manfred and his patrol dropped to the ground searching for cover, only to meet a withering blanket of fire. Manfred Schulz was killed when two rounds caught him in the chest, and his comrades died along with him and just as quickly.

Yianni ordered the men to stop firing and the andartes stood in silence, reviewing their carnage and feeling the adrenalin still pumping though their veins. Gun smoke hung listlessly in the still summer air, biting into Paul's throat and making him gag. Some of the Cretans began congratulating themselves on their easy victory, but Yianni ordered them to silence, and they listened in case more Germans were arriving. But there was only silence, and the Cretans turned back to the dead bodies. Each German was meticulously searched and everything of value was taken. One of the Germans twitched and a slight groan escaped his lips. Yianni took Paul by the shoulders and dragged him over. He pointed his fingers at the German, pretended to shoot him and pulled up Paul's hand still holding the Webley and nodded.

Yianni pointed Paul's hand at the German. He nodded again at Paul. The young Englishman felt every eye on him, especially the German's. He pulled the trigger. The German's chest heaved as the bullet entered, and a low gasp as the German died. Yianni gave Paul a small flask of raki, which he drank, in one gulp. The interpreter, Anesti Mandrakis, spoke. 'Now, you are true man, one of us.' Paul lent against a boulder and threw up, but another mouthful of raki washed away the taste. Yianni wordlessly nodded his approval; even Christo patted him on his back.

The next three days increased Paul's fear for the success of the ambush had made the andartes reckless. They no longer kept off the major trails or took hours of observation before entering a village, and they made only half-hearted attempts at hiding whenever a German spotter plane came too close. They had never acted this way before and not even Yianni could fully control them. Paul was unsure whether this recklessness came from their success with the German patrol or simply because of the lack of discipline that only well-trained soldiers can keep up for day after day. He feared it was both.

A Sunday morning, and the men had decided to attend church service in a small hill village. It was a bright, cloudless morning and in the distance the Aegean glistened a silvery blue. The men were boisterous. Some had already started on their raki, something just a week ago Yianni would never have allowed. The men began to sing a war song, about how the Cretans had killed the Turks many years ago, but their boisterousness was too much for Yianni and he ordered them to shut up.

The men obeyed their leader but not for long. 'Hey, little Alexi Doukakis, you call that a beard? My goat has better hair than you,' one of them yelled. Christo, ignoring Yianni's orders, laughed uproariously with the rest of the men as young Alexi turned bright red. He muttered something under his breath as Anesti ran by him and grabbed his cloth cap and threw it high into a tree.

'You are all malakas, ba-ba-bastards,' Alexi stuttered, 'and that was only my only cap, damn you, Anesti Mandrakis. Your brother fu-fu-fucks goats, did you know?'

'Well, better than fuckin' your sister,' Anesti retorted. The other men laughed, and even Alexi smiled. Argyro Doukakis was not the prettiest woman in their village, her brother had to admit.

'Here, Anesti, give me a hoist up,' Alexi ordered. 'I need that cap. My mother will kill me if I lose it.' Anesti grudgingly made a stirrup with his hands, and Alexi hoisted himself up the tree to retrieve his mother's gift.

'Good,' Alexi said with a smile, 'Now I duh-duh-don't worry about going home.' He placed the cap back on his head and with the others made his way down a narrow defile that opened onto a wide expanse of fields.

Paul let the other men pass him and peed against a bush, the steam rising from the leaves he spattered. Yianni turned around and joined him. 'Good idea,' he joked. Paul laughed to himself, catching against his better instincts the carefree mood of the men. The Cretans continued their Sunday morning stroll, and Paul and Yianni hurried to catch up with the tail end of the band as they approached the defile. The two men smiled at each other, enjoying the happiness of the morning almost as much as the physical pleasure of an empty bladder.

Chapter 26

If I'd been in charge, Dieter Lehmann angrily told himself, I'd have ordered my men to wait until the women and children of Ayios Stefanos had entered the church for their early Sunday service. But he wasn't in charge and so it was the villagers who'd had to postpone their worship until he and about thirty paratroopers, together with as many Wehrmacht regulars, had climbed into their lorries. The village women had grumbled, but as usual they had realized there was nothing they could do about it—just another inconvenience courtesy of the damned Germans.

The men on the lorries had been told nothing—even the sergeants who could normally be relied upon for at least an inkling of the missions shrugged their shoulders with the rest of them—and after they had debussed, following a short drive into the hills, they stood in a silence broken only by the clicking of the cicadas. A wait of fifteen minutes brought Lieutenant Maier in a staff car, and it was not only Dieter Lehmann's heart that sank as he clambered onto the bonnet. With him in the staff car was Lieutenant Schneider, who simply got out the car and waited for Maier to speak. The officer ordered four men to position themselves as lookouts for any stray Cretan. A sergeant ordered the rest of the unit to gather around the staff car.

'We may have a long walk ahead of us,' Maier said. 'We must keep out of sight, so we'll stay away from the open fields as much as we can.' Maier spoke in a low voice as though concerned that even the olive trees were spies and would pass on the information.

'We have it on good authority,' Maier explained, 'that a band of insurgents is in this general area. We've been informed it's the same band that ambushed the patrol from Ayios Stefanos. We have to thank Lieutenant Schneider for this information.' He nodded patronizingly at Schneider. 'Last night a spotter plane thinks it saw them a few miles south of here. You know what happened to our patrol.' The paratroopers nodded their heads and growled threats and insults. 'Shut up, men, and listen. Command has given us the special honour of going after them,' he concluded. 'Maybe we wait for them, like they wait for us, or better yet catch them unaware. And when we find them, well, you'll know what to do.'

Schneider's intelligence did not let him down. Just two hours after they had climbed down from their lorries the Germans ran into the andartes. Dieter was surprised by how careless the Greeks were, pouring out of a defile into an open shrub-covered field with nobody on point. The Germans, emerging from a copse, got over their surprise before the andartes, and they opened fire while the Cretans were still joking with each other or lifting their rifles to their shoulders at the Germans who had suddenly appeared in front of them. The volleys from the Schmeissers were disciplined and accurate. Dieter's own line of fire was blocked by the press of paratroopers in front of him, so he ran to the side of the column, hoping to train his machine pistol on any Cretan trying to get back into the defile, but the opening remained empty. He sprayed a burst into the defile for good measure before turning back to deal with the remaining andartes. He saw Cretans fall in front of him. Christo Papadakis was at the front of the band, and he was the first to fall as bullets ripped into his abdomen. Anesti Mandrakis's head was half blown away, and young Alexi Doukakis's body was spun like a top by the bullets slicing into him. His cap was tossed into the air before it too was riddled with bullets. The other men fell as quickly. The Germans stopped firing, the smell of cordite curdling in their nostrils. Hearing the groans of wounded men, the NCOs ordered their men to shoot any Cretan who had not yet died. Single luger shots fired into the skulls splashed blood onto the troopers' boots, but finally the battlefield was quiet.

At the sound of the firefight, Paul started to run into the open field to help, but Yianni pulled him back to the cover of the defile. The Cretan was too late, however, and the Englishman felt a heavy punch in his side and then an intense burning. He fell to the ground and tried to sit up, but the burning returned even worse than before, and he gasped through clenched teeth. Yianni grabbed him by the shirt and pulled him deeper into the defile. Then Paul felt a curious sensation as though he were being lifted, high above the ground, above the fray, and then nothing, just a peaceful nothing as though time and space had melded into something indeterminate.

Yianni hoisted Paul onto his back and staggered back up the defile, stumbling over the rocks and straining under Paul's weight. They took shelter in a grove of pine trees and listened as the chatter of machine pistols was replaced by single pistol shots. He began to put the flask of water to his lips but on seeing Paul's drawn face immediately offered it to the Englishman. Paul choked on it, so Yianni eased back the flask's neck to allow Paul to swallow a small amount of the warm liquid without gagging. Yianni then poured a small shot of raki into Paul's mouth. It burnt and the Englishman coughed hard, sending an earthquake of pain through his body. 'Sorry,' Yianni whispered. 'I should not have done that.' The Cretan thoroughly examined Paul's body and found only an entry wound and a larger exit wound, in Paul's right side. He pulled a shirt from his sakkouli and ripped it into a makeshift bandage to wrap around Paul's ribs. He kept the pressure on the wound until the blood flow had almost stopped.

Yianni sputtered in broken English. 'Germans, kill us, you, me okay. I go. Help. I come back. You safe.' The Cretan picked up his sakkouli and rifle, kissed Paul on the forehead and crept away.

Paul lay back. His head was spinning with the pain and the buzz of cicadas, and although he could see the sun bright overhead, an iciness had gripped his whole body. He moved his hand slowly down the right side of his chest where his body seemed the coldest, and his fingers touched a folded rag, warm and sticky. He saw blood on his fingers. His eyelids became heavy and he closed them as unconsciousness took away his pain.

It was night when Paul opened his eyes. Gingerly moving his fingers down his ribs he touched congealed blood. He felt around for his canteen, which Yianni had left on the ground next to him, and drank. The water was warm and tasted of metal, bitter and harsh, but it made him feel slightly better. He was not sure Yianni would come back and so alone once more he made his decision. Drake had told him in what seemed an eternity ago that if you were lost on an island you should just go downhill until you reach a coast; then at least you would have a bearing. He lifted himself slowly onto his knees and after he assured himself that the wound had not opened, he raised himself upright and tried a few halting steps. Pain twisted into his side like a knife but he felt confident enough to continue, and so Paul Cuthbertson, late of Liverpool, England, staggered on through the Cretan night with a German hole in his guts, tripping on rocks and catching his clothes on branches and bushes. The rocky ground was treacherous but he kept on going downhill, mentally tired by the need to stay alert and physically exhausted by the constant stumbling and the ever-present stone walls he had to climb. Where he was going, other than downhill, Paul had no idea. His right foot caught a root, his ankle buckling beneath him, and unable to stop himself he fell heavily. He lay still to catch his breath, the dewy soil pressing into his lips, and then got to his feet. He put weight on the ankle. It burnt. He felt blood trickle down the inside of his shirt—his greatest fear had come true—and he knew he had to hide and rest and stop the bleeding before daylight broke fully over the island. Ahead of him, a white smudge through the trees reveled itself. Closer, the smudge became the wall of a small building. Paul dragged himself through the front door and lay down by a small altar. He felt a pile of netting in the corner and he pulled it over himself. His mind registered curious doll parts hanging on the walls, but he was too tired to wonder what they meant, and he fell into a fitful sleep.

Chapter 27

The Germans' boisterousness after a well-executed action infected Dieter on the road back to Ayios Stefanos, for despite his having killed civilians—something he had previously rebelled against—he had also killed the enemy and that was what he had been trained to do. The paratroopers and the regular soldiers, as they always did, went their own way after debussing in the square, the latter drifting back to the billets. But the paratroopers were ordered to congregate in front of the church. Lieutenant Maier stood on the bonnet of his staff car and cleared his throat. 'My boys,' he shouted. 'Tonight we enjoy a good meal and a good sleep. Today was only a small victory for the Führer and our beloved Fatherland, but it is one of many. The enemy are beaten here, and soon we will beat the damned British everywhere and piss on Mister Churchill's head.' The men brayed their agreement. 'Now then, men, I can tell you something else, now that we're away from those puffed-up Wehrmacht fellows. High Command chose you for this last operation,' he continued, 'because we're the last paratroopers on the island, so we're the best they've got.' He paused for a few seconds and then continued. 'Probably next week, we're all being transferred back to Athens. The Führer has something new for us to do.' He grinned, letting the news filter into his men. 'Yeah, that's right. We're off to do some real fighting again.' The men looked at each other and began to grin as they realized what he was saying.

'Soon, we will leave this accursed island for good. Gentlemen, a toast. To the Fallschirmjäger, to the Fatherland, to the Führer. Sieg Heil, Sieg Heil, Sieg Heil.' The salutes reverberated around the plateia and escaped down the narrow streets encasing the village in the sound of a triumphant Nazism.

That evening, the village of Ayios Stefanos rang with the

drunken revelry of German soldiery. The paratroopers and the regular Wehrmacht had been ordered to stay away from each other and as a result there were only two minor brawls when two regulars tried to prove they were as tough as the paratroopers. Dieter joined in the drinking, glad of the camaraderie and quietly and pleasantly surprised at how much alcohol he had drunk. He felt giddy and even led the tavern in a round of the Horst Wessel. Thirsty after his solo, he grasped one of the many bottles of beer in the middle of the table and immediately felt a stickiness on his hand. It was covered in blood and he wiped it away to see a cut on the side. He was surprised that he had not noticed it before, let alone felt it, for it was deep. He took out a handkerchief, wrapped it around the wound tightly and thought no more of it.

Yet as the night wore on, Dieter's elation became more and more forced. He felt his eyelids drooping as the adrenalin of the day's fighting worked its way out of his bloodstream to be replaced by beer and wine. The alcohol, as it always did when he had drunk too much, began to depress him, and after hearing one too many times a sergeant and the lieutenant argue about the best way to screw a woman, he grabbed his machine pistol and headed for the groves surrounding the village. He noticed that the wound on his hand—maybe he had been hit by a ricochet during the firefight, though he hadn't felt it at the time—had opened up again and he wrapped his handkerchief more tightly around the wound. Through the dawn's light he caught sight of the small chapel that overlooked the village. Consoled by the notion that sometimes a walk is made more enjoyable by having a destination, even if the destination is not in itself particularly important, Dieter, half-staggering, made for the chapel. The walk had started to clear his head of the alcohol's mugginess, and he reflected that he was a good soldier, a good paratrooper, and that he had not hesitated to kill the enemy, even when they were Cretan males. Yet, exacerbated by the depressive effects of the alcohol, still there lurked the fear that for all his good soldiering he would never be able fully to erase what he had seen since he landed on the island. He was ashamed of his passiveness in not resisting the massacres or the other brutalities he had witnessed. Was it enough, he wondered, simply to have avoided shooting the unarmed men of Ayios Stefanos in the olive grove? What could he have done to prevent the murders of the two women at Apostoli? Should he at least have tried? Dieter knew he was simply one individual in a huge machine of war. But his father's words at that final dinner reverberated. Had he, as his father suspected, been corrupted beyond redemption? And was that acknowledgment of doubt, he asked himself, simply a reflection of reality or was it an excuse to wrap around himself as a shield against his own moral cowardice?

The women of Ayios Stefanos learnt of the firefight that same day by the curious manner in which all news filters through a rural society, but Anastasia was careful to keep the news of the massacre away from Elpida. It was likely that the little girl's father had been killed, for the old woman sensed, though without certainty, that her son had been involved. Until she had more information there was no point in sharing what little she knew with her granddaughter. Anastasia herself felt numb to the probability that now her son too had been murdered, his escape from the massacre merely a reprieve before God's plan for her family was fully executed. But she could not understand her indifference or the lassitude that kept her from her daily chores for they had to be done. Perhaps, she thought, life had finally got too much for her. The old woman sat in her living room, absent-mindedly stroking Wawa who lay contentedly on her lap. Occasionally she would chop up a vegetable or two, but her heart was not in it. She looked at Elpida asleep on the floor and smiled. Anastasia heard a gentle knock on the door and immediately rushed across the room, hoping against all realistic hope that it might be Yianni. But it was only Sophia Theodorakis.

'Come with me, now, Ana.' the old woman ordered in a barely audible voice, 'Leave Elpida here. All the Germans are in the plateia drunk, nobody will see you in the dark anyway. And hurry, for Jesus' sake. Something bad is happening, at my house.'

Anastasia, with no idea of what that 'something' was, made sure Elpida was still asleep, quietly closed the door, and she and Sophia walked as fast as they could through the evening gloom to Sophia's house, Anastasia still clutching her vegetable knife. Sophia's living room was filled with the village women, all of them crowded around a hard wooden chair on which sat Eleni Apostolakis. The young woman's blouse was torn, and a trickle of blood ran from the corner of her mouth.

'What is going on?' Anastasia asked, her voice pitched high with confusion.

One of the women, anonymous in the half light of the room, spoke. 'That bitch is a traitor. How did the Germans know where the men were? How did the Germans find them so easily when they usually don't even bother to try? You see how they like to hang around the village, like they're frightened to go up into the hills. No, the Germans knew where the men were going to be, and they waited for them. And we know who told them.'

There was a murmur of agreement from the women and one of them grabbed Eleni's hair and pulled her head back sharply, exposing her neck.

Eleni screamed. 'Let me speak, for God's sake, let me speak.'

One of the women pulled out a long hunting knife and stepped over to Eleni, but Anastasia, without really knowing why, stood in front of the terrified woman.

Anastasia spoke harshly. 'Eleni Apostolakis, I do not know if what they say is true, but it doesn't really matter now does it? You have been shunned by the village. These women have already passed judgment on you. You are no longer welcome here, and I will not be able to protect you even if I wanted to. And your boyfriend won't help, either. He's getting drunk with all the other German bastards. My advice is to leave now and never come back.'

Eleni spat at Anastasia and watched the spittle make its slow way down a wrinkle in Anastasia's cheek. 'I have done nothing wrong. It was not me who told the Germans about the men. I don't care if you believe or not. You are all stupid, weak women,' she cried, the words tumbling out uncontrollably. 'You do not see the reality, do you? The Germans are here to stay. And yes, I slept with the officer. How else was I to survive? You all have something to give them and you take from them, as well. You, Anastasia Manoulakis, I see your little Elpida take chocolate from the Germans. You, Sophia Theodorakis, do you deny you sell goat milk to the Germans and they give you extra rations? And you, Olga—' Her words were cut off as Anastasia slapped her across the cheek.

'Shut up, you fool, I am trying to help you.' Anastasia ordered, the spittle still making its way down her cheek.

'I don't need your help,' Eleni retorted, her face twisted in a grimace of contempt. 'And Yianni, your glorious son, who you think walks on water, was as weak as you.' Eleni Apostolakis's years of anger and frustration spilled out. 'He could have had me as his wife, but he insulted me, made me feel as though I was nothing. I think it's because he knew he wasn't man enough for me. Couldn't take a real woman, not like that feeble little kitten he doted on. And where is your darling son now? Lying dead in a field somewhere. For what? To stop what's going to happen regardless of what he did anyway? You're all fools, weak fools who can't see the future right in front of their noses.'

Eleni paused and looked around her as though willing the other women to make a move.

'Anyway, you cannot touch me,' she continued. 'Schneider will protect me. I don't need you. Now let me go before you really get into trouble.' Her words, interrupted by sobs of anger, bounced off the walls of the house.

Anastasia whispered into Eleni's ear. 'Did you tell the Germans where the men were? Well, did you?'

Eleni said nothing, just grinned and raised her head in defiance.

The memories of her lost family flooded unbidden into Anastasia's brain, and she swiftly swiped the blade of her vegetable knife across the woman's throat. Blood spurted out of the gash and poured down onto Eleni's blouse. The woman made a gurgling noise as she tried to suck in the precious air. Then her body slumped off the chair onto the stone floor. The women gasped at Eleni's body, blood still oozing out of her neck.

Anastasia took command. 'Sophia, clean this mess up as soon as we are gone. You two,' she said, pointing at two of the women, 'help Sophia. No one must know what happened. Now, who will help me take her away?' Three of the women stepped forward and picked the limp body up.

Anastasia looked at the other women. 'Remember, not a word. And if it gets out, I will find the traitor and do to them what I did to her.' She pointed at the corpse with her vegetable knife. She slowly poked her head out into the street. She heard the drunken reveling of the soldiers in the square but saw nobody. She motioned to the three women to follow her, and they slipped through the empty streets, half-carrying, half-dragging the corpse to the ravine that the villagers used as their rubbish dump. The bottom of the ravine was thick with discarded chairs, worn out crockery that could no longer be repaired, the trimmings from last winter's olive harvest, sheep and goat carcasses stripped bare of everything humanly edible, a couple of dead dogs and cats half eaten by the rats who thrived there. The four women swung Eleni's body twice then heaved it into the ravine. It slithered down a rotting mattress and then crashed into the junk. Anastasia knew that the bottom of the ravine could not be seen from its lip, and she satisfied herself that the body was well hidden. She knew too that the smell of the rotting animal carcasses would hide Eleni's own putrefaction. Anastasia and the three women retraced their way back to Ayios Stefanos.

At her front door, Anastasia halted, looking up and down the alley as though expecting something unknown. She stared at the door, wondering what might confront her. Perhaps the Germans, or worse, a demon come to punish her for her mortal sin. She steeled herself, knowing that her granddaughter was across the threshold. She gingerly entered the door, and said a prayer in gratitude when she found everything as she had left it. Even Elpida was still asleep where she had left her, curled up in a ball on her bed. Anastasia poured herself a large shot of raki as the shock of what she had just done began to wear off. Suddenly a sharp pain stabbed into her chest, as though someone was grabbing her insides and squeezing them. She gasped for breath and stumbled against the table. But as quickly as it had come, the pain vanished. She crossed herself. These attacks had happened before, and she had ignored them. But tonight she was frightened that it might be punishment from God. Elpida still slept, undisturbed in the peacefulness of childhood, and so Anastasia, silently begging her God to forgive her, stepped outside into the balmy night air and made her way slowly to the little chapel where she could find, perhaps, some peace and solitude.

Chapter 28

Thirty minutes before Anastasia Manoulakis had decided to ask her God for forgiveness, Dieter Lehmann opened the door to the little chapel that overlooked the village and stepped inside, the cloying dampness and the sweet incense of the interior clinging to his nostrils. There was a noise in the corner, and the German raised his machine pistol in defence. He saw two legs protruding from a pile of netting. Still pointing the gun at the lump he kicked the legs. Paul groaned and moved the netting from over his face to see Dieter staring at him. He groped for his rifle until he remembered he had long ago abandoned it. Dieter kept his gun trained on Paul and quickly pulled the netting away from the Englishman. Paul slowly raised his arms as far as he could but he felt his gut tighten and so he let his arms drop uselessly to his side. Never relaxing his gaze, Dieter patted Paul down and then slumped against the opposite wall. He kept his gun pointed at Paul's gut.

'Please,' Paul's voice was thick as blood oozed from the side of his mouth. 'Please, put the gun down. I...' He coughed. 'I cannot hurt you.'

Dieter pulled the gun away but kept his finger on the trigger.

'You are not Greek, true?' Dieter said. 'I think you are a Tommy, yes?'

Paul nodded.

'You have no uniform, I could kill you.' The Englishman's body stiffened. 'It is okay. Tommy. I have done enough killing for today.' He half smiled. 'Perhaps forever. You are bleeding bad, Tommy. We are both soldiers. Let us truce, is that the right word?'

'I, yes, I am a, and you...' Paul hesitated. His face pursed. 'But you're a Jerry.'

'Ah, yes. A Jerry. I like that name.' Dieter smiled. 'A Jerry and a Tommy.'

'Are you in pain, Tommy?'

'What do you think? Some bastards…' But he stopped, as his befuddled brain cleared enough to realise the German in front of him might have been involved in the firefight.

'You speak good English.' Paul's hooded eyes burrowed into the young German's face.

'Yes, I went to a good school. I learnt all about England. Its writers.' The German hesitated. 'Its empire. I grew up thinking we should be friends, our two countries. We should have been fighting the French together.' Dieter placed his gun across his lap.

'You sound like my Dad. He thought that too. He even read that book your Hitler wrote. Can't remember the name. Camp or something.' Paul coughed.

Dieter smiled. '*Mein Kampf*. You see, Tommy, we didn't have to fight, so why did we?'

'I suppose we had to stop you lot.' Paul settled back into the netting, and Dieter leant forward to catch Paul's words.

Dieter raised his voice. 'But, Tommy, we are the same people.'

'No, we're not.' Paul's laboured breathing made it difficult for Dieter to hear and he bent forward even closer. 'We're not the same people, Jerry, we're not.' Paul's face froze in a rictus of pain.

Dieter's eyes narrowed. 'And is that why you started it? Because we're different? You bombed our cities, and all we wanted was to be your friends.'

Paul closed his eyes and the image of Mary McGinley's severed head jumped into his consciousness. He opened his mouth to speak but no words came.

'You have lots of people fighting for you, Tommy,' Dieter said. 'From your empire, from all over the world.'

Paul shrugged. 'I suppose they thought the fight was worth it.'

'And yet still you lost.'

The young Englishman turned his head away as tears filled his eyes.

'I'm not clever like you,' Paul whispered. 'But I'm not stupid either. And if you think we started this war, then maybe being clever isn't worth the effort because you're so bloody wrong. I've seen friends killed here and at home, and I just don't understand what you're trying to do. Nobody does. Has all the killing been worth it? Why couldn't you just leave everythin' alone. Like it's always been.'

Dieter stiffened, and for a moment Paul thought he had gone too far.

'Englishman, I think you need to remember how you got your empire.' But as quickly as his temper had flared, the German relaxed and leant back against the wall.

'I'm too tired to argue with you, Tommy. I suppose we all have different ways of looking at the truth.' He scratched the scar on his cheek. 'But do you think this war has not been hard for me? I've seen my friends killed, in horrible ways as well. It might be easy for you to think we are just killers, that all we want to do is kill. But we're not, you know.' Dieter wondered if he was trying to convince just Paul or himself as well.

The two settled back into a silence broken only by Paul's racking cough.

Tears clogged Paul's eyes and the German became just a misty blur. 'I'm dying,' he said, 'and I don't want to. And all because your country wants to rule the world. I don't know, Jerry. I suppose you don't see it that way, like you said. I suppose you think that we had an empire and now it's your turn. You know, I read a little back home about the Romans and the Greeks. Alexander, that sort of stuff. Didn't understand a lot, but I do know that all empires fall. And when they do, it's a bloody mess. It's all a bloody mess, isn't it?'

Paul's face was ashen and drawn, fresh blood stained his

lips and the dark stain on his shirt grew larger and deeper as he spoke. He closed his eyes. He knew he was dying, had seen enough death already to know he was beyond help. He tried to think of a prayer, but none came right away. He had gone to church each Sunday morning, but he had never really believed, at least not with his mother's almost childlike simplicity. He had never imagined that one day he would envy her for her faith, but now, lying under dirty netting as a German watched him bleed to death, he… His thoughts trailed away to nothing.

Dieter spoke. 'Yes, it is a bloody mess. Yes, I think you are dying. I am sorry, Tommy.'

Paul allowed Dieter to light a cigarette for him, but choked as he tried to inhale the bitter tobacco smoke. 'I've never smoked. This is the first one. Stupid, ain't it? Never smoked, never even kissed a girl. And now here I am. Like this. Bloody pathetic.'

Dieter leaned over and lifted the cigarette from Paul's shirt where it had fallen from his lips. 'No need to waste it.' He half-smiled.

Just before the ash burnt his fingers, Dieter stubbed the cigarette out on the chapel wall.

'I think we're all dying, Tommy.' The German spoke quietly. 'We are all dying. It's just that some of us will die sooner than others.'

'So, what will happen to you, Jerry?' Paul coughed, and another small trickle of blood ran down his chin.

Dieter lit another cigarette and stared at the smoke rings as they floated lazily to the chapel roof. 'What will happen to me? I am a paratrooper, and I suppose I'll be sent somewhere else. But after this is all over? And supposing I'm not dead somewhere? Well, that's a good question. Perhaps I'll become a pastor. My friend Hans always did say I could talk him to sleep in five minutes. But I don't know. The future seems too far away. I just don't know.' The young German smiled at the memory of his dead friend.

He stood up and flicked cigarette ash off his shirt. "I think I need to get you help. I will take you to the village. It's not far.'

Paul's voice quivered. 'No, You…they'll kill me. I'm out of uniform. They'll think I'm a spy or summat.' Dieter nodded. 'Look, just leave me here.' Paul hesitated a moment. 'Please. Anyway, why are you being so good to me, Jerry?'

Dieter watched the cigarette smoke waft up to the chapel roof where it hovered like a cloud before a rainstorm.

'I don't know. Maybe because you will die soon, and no man should meet his God alone and frightened. Maybe so you know we are not the monsters you think we are. Maybe because I like you, maybe because…' He stopped and smiled at Paul. 'Maybe because I need to know I haven't changed too much.'

Paul coughed, and a gobbet of blood spilled from his lips. Dieter wiped it away from Paul's chin and then unwrapped the blood-caked cloth from Paul's torso. Below the rib cage there was a circular hole with small red bubbles frothing from it.

'Let me help you.' Dieter padded his handkerchief against the wound before retying the bandage.

'Thank you,' Paul said.

'I remember, Tommy, a line from one of your poets. Something about the turbid ebb and flow of human misery. I have always liked that line. Do you know it too?'

'No,' Paul coughed. 'I never got that far in school.'

'Well,' Dieter said, 'it means…'

'I know what it means, I think. It means we're all fucked sooner or later, one way or another.' Paul's laugh turned into a cough that convulsed his whole body.

Dieter smiled. 'Yes, that's exactly what it means, I think. Here, drink this water. I should've given it to you before. I am sorry.' He put his canteen to Paul's lips.

Paul risked a small sip and felt the warm water on his cracked lips. He lay back against the netting.

The door of the chapel creaked open, and the two soldiers

looked with a start at Anastasia Manoulakis standing on the threshold, her mouth wide open. She turned as though to run away, but when she saw the young man sitting by the altar, the blood oozing through his shirt she hurried over, for she realized it was the young man whom Yianni had invited to their house just a short while ago, the shy young man who had been so scared.

She looked at Dieter briefly who nodded his approval, and she quickly cleaned away as much of Paul's wound as she could. As she worked on the wound, her face close to Paul's, she heard a whisper, so low as to be almost inaudible. 'Yianni is safe. He will return. Ine kala.' The old woman did not understand most of what the young Englishman was saying but the last two words were all she needed to hear. Her son was well.

Anastasia ripped a long strip off her skirt and wrapped it around Paul's body. But his weight, slight though the Englishman was, was too much for her, and she motioned Dieter to help. Wiping away the sweat from his eyes, he took the limp body in his arms so that Anastasia could wrap the strip around. The two of them laid Paul's body gently down onto the netting. Dieter felt a warm sticky wetness on his hand and saw that his own wound had opened up again. He inexpertly tried to retie the bandage but felt his hand being held by the old woman's, and he looked on in silence as Anastasia unwrapped the bandage and then retied it properly around his hand. He nodded his thanks, but she said nothing and as quickly as she had entered the chapel she left.

Paul settled back against the wall. 'I feel cold,' he said.

'Perhaps this will help.' Dieter lay more of the netting over him. "I must go now. My sergeant will want to know where I am. Do not worry. I will not tell anyone. I am Dieter Lehmann. Tell me. What is your name?'

Paul slowly whispered the two words.

'Paul I will remember. My uncle is called Paul. But that last one? I will never remember that,' Dieter said. He opened his diary and on the first page he underlined the first 'C' he came to. On the next page, he underlined the first 'U' until all the letters of Paul's surname had been marked.

The German stood up and Paul held out his hand. 'Please,' Paul said, 'Please stay. I don't want to...' His voice trailed off.

Dieter took hold of the young Englishman's hands and quietly recited the Lord's Prayer.

'Thank you, Jerry.' Paul's words were interspersed with a bloody phlegm. He closed his eyes, and Dieter repeated the prayer again until the laboured breathing had stopped. The German gently closed the Englishman's eyes and slipped out of the chapel.

Chapter 29

Anastasia still lay in bed, half asleep. The odour of Antoni's cigarettes still clung to the room but even that was fading, and she knew the presence of her beloved husband in their home was receding every day until only memories would be left. Then the dread recollection of last night forced her into consciousness. Down below, she heard Wawa chasing a mouse, and grateful for the interruption to her thoughts, got out of bed as quickly as she could before the cat did some real damage

'Hush, you silly cat,' she said through a huge yawn, as Wawa finally gave up. She poured out a little water for the cat, seeing with satisfaction that the wound in Wawa's side, where the German had kicked her, had almost healed.

Elpida rolled over and out of her bed on the kitchen floor. She rubbed the sleep from her eyes and yawned.

'Come on, little girl, we've got a lot to do today,' her grandmother said.

The two ate a small piece of bread as they walked to the cemetery. The village was silent except for the first of the early risers starting their daily routines. Anastasia and Elpida stood before Antoni's grave and Anastasia said a short prayer. Elpida crossed herself and told her papouka that she would be a good girl for her baba when he came home and that she missed him a lot. Anastasia wiped away her tears as she listened to her granddaughter.

'Come, pedhi mou. How about a little walk before we start the day, yes? Elpida,' her grandmother said softly, 'there is something special we must do at the chapel. But first I must tell you something, something you must promise never to tell anybody.' Elpida nodded solemnly. 'Do you promise?' Anastasia persisted.

'Yes, Yiayia, I promise.'

'Well then, little girl. Soon, I think, you will see your baba again. I know it has been a long time, but I think he is fine and he will return to us soon.'

Elpida's face broke into a huge smile. 'But when, Yiayiaka, when?' Her voice raised an octave and her grandmother hushed her. 'When, Yiayiaka, when?'

'Soon, little girl, soon. Now, hush before the whole village hears you.'

Elpida grabbed her grandmother's hand and danced down the street.

As they came nearer to the chapel, Anastasia slowed down. 'Elpida, I want you to stay outside, okay?' The little girl nodded.

Anastasia, after checking to make sure Elpida was still standing back, opened the chapel door, wrinkling her nose at the slightly sweet odour that confronted her. By the altar lay the body of the young Englishman, still covered in the netting Dieter had draped back over him. She removed the netting and knelt over the body. The blood on his shirt was dry. At first she thought she saw some motion in his chest, as though the Englishman was still breathing, but she realized it was a trick of the light. She placed her cheek over Paul's mouth but felt no breath, no sign of life.

She crossed herself and shouted to her granddaughter outside. 'Elpida, run to the village and tell Sophia that there is a dead Englishman here. She'll know what to do. Tell her we need help to move him. But do not tell anybody else, just Sophia.'

While she waited, she laid out Paul's body and gently cushioned his head on the netting. She wet the hem of her pinafore with spit and rubbed as much of the dirt off his face as she could. She kissed him on the forehead and hoped that his soul would think his own mother was kissing him Good Morning. And then she raised herself onto her knees and prayed for the young man's soul, that he would find eternal salvation and that he might be the last young man to die in this accursed war. Thirty minutes later, Elpida, Sophia and two other women returned with a small donkey-drawn cart. The women carried Paul's body out of the chapel and gently placed it in the back of the cart. The makeshift funeral cortege made its way to a small dell hidden from view of the village, and there they dug a shallow grave and laid Paul Cuthbertson's body to rest. Anastasia covered his face with her pinafore, and Elpida, tears rolling down her cheeks for she had liked this nice foreigner, laid a posy of wilted wildflowers on his chest. The women gently placed the soil over his body and then covered his grave with rocks. They stood and said a prayer for him and the hope that his English friends would soon find him and give him a proper Christian burial. Then they crossed themselves and made their way back to the village.

Chapter 30

A mourning dove cooed its first dirge of the day as if to bid Dieter Lehmann farewell. The young German was leaving Ayios Stefanos. Too much had happened there, and most of it bad, for him to feel anything but relief. Let the Wehrmacht have the village. And good luck to them, he kept telling himself. It was a week after the successful ambush of the andartes, and although the paratroopers had heard of the rumours about being transported to the Russian campaign, the orders to leave the island had come through only the day before. It had not taken long for Dieter and the other paratroopers to pack.

That final evening the paratroopers had decided to end their stay in Crete with a monumental binge. Dieter had joined them, from boredom if for no other reason. As he had waited for the first of the beers to arrive, he had pulled out a letter he had recently received from his mother. She had emphasized the positive events in the news. Rommel was still doing brilliantly well in North Africa, the Luftwaffe continued to bomb British cities and the U-boats (Please be safe, Otto, Dieter prayed) were devastating the British convoys in the north Atlantic. But the fate of the *Bismarck* was now well known in Germany, and the country was still trying to come to grips with the defection of the Deputy Führer, Rudolf Hess, to the British. The official news release was that Hess was insane, but like other Germans Dieter wondered what was really behind his defection. Little Liesl had just passed her latest piano proficiency certificate with a wonderful rendition of a Beethoven sonata, Magda was still as unreliable as ever, but where, his mother fretted, could she find someone else to work for so little, and Father was the same as ever, griping if he could not buy his favourite tobacco from the corner shop or if the newspaper boy was late in delivery. Dieter smiled. At least some things never changed.

The paratrooper next to him had punched his arm. 'A little letter from your girl, Lehmann? I saw you smiling. Well, I wouldn't dote on her. She's probably getting screwed by some big, beefy firefighter back home. The girls love those uniforms, you know.' The paratrooper started laughing, and Dieter had tried to laugh along with him, striving in vain to enjoy the camaraderie and the first deep gulp of the newly arrived beer.

The next morning, with heads pounding, the paratroopers lined up in the village square and waited to board the lorries. As they pulled away from the square, the men cheered. The lorries passed through the fields where, for better or worse, Dieter had become a man. The threshing floor, the dead, mustached New Zealand officer, the tree where Hans's head had finally come to rest, the grove where he and his friend had landed, scared beyond his comprehension until Hans had taken things in hand and brought Dieter back to his senses. From the lorry he could even catch a glimpse of where they had massacred the village men. For even though he had not killed anyone that day, that knowledge was not enough to assuage the embers of guilt that continued to burn his conscience. He knew that his schoolboy fantasy of this being a good war for the sake of the Fatherland had been crushed, but he still hoped to find some personal salvation in going to the Russian Front where he could at least fight real soldiers. Hans had once told him that the Slavs were savages, a real threat to his country, and that he was mystified that the Führer had ever allied with them in the first place. But at least now the sides for a proper war had been set, and Dieter hoped that he could do his duty and perhaps redeem himself for all the atrocities he had witnessed and not even tried to stop.

At the Maleme airfield he boarded a Junkers 52. It lifted him into the virginal blue sky, and Dieter Lehmann promised himself that he would never again set foot on the island of Crete.

◊

It had been two days since the paratroopers had left the village and Elpida awakened to another day of drudgery and loneliness. It was dark outside, and she could hear her grandmother snoring softly in the loft above her. The little girl opened two bleary eyes and rubbed away the sleep. Her eyes burned, as they always did first thing in the morning and she started to get up to slosh some water over her face. But this time something was different. She felt a presence in the room, a presence felt but not seen. Then a grey, shadowy figure crossed the end of the bed. Elpida drew her legs up, cowering in the corner of the tiny room. Was it Pappous, she wondered in fear, come to make sure they were safe. Yiayia had told her that he looked after them day and night. But there came a gentle voice from the shadow, a voice she loved.

'It is me, little girl. Baba, I'm home.'

Elpida shouted out in joy and jumped out of the bed. Hot tears ran down her cheeks as she drank in the familiar odor of sweat and tobacco of her father. Yianni lifted her up and she felt his rough beard scratching her cheek as he kissed her.

'What are you doing, silly child?' her grandmother called from above, and the two of them heard the bed and then the ladder creak as Anastasia started to come down. Then she too recognized her son's voice and she almost jumped down the final third of the ladder to hug her son tightly.

'I came as soon as I could, Mama,' Yianni said.

'Son, you know some of the Germans are still here, don't you? They haven't all gone.'

'I know, Mama, but I couldn't stay away any longer.'

'Baba,' Elpida's thin voice cut through the still air of the house. 'You can't leave again, Baba, no, you must stay here forever. Please.'

'She's right, Yianni.' Anastasia pursed her brow. 'What do you mean, my son,' she asked, 'for a little while at least.'

Yianni opened his mouth to reply but his mother cut him off.

'Son, no, you've done enough. Your daughter needs you, I

need you. You...'

'Mama, you must understand, it is too dangerous for me here, and that makes it too dangerous for you and Elpida too. I,' he hesitated, 'I, look, I will not be fighting anymore. I am to go to Egypt and help train the English. That's what the officer told me. So, I will not even be on the island all the time. Most of the time I'll be safer than you and Elpida.'

Elpida looked at her grandmother and settled back onto her father's chest as soon as Anastasia nodded at her son.

'I believe you. I suppose I have no choice. But you must promise me that you will look after yourself.'

'I promise you, Mama, I will look after myself. Now, I am starving, what do you have for breakfast?'

That evening, Anastasia made her son eat some soup, although it was difficult for him to get the spoon to his mouth, for Elpida refused to leave her father's lap. The little girl stared at him as he slurped his meal, his eyes flitting everywhere, his mind unable to focus on anything for more than a few seconds. Anastasia saw that the left side of his face twitched uncontrollably. She wanted to ask but was afraid to.

'Remember that young English boy you brought here?' she said.

Yianni nodded.

'Well, I found him in the chapel, with a German of all people. They were both hurt, and I took pity on them both. Maybe I shouldn't have, but what could I do?'

She waved down Yianni as he began to protest.

'I helped them both. The English boy really needed my help. Anyway, they both looked too tired to harm an old woman, and I have committed many sins to ask God for His forgiveness for.' Her mind flitted to Eleni's death. 'The boy died later that night, the English boy that is. But before he died he told me that you were still alive. I made sure that he got a proper burial.' She let her words linger. 'I wonder. Do you know how he got wounded,

Yianni?'

'He was a good English boy, Mama. I liked him. We all did. He was so shy when he came to us, and frightened like a little puppy but he proved himself a man. I am sorry he is dead. This war has taken too many good men.'

Despite Yianni's reluctance to answer her question, Anastasia probed further. 'You haven't answered my question? Do you know how he got hurt? I don't know why, but I'd like to know. He was a guest in my home. Maybe that's why I need to know.'

Yianni shook his head, and his eyes bored into his mother's.

'You never could lie to me, Yianni mou.'

'No, Mama, I never could. Yes, I was with him when he was wounded. And he fought bravely, like all the other men. I went to get help but couldn't find anybody. So I went back by myself but he had gone. I suppose he had wondered off.'

Desperate to change the subject, Yianni said, 'Mama, I want to visit Baba's grave later. I'll wait until it is dark. Just in case.'

Both of them seemed happy to move on to other things.

'Thank you, Son. We visit him every day, but I know he will like your company. He must get tired of two silly females blubbering over him.' She smiled and wiped away the tears that misted her eyes.

Yianni's eyes twinkled. 'What makes you think he was listening to you? Just a few months ago he told me he was glad he was going deaf. Wouldn't have to put up with your chattering all the time.'

Elpida sat upright. 'Baba, that's a terrible thing to say about Papouka.'

'Little girl, I'm only joking. Look, Yiayiaka is smiling as well.' Her father smiled at his daughter and kissed her cheek. 'I hope when you are a woman your husband loves you as much as Papouka loved your Yiayia.'

'Well, okay,' the little girl said. 'Okay.'

You know, Yianni,' Anastasia said, 'the German who helped

Paul, yes, Paul, that was his name, I couldn't remember it, well, the German in the chapel was, I think, a good man. He could have killed Paul or taken him back to the village as a prisoner. But he didn't. So maybe the Germans can be good after all, or maybe some of them.'

'No, Mama, no.' He banged his fist on the table so hard that Elpida almost fell off his lap. 'No, Mama. I've seen what they've done to villages all across the island. I've seen what they've done to women and children, innocent women and children. They slaughtered Christo, Alexi, all of them. Have you forgotten what they did to Baba?'

Anastasia's face hardened. 'Do not speak like that to me, my son. Do you think I could ever forget holding my husband's body in my arms, crying over his corpse until I had no more tears to cry? Well, do you?'

Yianni stretched out his hand to take his mother's. 'I am so sorry, Mama. What I said was unforgiveable. It was stupid of me. Please, forgive me. It's just I've been away so long, I'm becoming as wild as the sheep in the hills.'

'Of course, my son, of course I forgive you. These are terrible times, and sometimes I think we've all gone a little mad. Come on, it is dark enough for us to go to the cemetery. I know Baba is looking forward to talking to you.'

Yianni Manoulakis left his mother and daughter the next morning before either of them had awakened, and later that same day he stepped onto the terrace in front of his old cave. Cranford sat in front of the embers of a fire, conversing quietly with Ari, his runner.

'Yianni, I'm glad to see you. How is your daughter, and your mother too? Well, I hope. Come and have some raki.'

Yianni nodded and sat down. He rolled around a mouthful of

raki from the flask Ari gave him, enjoyed a large belch, and then started on a large chunk of bread and a chop that he ripped from the carcass suspended over the fire.

'He's dead. They're all dead,' Yianni stared at the ground.

'I know, Yianni, and I am sorry. This damned...'

'They're all dead.' Yianni interrupted. 'Even your Englishman, Paul.'

Cranford shook his head. 'I thought so. I know all about the ambush. I guessed he had been killed. I'm just glad you survived.'

Yianni looked at the Englishman, half angry, half afraid, at his callousness towards so many deaths.

Cranford stared back, his brow wrinkled. 'Are you ready, Yianni? I need to know. Neither of us can afford feelings. They get in our way. Time for them when we've won. Okay?'

The Cretan said nothing and looked at the Englishman. 'Of course, I am ready. Do you think I'd have come, if I wasn't?'

'I just had to make sure. What did you tell them by the way?'

'Oh, that I was off to Egypt where it was safe. They believed me...I think.'

'Okay. The three of us will leave in an hour. It'll take us most of the day but we'll be safe up in the mountains. And then you can meet your new band.'

Yianni nodded and this time tore off a large chunk of meat from the carcass, which he devoured in three bites. He had already stuffed his family back into the darkest recesses of his memory, where they would stay until the war was over.

November 1941

Chapter 31

Under a louring sky the first storm of winter had driven the women and children of Ayios Stefanos indoors, and not even the dogs and cats cared to stray from their shelters. The small German garrison huddled in their billets, and the sentries hid under the eaves to avoid the worst of the deluge. Anastasia chopped up some celery to throw into a rabbit stew and hummed an unnamed aria memorized from her evening of culture those many years ago. Just three days ago, Yianni had once more slipped into the house and reassured his mother and daughter that he was safe, and that he was off again to Egypt to train more English. His mother knew it was a lie, that he had never left the island at all, but she had convinced herself for Elpida's sake—and perhaps her own—that some things were best left unexamined. Perhaps it was a false comfort, but Anastasia took such small comforts willingly and enjoyed his brief overnight visits as much as she could.

Wawa sat under the table nestled on Anastasia's feet, the cat's shallow breathing barely moving its body, while Elpida washed the plates for their supper. Despite all that had happened, the mundanity of the scene in front of her, and the coziness of the fire as it fought against the coldness of the rain splattering the windows made Anastasia feel something akin to happiness. Still, every day she wept for her beloved Antoni and hoped that her only son would survive to have grandchildren. The old woman stood up and placed the bowl of greens on the table. She felt a twinge in her chest, but they were so common now that it hardly bothered her.

'Come, little girl, I think it's time,' she said gently. 'I think the rain is lessening.'

The two of them took down their coats from the nail on the back of the door and taking each other's hands they walked to the little cemetery.

Anastasia knelt in front of her husband. 'My dear husband,' she whispered, 'we saw Yianni three days ago, but you probably already know this. He is well, but he misses his daughter. Still, he believes that the war will be over soon, and we will all be reunited. I know little Elpida misses him too, but she is a very brave little girl. Husband, there is not a day goes by without thinking of you and the wonderful life we had together. I'm feeling old, Antoni, and my heart sometimes seems as though it too is tired. I will see you again, perhaps sooner than I thought.' She smiled. 'But maybe not. It is all in God's hands. God willing, I will survive the winter, and perhaps the spring will bring all of us happiness. God knows that we deserve it. God sees everything, and I know he is watching over us just like you do. Well, my love, we must go back now. I will say a prayer for you this evening in the church, and light a candle for your soul.'

Anastasia motioned to Elpida to join her, but first the little girl laid a small doll made of twine and corn husks on her pappous's grave, telling him that she hoped he liked her little gift. The two stood up and made their way back home. The path up to their house still flowed with the remnants of the rain, and they had to pick their way carefully. They passed the front of a deserted house, its door hanging off its hinges, when Wawa, who had taken shelter there, jumped from inside the doorway and hit Anastasia full in the chest. The old woman was startled and she reflexively jumped back. Suddenly she felt a squeezing in her chest and a tingling that ran down both her arms. She gasped for breath and leant again the house wall. Elpida grabbed her by the arm to support her, but the pain eased, and Anastasia was able to give a weak smile to her granddaughter.

'It's okay, my love,' she murmured, 'nothing serious.' But no sooner were her words spoken then her whole body was racked by a pressure that seemed to force the air from her lungs. Her face twisted in agony, and she clutched at her chest as through trying to push the pain out of her body. Another bolt of pain, like nothing Anastasia had ever known, pulsed through her body, and now it was unbearable. She slumped back against the wall and fell heavily to the ground. Elpida cradled her grandmother's head and cried out for help. For what seemed an eternity, Elpida was alone with her grandmother, screaming for help as her sobs welled in her throat. After an age, or so it seemed to Elpida, Sophia Theodorakis heard the little girl's screams and she rushed out of her house. She gently lifted Elpida out of the way, and looked down at her old friend as the muddy water curled around her body. Sophia had seen this before on too many occasions; the facial rictus, the blue lips, the thick sweat on the brow. She stood up and held Elpida tightly.

'Now, little girl, go to the church. See if the new Papa is here. And if he is, bring him to me. Your Yiayia is with God now, and with your Papouka too. She is at peace now.' And she crossed herself and held her friend's hands as she said a prayer for the soul of Anastasia Manoulakis.

Too many funerals had been held at Ayios Stefanos, and even the priest wondered if the village was somehow cursed before he crossed himself and asked God for His forgiveness. Elpida was numb through the days of mourning and the burial of her beloved yiayia. She clung to Sophia, and the old lady held her tight each day until she could rock the little girl to a restless sleep.

A week after Anastasia had been laid to rest, Yianni slipped into the village. His face was drawn and his tic had become almost unbearable to look at. He spent only five minutes before the graves of his parents. At Sophia's house, where Elpida now lived, he drank coffee after coffee until Elpida had awakened from her fitful slumber. Their embrace was almost perfunctory, as though both had lost faith in the world and could no longer summon the love that was once so natural.

Elpida did not fight him when he laid her down and told her he had to go. He looked plaintively at Sophia, who could barely mumble that she would look after his daughter until he returned for good. He nodded to her and slipped away, as though he had never been there.

Elpida looked at the old woman. 'What can I do, Kyria Sophia? Life must continue, yes?'

Sophia nodded towards the water jug waiting to be filled, and wondered when, if ever, would this nightmare be over.

May 1990

Chapter 32

The commercial turbo-prop banked lazily and followed the coastline in its descent to the airport on the rocky peninsula north of Chania. Dieter Lehmann leant over his wife and his eight-year-old granddaughter, Angela, and caught his first glimpse of the island. It doesn't look much different, it crossed his mind, but then again why should it. As the plane had droned southwards from Athens he had become quieter—even little Angela had noticed it. His wife, Frieda, did not need to ask why, for she knew the events of many years ago were overwhelming her husband. As the plane made its final turn for landing, it traversed the airfield at Maleme, and Dieter thought he spied the hill village where his life had changed. But now Angela was pulling on his sleeve and he came back to the present to share her excitement at the adventure awaiting her.

On the urging of friends who had enjoyed the island's tourist attractions, a few years ago Frieda had suggested a family holiday in Crete, but Dieter had refused. He had told his family that he could not afford the time from his parish, although it had never stopped him from taking holidays to France or even to England. It was not, he confided in his wife, that he was afraid of returning to the island, at least not in the way she would understand it. Rather—and he had kept this to himself—he was afraid that returning to the island might no longer hold him in thrall, and invalidate, or at least dilute, the memory of what had happened to him there and with it everything that had made him the man he was. But this time, everything was different in ways only he knew, for he had confided in nobody, not even his wife, with whom he shared everything. He had to come back—he had no choice—and confront the island and its ghosts, good and bad.

He felt Angela pulling his sleeve again, and he pointed out the beaches where they would swim and the mountains where she would see wild goats. He told her they could visit archaeological sites and old churches — Angela pulled a face at that. The wheels dropped for landing, and then the wing spoilers noisily reduced airspeed as the flaps went down. There was a heavy bump as the plane touched the concrete runway, and at last it rolled to a halt in front of the terminal.

As Dieter stepped from the charter plane onto the mobile stairs, the hot petrol-fumed blast of summer caught him unawares, and he physically recoiled not just from the heat itself but from the memories that flooded over him. Gingerly, despite Angela's pulling, he walked down the stairs to the tarmac and for the first time in almost fifty years stood on the island of Crete.

After they had gone through customs and retrieved their suitcases, they were ushered along with other tourists to the buses that would take them to their destinations. Their hotel was located in a village just west of Chania, part of the coastal development that had turned the island into a popular tourist destination for north Europeans. The hotel had only opened at the start of the summer season, and the smell of fresh paint and newly applied plaster lingered in the foyer. At the reception desk Dieter was given their room key and the three of them took the tiny lift to their room while a porter carried their suitcases up the marble staircase. Their room was barely large enough for their two beds, and while Frieda and Angela unpacked their clothes, sometimes bumping into each other in their haste to be done, Dieter stepped outside onto the small balcony. He had bought a pair of binoculars especially for the trip and with them he could see all along the coast to Maleme. As his gaze turned inland, he was able to pick out particular locales, the area where he had landed, the hill where Hans had been killed during the attack by the Maori New Zealanders, their blood-thirsty war chants indelibly etched into his memory. He replayed how his squad had at first run away but had regrouped and eventually taken the village. Was he wrong, Dieter wondered, to have returned after all these years? Soon, he knew, he would find out.

The family went downstairs, and while Angela splashed in the hotel pool, Dieter and Frieda planned the next few days over iced coffees. Idly watching Angela, the two became silent. At last, Frieda spoke. 'Dieter, you are sure about this, aren't you? I'll understand if you decide it's too much. There's really no need, you do know that, don't you?'

'I know, my dear, I know. But we've come this far, and surprisingly I do not feel in any way apprehensive. I did, you know, on the plane. But now? Well, I'm here, and I'm ready. But I think I want to do this by myself. I certainly don't want to drag little Angela along. It would be really boring and anyway,' he allowed himself a smile, 'who knows how her grandpa might act. No, you stay with her. I'll be fine, and then we can have a nice dinner at that taverna we passed on the way in. Come on. Let's get this little liebchen to bed. It's been a long day for all of us.'

The morning sun flooded into the hotel foyer and warmed Dieter's old bones as he waited for his rental car. Sinking into a luxurious faux leather chair he looked once more at his map. His plan was simple: to visit the places that had grown into his soul when he was still a callow youth. A discreet cough made him turn. Looming over him was a young man, elegantly attired in an open-necked shirt and creased trousers and equipped with a clipboard and a monstrous stack of papers. Dieter smiled at the man, idly wondering if perhaps he was the son or grandson of someone he had fought against all those years ago. Fifteen minutes later, his hand sore from the signatures he had written, Dieter started on his quest.

The German cemetery at Maleme, his first port of call, was only a few kilometres away, but even so the aging Fiat seemed barely up to that small a distance. He passed through the small village of Maleme, unrecognizable from the village he had known for now virtually every shop along the village's main road catered to the tourists: inflatable beach beds, sunglasses, suntan lotion, hats and strangely incomplete plastic sandals that Angela called flip-flops. On billboards set up in the middle of the pavements and stopping window-shopping tourists dead in their tracks, tavernas proclaimed the best Greek salads and moussaka on the island. And lots of people in all states of dress, but most of them almost naked save for scanty swimsuits and bikinis. Dieter shook his head, unable to comprehend what the village had become. Did these people know, he grumbled to himself, what had happened here long ago? But then he stopped and smiled to himself, realising that he really was becoming the crusty old pensioner his children teased him about.

At the far end of the village Dieter saw a sign directing him to the cemetery, and he dutifully drove along a track that ran through open fields before climbing onto a terrace. Dieter turned into a small car park and parked his Fiat under the shade of a tree. Taking his walking stick, he limped up a flight of stone steps. At the top he stopped. Laid out in front of him on a series of small terraces were the graves, row upon row, each marked by a flat stone slab sunk into the earth. He wandered amongst the graves, lost in thought, and read the names of the dead men, their ages, the different regiments, the men who had come to the island fearlessly, ready to do the Führer's work. He had known some of the men who now slept here but he did not deliberately seek out their graves, not even Hans's, for he was afraid that confronting the mundanity of their resting places might somehow lessen the sanctity of their memory. Around him lay young men, mouldering in graves far from home. Killed by other young men, from New Zealand, Australia, Great

Britain. Young men who simply wanted life. None of us wanted to be here, Dieter thought, although some of us had deluded ourselves into thinking otherwise. No, he concluded, none of wanted to be here, to fight here, and certainly not to die here. The anger that never quite left Dieter bubbled up. His heart raced and his breathing was harsh and laboured. He was angry, more angry than he had been for many years. He wanted to shout at the top of his lungs: 'This is not right.' But even if he could have managed it, who would have heard anyway? He cursed the stupidity of a species that sacrifices its young so readily. Yet he knew, standing on that serenely beautiful hill, that nothing would ever change. Old men do not go to war, and all young men think they will return.

There was a wooden bench halfway up the terracing and he sat down, exhausted by his exertions and his emotions. Taking deep breaths to calm his heart, he gazed out to sea. The cemetery looked directly onto Maleme aerodrome, only a kilometre or two away, the cause of all those deaths years ago. Of course, it hit him, wasn't he standing on the hill that covered the runway? Wasn't this the hill the paratroopers who had landed by glider along the Tavronitis River had been ordered to take? They had faced withering fire from the New Zealanders—my God, there were brave men on both sides—but in the end the paratroopers had prevailed. Dieter asked himself again the question he never could answer. Why did the British allow this hill to fall? If they had held it, he and all the other Germans would have been slaughtered or captured. His mind slipped back to the horror of the landings. He heard the rattle of small arms fire, smelt the cordite of exploding shells, saw the parachutes being blasted out of the sky. Dieter's body shook, but at last he was able to force the memories back into the recesses of his mind.

A voice brought him out of his trance. He heard heavily accented English. 'Are you all right? Would you like some water?' Dieter turned to see a Greek, his own age. The man wore trousers held up with a piece of rough string. From a dirty and torn shirt there dangled some sort of military medal. He wore a tattered British Army beret, perched jauntily on the back of his head.

'No, thank you, no, I'm fine,' Dieter replied, his accent unable to hide his origins. 'You see, I was, well you know why I'm here.'

The Greek smiled. 'Yes, your people come here now. It is a good thing. I too remember the war. I...we were all in it and we were so young. So full of life.'

Dieter nodded.

'I'm the caretaker here,' the Greek explained. 'I have a little hut over there. If you need anything, please come by. My name is Aristotle, but everyone calls me Ari.' He grinned like a schoolboy. 'This is why I am here, to help people like you and keep these tidy for them.' He nodded towards the graves. 'I am the only worker here right now. We only opened the cemetery a few years ago so you must forgive me if it is not yet what I want it to be.'

'Thank you,' Dieter smiled. 'But I would just like to sit here a little and get my breath. I think this cemetery is very beautiful, if that is the right word. It is peaceful, as I hoped it would be.'

The Greek nodded and left Dieter alone.

Dieter was glad the caretaker had visited him. He must have fought against him, surely, but here he was, keeping clean the graves of the very men who had tried to kill him. Now that the spell was broken, Dieter could walk around again, and he felt sufficiently recovered to take some photographs of the cemetery and the surrounding countryside. As he walked back to his car he looked for the old Greek, but he was nowhere to be seen, and so Dieter got into the Fiat and drove back down the hill.

He headed the Fiat east along the narrow coastal road towards Chania, passing his hotel and hoping that his family would not see him. The traffic grew heavier the closer he got to the city, and he was forced to stop often for buses and delivery trucks. He was unsettled by the scooters and motorcycles that passed him, often alarmingly close to his wing mirrors, and Dieter prayed that he might get through the city without a serious accident for he had little trust in the insurance the young Cretan agent had insisted he buy. At one forced stop, caused by a tanker that was having trouble getting into the forecourt of the petrol station, he was able to look around at his surroundings. His breath was forced from his lungs, for set back from the highway and almost hidden by cheap concrete buildings, was a large war memorial crowned with a statue of an eagle, its wings spread wide, as though landing on its victim. It was the memorial to the German Parachute Regiment that had been erected soon after the island had fallen. He had seen pictures of this when he had returned to Germany after the war, but they had been taken soon after its construction, when the hill on which it stood was still not surrounded by the expanding suburbs of Chania and the monument dominated the landscape. He managed to pull the Fiat over to the side of the road and climbed out to get a closer look. It all looked rather pathetic. The stone-lined walkway to the memorial was overgrown and some vandal had splashed paint on the memorial plaque. Even the eagle looked precarious, as though a good wind might blow it off its pedestal. The apathy with which this memorial was tended was in stark contrast to the cemetery at Maleme. But who could blame the Cretans, Dieter asked himself. Yet the monument moved him in ways the cemetery had not. Perhaps its dilapidation was a poignant reminder that what had happened, what he had done, did not deserve glorification, that perhaps it would be right for the monument to disappear and take with it all reminder of that time. He walked to his car, not deigning a backward glance at the monument to him, Hans and all his comrades.

Dieter had discovered in the first ten minutes behind the wheel that while the first two gears of the rental car were where they should be, third gear was difficult to find, and fourth was well-nigh impossible, and he was grateful that the drive through Chania was stop-and-start. The slow pace also allowed him to get a feel for the town. Cars and municipal buses, plus a few tourist buses that looked impossibly large to navigate through the narrow streets, shared the road with donkeys carrying old men and women on their backs or pulling them in small carts. The sweet smell of petrol fumes hung over everything. Garish shop signs in Greek, some even in English, hawked wares of all sorts, and the careless street habits of the Chaniote shoppers forced Dieter to constantly ram on his brakes. The gaps in the shop fronts and the ugly cement apartment buildings that had been hastily thrown up reminded Dieter of exactly what he and his countrymen had done fifty years ago. A bus driver who could not find the right gear—Dieter smiled, he knew the feeling—forced him to stop the Fiat in front of a large stone building with a monumental entry. It bustled with Greeks of all ages coming in and out, loaded down with fresh fish, cheeses, vegetables and large jugs of wine. He wondered if the building had been there during the war. An impatient car horn from behind broke his spell, and Dieter depressed the accelerator pedal and moved slowly away. A small hill taxed the Fiat's engine—its tiny engine struggling against the incline—and he had time to admire a large and gaudily decorated church to his right. But suddenly, as though the town had never existed, the road dropped down a steep hill and entered an area of flat, empty fields that stretched down to the Bay of Souda. At the side of the road a small sign said, "Allied War Cemetery," and gratefully, for the Fiat was still not behaving, Dieter followed its directions.

Dieter parked the car and walked through a small iron gate. In front of him, stretching down to the western shore of Souda bay, were row upon row of small white crosses. Except for the distant sound of the occasional motorcycle, all was quiet as he walked towards the large stone cross in the middle of the grounds to get his bearings. A gentle breeze blew in from the bay, a pleasant change from the stuffy heat of the city. Dieter scarcely knew where to begin; there were so many graves, but he was called to one of them. He pulled from his pocket a letter that the War Graves Commission in England had sent him, which gave the precise reference of the grave he sought. Almost reluctant to find it, he walked slowly through the rows. He had to stop repeatedly for his leg was hurting from having to push the stiff clutch to find the right gear, and although he had vowed not to do so he found himself taking a short cut by walking over the graves themselves. But he comforted himself with the knowledge that he was one of them, a comrade-in-arms, albeit from the other side, and he hoped—he knew—that the men he trod on would not mind too much his inconvenience to their slumber.

He arrived at a grave, its inscription, like all the others, very simple. Paul Cuthbertson, Royal Artillery, 1941. He sat down at the end of the grave, slowly in order to favour his aching leg. Apart from a worker pushing a lawn mower at the far end of the cemetery, Dieter was alone.

'Well, my friend,' Dieter whispered, 'because we are friends I hope, I promised myself I would do this, to come back to see how you are. I am sorry it has taken me so long, and I ask your forgiveness. After I left you, my company was moved out of the village soon after, if I recall correctly, and I never got a chance to come back and see what had happened to you. But I am sure the old lady looked after you, and you found rest. I was sent to Russia, and only God knows how I survived but I did. I saw too many of my comrades slaughtered or maimed with frostbite. But all I suffered was a wound in my leg, so I am grateful it was nothing worse. As the campaign got worse and worse for us, and the brutality on both sides matched nothing the world had ever seen before, I found I could not kill anymore. I had been a good soldier but with my bad leg, I wasn't much use anyway, so I replaced our unit's medic when he was killed in a horrible bayonet fight. I wasn't much use as a medic. It was so cold and we had no supplies. But I tried, and at least I didn't have any more blood on my hands.

'I am here, at last, Paul, but I'm not sure I know what to say to you. And I do not know why it was important to visit you when I could not even bring myself to visit Hans's grave. He was my best friend and he died on the first day. Hans was a good man, better than me. Maybe when I see him he can explain. He knew me better than I knew myself.'

Dieter smiled and remained silent for a few moments. He stretched his sore leg and looked around, breathing in with relish the sweetness of the freshly cut grass.

'Paul,' he continued, 'we met only for a brief moment, we were both young and scared, and we should have hated each other, for that's what they'd taught us, but I couldn't. And you couldn't either. I knew that as we talked. You remember that old woman in the chapel who helped us, don't you? I never told you this back then, I didn't have time, but I am sure that I had killed her husband and son in an act that I am still ashamed of. Not me directly, but I was part of the squad that did it. And, you know, Paul, I know she knew I was their murderer. God knows how she did, but she did. That old woman forgave me. Remember how she wrapped up the cut on my hand? She never said anything, but still she forgave me. And everything I had done in my life up to that point became meaningless. I realised that later, but only too many years later, I am afraid. It was she who gave me, at last, the courage to change, to ask God's forgiveness for killing people for ideas that I never really believed in.

'When I was young, Paul, I believed in this thing called predestination, that somehow our lives were all planned out for us. But I know now how silly that was. I was responsible, and I alone, for everything I did, and I have had to live with that all my life. I have tried to make amends for what I did. Perhaps God will forgive me for his mercy is endless, but sometimes I am not sure. My life is almost over, Paul. Two months ago my doctor told me I had a cancer. I have perhaps another six months because it is inoperable. Not even Frieda, my wife, knows this. I haven't told her yet. I still search for the strength of that old lady in the chapel.

'Paul, I believe I will see you soon. I hope that you can greet me and we can be the friends that we could not be all those years ago. Paul, I am going to visit our little chapel and the village. I don't know why but I have to go there. I just know I have to do it.

'Goodbye, Paul. And thank you.' Dieter kissed two fingers on his right hand and gently placed them over Paul's name on the headstone. He wiped away his tears and limped slowly back to his car.

Dieter turned off the engine and looked up at the village of Ayios Stefanos, his eyes squinting in the harsh Cretan sun. To his left there was an open olive grove surrounded by stone walls. It was like so many others around the island, but Dieter sensed, rather than knew, that this was where Hans had been killed, where he himself had almost met his Maker. He straddled a low wall, ignoring the throbbing pain in his leg, and walked to the centre of the field. Was this where it all took place, was that not in fact the very tree that Han's head had rolled against?

Dieter made his way slowly through the grove. He sensed that somebody was watching him. He stopped and looked around, but he could not see who is it was. He felt no fear. Indeed, Dieter felt almost a comfort knowing he was not alone. As he turned to continue his climb, out of the corner of his eye he saw him. Dieter froze. The man stood almost at attention, and with his left elbow he leant against an olive tree. He was in his early twenties, and his short hair was sandy-coloured and parted on the right side of his head. His grey shirt was rolled up to the elbows. It was grimy as though he had been living rough. His trousers, held up by a thick leather belt with a tarnished buckle emblazoned with the Swastika, were disheveled and were tucked into parachutist boots. His right sleeve bore badges, but Dieter could not make out what they signified. The soldier looked at Dieter quizzically, as though mildly surprised by his presence and wanting to know what he was doing here but was too polite or too shy to ask. Dieter turned his head to confront the soldier straight on, but immediately he disappeared. Only when Dieter turned his head away did he see him again, not as a transparency but clearly and distinctly. Still, Dieter felt no fear, rather an enormous sense of comfort and peace. Dieter nodded towards the soldier—he could not tell if it was Hans but hoped it was—but the wraith had already disappeared, whether into the shadows between life and death or merely into the recesses of his own imagination Dieter did not know. How curious, Dieter thought, that I, a man who dedicated himself to Christ so many years ago, who believes in eternal life because of Him, should be so skeptical of what I think I just saw; we are too weak, he realized, for faith alone and so we ask for proof. Yet we reject that very proof or fail to recognize it when it is presented to us. Dieter smiled, knowing that his sermon about Doubting Thomas would have a new twist next time he gave it to his congregation, should he ever have the chance.

Dieter continued up the slope to the first of the village's houses and entered its narrow main street. He came to a small war memorial, set back off the street. It consisted of a small, paved courtyard framed by three low stone walls. He entered the courtyard and saw on one wall a list of names carved into white marble, and on the others, set inside glass panels, faded black-and-white photographs. Dieter choked on bile that rose from the depths of his stomach as he realized the pictures were of the massacre, the village men pleading with Lieutenant Maier for mercy, the men standing in the olive grove and falling as the bullets hammered into them, with clouds of dust from errant bullets kicked up all around. Dieter prayed that his own image was not present in the photographs but he was too weak to look at the pictures again. He closed his eyes and grasped the top of the wall to steady himself. He felt his heart racing and struggled for breath. But eventually his body settled down and he sat down on a low stone bench. All was quiet except for the cicadas. Dieter forced himself on.

Dieter walked into the plateia, and now everything was as he had remembered it. There was the small church and through a gap in the houses he saw, nestled on the far hillside, the little whitewashed chapel where his life had changed. Dieter knew that the chapel was out of the reach of a sick old man and so he turned towards the small kafeneio. The coffee shop had not changed at all, he fancied. He smiled, thinking that even the men drinking coffee were the same ones of fifty years ago. His leg continued to bother him, and he limped stiffly across to the nearest table and sat down. The men looked at him with some interest but said nothing. The waiter brought him some water in a cracked and dusty glass, together with a bowl of nuts, and then sat down again with the others to continue their conversation. Dieter ordered a coffee in halting Greek.

A middle-aged woman brought a small cup of coffee to him. She pulled at a lock of hair that had fallen over her eyes, smiled and patted her chest twice. 'Elpida, Elpida. I live here. All my life. Very beautiful, yes? My village. Sugar for coffee? I learn English for visitors.' She spoke slowly. Dieter smiled, glad that he could follow what she was saying at least a little, and he sipped the coffee, slowly gathering his strength and wondering if he had known Elpida when she was a little girl, all those years ago.

Long ago, Dieter knew, God had forgiven him for what he had done in his youth. He knew too, although vanity was a sin he recognized all too fully in himself, that he would be received into Heaven for he had tried all his life to make right the madness of his actions. But, Dieter, he asked himself, as the coffee brought some life back to him, what exactly do you want now? Here, in this village. Now. He found no answer he could articulate, but as he sat at the table, sipping the grainy coffee, he experienced a feeling of peace, almost physical in its force, welling up in him, identical to the warmth and safety he remembered as a child in his mother's arms. It was as if the Holy Spirit itself was suffusing through his body and soul.

Dieter rubbed the scar on his cheek. He sensed a man staring at him, his eyes seeming to bore into Dieter's own. He was about the same age as Dieter, perhaps a little older. He noticed that the man's cheek twitched continuously. The German looked at him and nodded, but the Cretan continued to stare until he stood up and walked away brusquely. He turned around and gave Dieter one more look before leaving the plateia.

Dieter looked at his watch and decided it was time to return to the hotel. There was nothing more for him here. He had promised Angela a swim in the hotel pool and he did not want to disappoint her. He placed a wad of drachma notes on the table, hoping that it was the right amount. He smiled at Elpida who was leaning against the bar smoking a cigarette, nodded to the men, and started his slow walk out of the village.

At the memorial he stopped to catch his breath. A man stepped out from behind a wall, the same man who had been staring at him in the kafeneio, and blocked the German's path. The Cretan pointed a pistol, an old British Webley, at Dieter and pulled the trigger. The bullet entered Dieter's chest and he fell to the ground. The man straddled Dieter, stepping carefully to avoid the pool of blood, and whispered, 'I am Yianni Manoulakis. You killed my father. And now I have my revenge.' Yianni stepped over Dieter and casually walked away. Dieter heard the chirpings of the cicadas fade into eternity. Somewhere a dove cooed but that too soon ceased its melody. The blue sky turned misty, and soon all was black as the light shone from Dieter Lehmann's eyes one last time.

Author's Note

The Battle of Crete began on 20 May 1941, after the Germans had swept through mainland Greece and forced the evacuation of the British Expeditionary Force. Operation Mercury, the name given by the German High Command, was intended to secure the occupation of Crete, thereby tightening German control of the Eastern Mediterranean and threatening British forces in North Africa. The Germans targeted the north-coast airfields at Iraklion, Rethymno, and Maleme, a small village west of Chania, and committed the regime's finest troops, the Fallschirmjäger (Paratroopers), to the operation. The Allies comprised a force of about 40,000 Greeks, British, Australian, and New Zealanders (the Cretans tended to refer to all the Allies as English, regardless of their nationality). It is worth noting that the elite Cretan 5th Division was not available for the defence of the island as it had been sent to northern Greece against the Italian and later German invasion of the mainland. So, at the time of the Cretan invasion, there were only about 4,000 Greek troops on the island, and most of these, like the rest of the Allied contingents, were woefully under equipped. Nevertheless, these soldiers, together with Greek civilians alone or in small groups, inflicted such losses on the paratroopers, especially on the first day, that General Student, in command of the Fallschirmjäger, considered calling the whole operation off. These losses were even more significant given that the combined German force was considerably smaller than the Allies facing them. The Germans were nonplussed, to say the least, by the resistance the paratroopers faced, even when they were still in the air; at least one German officer believed that the paratroopers should have been allowed to land and organize themselves into battle formations so that a "proper" battle could be fought.

Unfortunately, General Freyberg, the New Zealander in

overall command of the Allied defence forces, was unable, despite his access to Ultra intercepts of coded German messages, to prioritise an airborne or a seaborne assault; was the airborne attack the real thing or merely a ploy to divert him and the coastal defences from where the real invasion was coming? It was this indecision that ultimately caused the Allies' defeat. Once the airfield of Maleme fell on 22 May, the Germans were able to bring in an almost constant supply of men and material from the Greek mainland unhindered—the Royal Air Force presence on Crete was negligible—and they quickly overwhelmed the defenders' resistance. Freyberg ordered the evacuation of the island on 27 May, the same day that Chania fell. Thousands of allied troops did make it to the south coast where many were picked up by the Royal Navy and transported to Egypt. The Navy ceased transport on 31 May, and although many soldiers complained bitterly about this the Royal Navy did a magnificent job in running the gauntlet of almost constant attacks by the Luftwaffe to pick up as many men as they could.

The Cretans, however, were not so lucky. The Germans had never before faced such widespread and savage resistance, and they quickly branded the Cretans as guerrillas outside the bounds of the Geneva Conventions (not that adherence to the conventions had previously bothered the Nazis). Thousands of Cretans were summarily executed, thousands more imprisoned, and whole villages razed. The brutality began almost as soon as the Allies had abandoned the island, but the Cretans never wilted in their implacable resistance and right up to the German withdrawal in the summer of 1944 they continued a war of attrition against the forces of occupation. The exception to this fierce resistance was in the east of the island where the Italians, much more prone than the Germans to a *laissez-faire* attitude towards the Cretans, met much less resistance. As the German occupation of Crete wore on and the tide of war turned against the Germans, the andartes became increasingly politically factionalized as they vied for future control of the post-war island.

The village of Ayios Stefanos (Saint Stephen) is a composite of any number of villages that dot the island. For the first battle that Dieter engaged in, I relied, but only for the broadest of strokes, on the battle for Galatas, which saw some of the fiercest fighting. This sector of the island was defended mainly by New Zealanders, which included a contingent of Maoris. It is certainly true that the Cretans attacked the paratroopers with anything they had to hand, and both sides committed atrocities, but it is undeniable that the scale of the German depredations was far, far greater than anything the Cretans committed. Paul's adventures are entirely fictional, although similar journeys to the south coast are well documented in memoirs.

The massacre of the Ayios Stefanos men by the Germans is based on the execution of civilians at the small village of Kondomari, which took place on 2 June 1941. Estimates of the number killed vary, from as few as twenty-three (the number of names on the village memorial, as well as in the official German records) to as many as seventy.

The second massacre in the novel — the burning alive of the women — also has a basis in truth. Some of the old women from the village of Kali-Sykia were thrown into burning houses when they tried to escape.

A grammarian will note that I have simplified the case endings for single masculine proper nouns like Yianni so that the nominative has the same ending as the vocative and accusative. I followed this convention in *A Terrible Unrest*, my previous novel about Anastasia's family, the Andrakises. The Cretan dialect is quite distinct and is looked down upon by many mainland Greeks. The Cretans, of course, hold to it as a matter of pride; their spirit of independence is as strong today as it was seventy-five years ago. The majority of Cretan surnames end in "-akis," a diminutive that became common during the Ottoman occupation, but which actually goes back as far as the Venetian period. The diminutive is also added to common nouns.

Suggested Reading

Many books are available on the invasion and the occupation, ranging from historical analyses and personal memoirs to historical fiction.

I found the following sources especially useful:

Anthony Beevor. *Crete. The Battle and the Resistance.*

Alan Clark. *The Fall of Crete.*

Clark's and Beevor's books provide the reader with very well researched analyses of the buildup to the invasion, the invasion itself, and the occupation. These two studies are essential starting points for any reader wishing to understand the invasion and occupation.

W. Stanley Moss. *Ill Met by Moonlight.* A youthfully exuberant account of the kidnapping of General Kreipe by British and Greek soldiers in 1944, an operation concocted and led by Patrick Leigh Fermor and Moss, British resistance officers assigned to Crete. A feature film was subsequently made of the kidnapping, starring Dirk Bogarde at his swashbuckling best.

George I. Panayiotakis. *The Battle of Crete.* A photographic history of the invasion and occupation. Some of the photographs are graphic and moving.

George Psychoundakis. *The Cretan Runner.* Psychoundakis was a runner, responsible for taking messages, often at great personal risk, between British intelligence officers on the island. Brilliantly written and very difficult to put down.

Costas Hadjipateras and Maria S. Fafalios. *Crete 1941 Eyewitnessed.* A compilation of first-hand accounts of the invasion from both sides of the struggle.

Evelyn Waugh. *Officers and Gentlemen.* Waugh was attached

to a commando unit on Crete during the invasion, and this is a fictionalized and highly sardonic account of the invasion and evacuation written in typical *Waughian* style.

Jurgen Herbst. *Requiem for a German Past. A Boyhood among the Nazis*. An honest and beautifully written autobiography that shows the moral and ethical conflicts of growing up in Nazi Germany.

Spike Milligan. *Adolf Hitler. My Part in his Downfall*. (No, really, I'm serious.) This and the succeeding volumes follow Spike's service in the Royal Artillery in Africa and Italy. Although they are hilarious — as one would expect — they also provide accurate and poignant descriptions of what it was like to be a "common soldier" during two of the great campaigns of the Second World War.

Places to Visit

Crete is an atmospheric island, and it is very easy to move through the landscape to get a real sense of the battle that was fought here. Despite the summer tourists who now take over many of the coastal villages, it is still easy to imagine the Germans swarming through Souda, Kondomari, Galatas, Platanias or Maleme as they pushed the Allies back. The small village of Stylos has changed little and one can picture the soldiers lounging in the village as they await orders for the evacuation. The spring still exists and is the source of the bottled water that is sold everywhere. The road from Stylos to the Askifou Plain is only about twenty-five kilometers, and the new road makes the drive easy and very pleasant. Passing through the plain, the view farther on, as the Libyan Sea appears for the first time, is breathtaking. But imagine the plight of the soldiers who still had to make it down to the coast in boots that often were falling apart, hungry and thirsty, ever mindful of the threat of attack, and unsure of whether they would even be rescued by the Navy.

Chania remains one of the most beautiful cities in Europe. The center of Chaniote life is the magnificent old harbour, dominated by the pharos lighthouse at the end of the mole. Many of the historic buildings surrounding the harbour were destroyed by the Luftwaffe, but much of the famed Old Town remains, and one can see Ottoman minarets and domes next to Venetian churches and stately houses. If one looks past the tourist shops that sprout everywhere in the summer, one can easily get a feel of what it must have been like all those years ago.

I recommend the following to those who wish to understand the full tragedy of the battle.

The Allied Cemetery is located at the west end of Souda Bay and is accessible off the road from Souda to the Akrotiri. The small upright headstones, and the many men who lie there, all of them too young to die, will leave visitors with a profound sense of sadness, and perhaps anger too.

The turn-off to the German War Cemetery is just west of the village of Maleme. The cemetery is situated on Hill 107, the rise that overlooks the airfield at Maleme, a strategically vital objective for the Germans. Like the Allied cemetery, it is serenely beautiful. The entrance to the cemetery has a very tasteful display about the invasion and its aftermath. Visitors should note that although the cemetery provides an excellent view of the airfield, now a Greek military facility, it is forbidden to take photographs of any military installation in Greece (the same restriction applies to the Naval Station at Souda).

I recommend three museums. I would start with The Naval Museum on the west side of Chania's Old Harbour. It has photographs and military equipment from the time of the invasion, as well as from other periods. The village of Galatas has a small one-room museum dedicated to the German attack on the village. Finally, war buffs should not miss a visit to a private museum in the Askifou Plain. There one will find well-preserved guns, equipment and other military paraphernalia that were salvaged after the fighting had ended. The Hatzidakis family, the museum's owners and whose grandfather was initially responsible for collecting the material that constitutes the museum, are charming and knowledgeable hosts.

Acknowledgements

My wife, Donna, and my friends, Murray Morison, Dr Paul Bahn, Dr Shaila Van Sickle and Charlotte Potter were kind enough to assiduously read the manuscript, and they pointed out numerous clangers—some small, some large—that left unchanged would have degraded the novel considerably. Sean Damer and Ian Bradley looked at an early draft and pointed out some preliminary errors. I thank them all. I am deeply indebted to Father Benjamin Huggins of the Holy Prophet Elijah Orthodox Mission of Durango, Colorado, for guiding me through the specific rites of the Orthodox burial service.

**TOP HAT
BOOKS**

Top Hat Books

Historical fiction that lives

We publish fiction that captures the contrasts, the achievements, the optimism and the radicalism of ordinary and extraordinary times across the world.

We're open to all time periods and we strive to go beyond the narrow, foggy slums of Victorian London. Where are the tales of the people of fifteenth century Australasia? The stories of eighth century India? The voices from Africa, Arabia, cities and forests, deserts and towns? Our books thrill, excite, delight and inspire.

The genres will be broad but clear. Whether we're publishing romance, thrillers, crime, or something else entirely, the unifying themes are timescale and enthusiasm. These books will be a celebration of the chaotic power of the human spirit in difficult times. The reader, when they finish, will snap the book closed with a satisfied smile.
If you have enjoyed this book, why not tell other readers by posting a review on your preferred book site.

Recent bestsellers from Tops Hat Books are:

Grendel's Mother

The Saga of the Wyrd-Wife

Susan Signe Morrison

Grendel's mother, a queen from Beowulf, threatens the fragile
political stability on this windswept land.

Paperback: 978-1-78535-009-2 ebook: 978-1-78535-010-8

Queen of Sparta

A Novel of Ancient Greece

T.S. Chaudhry

History has relegated her to the role of bystander, what if Gorgo,
Queen of Sparta, had played a central role in the Greek resistance
to the Persian invasion?

Paperback: 978-1-78279-750-0 ebook: 978-1-78279-749-4

Mercenary

R.J. Connor

Richard Longsword is a mercenary, but this time it's not for
money, this time it's for revenge...

Paperback: 978-1-78279-236-9 ebook: 978-1-78279-198-0

Black Tom

Terror on the Hudson

Ron Semple

A tale of sabotage, subterfuge and political shenanigans
in Jersey City in 1916; America is on the cusp of war and the fate of
the nation hinges on the decision of one young policeman.

Paperback: 978-1-78535-110-5 ebook: 978-1-78535-111-2

Destiny Between Two Worlds
A Novel about Okinawa
Jacques L. Fuqua, Jr.
A fateful October 1944 morning offered no inkling that the lives of
thousands of Okinawans would be profoundly changed—forever.
Paperback: 978-1-78279-892-7 ebook: 978-1-78279-893-4

Cowards
Trent Portigal
A family's life falls into turmoil when the parents' timid political
dissidence is discovered by their far more enterprising children.
Paperback: 978-1-78535-070-2 ebook: 978-1-78535-071-9

Godwine Kingmaker
Part One of The Last Great Saxon Earls
Mercedes Rochelle
The life of Earl Godwine is one of the enduring enigmas of English
history. Who was this Godwine, first Earl of Wessex;
unscrupulous schemer or protector of the English? The answer
depends on whom you ask...
Paperback: 978-1-78279-801-9 ebook: 978-1-78279-800-2

Readers of ebooks can buy or view any of these bestsellers by
clicking on the live link in the title. Most titles are published
in paperback and as an ebook. Paperbacks are available in
traditional bookshops. Both print and ebook formats are
available online.

Find more titles and sign up to our readers' newsletter at
http://www.johnhuntpublishing.com/fiction

Follow us on Facebook at https://www.facebook.com/JHPfiction
and Twitter at https://twitter.com/JHPFiction